SQUARE
LOVE

Julie,
Hello There and
How the heck are you?
Just wanted to share This
story with you. I hope you
make it. I also put your
name in the book and I
hope you don't mind. :)
Devonne Collins

M R .   D E V O N N E   C O L L I N S

ISBN: 1482555476
ISBN 13: 9781482555479
Library of Congress Control Number: 2015900573
CreateSpace Independent Publishing Platform
North Charleston, South Carolina

ACKNOWLEDGEMENTS

First, I would like to thank Ms. Terry Tanner Holdridge. Thank you for all you have done to help me bring this story to life. You are a true friend for taking on such a challenge. How many other editors in the world would say to an author "That character really gets on my nerves!" Thank you for always being you and keeping me in line. I appreciate it more than you can ever comprehend.

Second, I would like to thank Ms. Sherry McClellan for all of your editorial help. It was your own personal determination that showed me I could complete this project through any obstacle.

With more than twenty years of time between us I am very happy to be able to call you my friend.

Finally, I would like to thank the masses. In the last year I probably have come into contact with you at some point. I apologize now for taking up your time and talking about this book. I say this with a smile. To all of those who I asked "what do you think about this idea or name," I thank you! My family, friends, coworkers, even my barber, I thank all of you for listening to me at some point or another.

DEDICATION

I would like to dedicate this book to my beautiful mother, **Ms. Frankie M. Hill**. I love you for molding me into the person that I have become. Thank you for always being there for me and teaching me what true patience is. Thank you for always handing down your wisdom and guidance. Everyone who comes into contact with you feels your warmth and compassion for others.

p.s.

Mom, I am sorry for all the curse words you are about to read. I know you did not raise me to speak this way. Love You!

THE WAKEUP

Have you ever had the best dream of your life? You know the one when it is just you, Kerry Washington and Taraji P. Henson. The three of you are all oiled up eating grapes and strawberries. All while snuggling together as they playfully fight to see which will feed you flavored cheese slices next. Nothing too physical just a nice classy dream, you know. Naturally, you have some classic Luther playing softly in the background as the Cristal is chilling in the ice bucket.

And, then, you awake to a nightmare. You wake up to your wife taking pictures of you, as the dog licks your face. You wake up stretched out in the backseat of your car, with obvious vomit all over you and your car. Now you realize why the dog is licking you. It is because he is taking care of the vomit that is all over your face, of course.

"This damn Chad is just always into something," Zeke says to himself. For the record Chad is my one hundred and fifty pound pit bull. The wife is banging on the window with the, "Why don't you get out of there. I came out here to let the dog out and look what I find; you out here sleeping with the dog. I already called Sandra this morning telling her that you didn't come home last night. I told her that she and I are going to happy hour today. I didn't even know you were here," she says. "I have been trying to call you all night but now I know why you didn't answer your phone. It's dismantled and sitting on the dashboard. And speaking of dashboard!" as she points to a totally ruined dog chewed up dashboard.

Taylor then goes into the twenty questions. "How did this happen to you? How did you get home? What brought this on? Oh my God what happened to the dashboard? Next time, can you call or, shit, even text so I won't be worried?" All I want her to do is close her mouth at this point. My head is pounding and I was doing just fine out here with Chad before she came out here running her mouth. Well, she says one thing too much and here it comes, more vomit. I let it out all over the back seat floor. Taylor reaches in and takes the dog out of the car while mumbling something about "Come on Chad he doesn't deserve you."

I just rolled over and was happy that what I thought was the last little bit came out. Just when I thought I was good and asleep, here she comes again. "I am going to work I have a quick surgery scheduled at 11a.m. I took the dog out back so he is fine. Get up and get into the shower," Taylor announces. She backs out her new 2015 S Class Benz and heads to work. Only thing I can do is roll back over and go back to sleep. "At least she closed the garage door," is all I can think.

Three hours later I finally come to my senses and I am so damn ready to get out of this car. I realize why my head is hurting, I drank too damn much. All I can remember is someone ordering another bottle of Patron from the bar. There was something in there about a four way kiss, well, I think anyway. Yeah a four way kiss was in there some kind of way for sure. Then it starts to come back to me, we did VIP at The Stadium Club. Oh the ladies are so lovely there and they give such great service. So many models with bottles you just can't keep up. I see why I don't go there too often. My marriage would be over, he laughs to himself.

Then a nasty frown comes over Zeke's face. He now remembers why he got drunk in the first place. He flashes back about twenty four hours. Head still ringing he can't even think about it until he gets a glass of juice first. His stomach is feeling like a washing machine. He pulls himself out of the back seat. He grabs his cell phone that has been taken apart and left on the dash board of his car, well, what is left of the dashboard anyway. The only thing he can think is how in the hell did this happen? The dog has chewed on it and it has holes all ripped in it. He can tell his boys set him up for real. "I am glad ya'll had a good laugh at my expense" he thinks laughing to himself. I mean my wife wanted a new Benz so you know I had to cop something. I just picked up the 2015 four door Porsche Panorama. So who knows how much this is going to cost me to fix.

As he comes in from the garage, he heads straight for the fridge for some much needed orange juice. After taking a few good swallows, he decides to turn on MSNBC to check the markets. As he watches the news, his mind starts to fade back to how all of this started in the first place.

NOT A CARE IN THE WORLD

"Wow, how did this happen to me?" Is all Zeke could think to himself. He goes back in his memory to twenty four hours before. His wife was doing her normal thing getting ready to head off to work in the morning. He noticed she is looking extra special today and he even comments to her. "Baby, you are looking good today. What is the special occasion?" She looks in the mirror and says, "Well, I have a meeting with the protocol staff and I wanted to make sure I looked professional. So, what do you think?" she asks. Zeke looking at her with a definite gaze in his eyes, "Baby, you look fantastic! Get in there and knock them dead!" he gives her a kiss in support and heads to his home office.

Taylor continues to get dressed and when finished, gives her hubby a kiss on the forehead and heads off to work. Not having a care in the world, Zeke continues to work in his office on some things. He is at it for maybe a good half an hour and then it happens, batteries go dead for the laptop. After searching for his power cord in his office and in the laptop case, Zeke determines that his wife has taken his again and it is probably in her office. So he strolls down the hall to his wife's office. When he walks in he sees the cord instantly and where is it? It is plugged into her laptop of course. "How many times have I told her if you take something put it back?" he thinks to himself. As he is taking the cord off of the laptop the screen pops on. I guess the screen saver had blacked out the screen, but when machine moved it popped back on. It comes on and is open to a page of Yahoo! email. Shoot Zeke didn't even know she had a Yahoo! account. "So she has a Yahoo! account?" he thinks to himself as he sits down to see what email has been sent. To Zeke's surprise her screen name is Taylored4U. "Really Taylored4U is your screen name?" he says out loud. Zeke starts to go through the emails and realizes that his wife has been fucking around. Some asshole named Mitch is actually meeting her for lunch today. "So that is why she was looking so sexy this morning," he thinks to himself. "That bitch! After all I have done for her, this is what I get?" Zeke says to himself.

At this point Zeke is furious and just doesn't know what to do. As he is reading more and more email, he realizes that this has been going on for months. All he can think of is, "how did this happen and why?" After going through a few of the emails and sending a few to his phone. He closes down the email so she can't tell he has been going through it and goes back to his office for a drink. He makes a double Hennessey on ice and sits down. He puts his head into his hands and just keeps repeating "Why? Why? Why? Why has this happened to me? I thought I gave her everything." As bad as he wants to, he refuses to cry; he is too angry and too upset to shed any tears. He does the next best thing and calls his main man, Carlos. When he gets Carlos on the phone he says, "The bitch is cheating on me and I am going to kill her."

After hearing one line from Zeke, Carlos says "No don't do that and I am on the way to your house now. Are you at home?" Zeke says, "Yes, I'm here but I don't want to be." All Carlos can do is say "Don't leave I'm on the way. I'll be there in fifteen minutes. Just let me put some shoes on." Zeke replies with, "Ok, but I am looking for my pistol now." Carlos yells, "NO, and I'm on the way."

Carlos speeds over to the mini mansion and finds Zeke outside of the garage smoking a cigarette. Carlos gets out of his truck and says, "Man, I thought you gave up smoking?" Zeke replies with "Yeah, I did and then I found out my wife is cheating, so, I can do anything I want." Carlos replies with "Ok, ok, you say she is cheating; what proof do you have?" Zeke says "I stumbled into her email and I found out she has a man on the side that she has been seeing for awhile now. She is actually meeting this dude today for lunch." Carlos replies with, "Oh, hell no. Let's get the crew together and whip his ass. Give him one of those World Star Hip Hop beat downs." Zeke says, "OK. I'm down with that for sure, but for some reason I am more concerned about who he is and what he's about. I want to know why she chose this idiot over me. How about we go down there and just keep an eye on them and see what they do?" Carlos says, "Ok but I would rather just beat the shit out of him and show him how we get down in Colombia." Zeke replies with "Yeah, that was my idea at first too, but I need answers. You know what I mean?" Carlos says, "Ok but after you get your answers, can I peel his skin off?" Zeke just looks at Carlos with a devilish grin.

Zeke tells Carlos, "From what I read in the email, she is meeting him today for lunch at Morton's Steak House, downtown near Farragut North." "Well, looks like we need to be there too," Carlos replies. Zeke says "I have one even better. Let's go into the house and I will lay out my plan for now."

The two head into the house and go instantly to the man cave. As Zeke sits down Carlos pours them both a drink. Zeke says "So here is what I am thinking, it is a little after 9:00 a.m. now. How about I get a private investigator to watch them and find out what she has been up to? If you and I go there to watch her, we are going to stick out like a sore thumb and nothing will get accomplished but her rolling out as soon as she sees us." Carlos replies with, "Oh, something will get done for sure. Dude will get that ass kicked for messing with the wrong married woman." Zeke says "See that's what I am talking about. Dude might not even know she's married and if that's the case, I can't hold him responsible for this fiasco." Carlos says, "It don't matter, everyone involved gets a beat down on this one, her, him, the mailman, and anyone else involved." Zeke chimes in with "Look, I love your attitude but that is not the way to find answers. Let's get a private investigator over here and see what we can really find out. Pass me those yellow pages over there. Let's get this show on the road."

Zeke flips through the yellow pages and finds a private investigator in Prince Georges County. He looks for one close to his Upper Marlboro address so that the guy has no excuse not to come and see him today. He wants to find out what is going on now. Zeke picks one out and makes the call. As the phone rings, Zeke seems to get even more frustrated, Carlos can see it on his face. Carlos asks, "What's wrong now?" Zeke responds, "I can't believe I'm about to spend more money on this ungrateful woman." Carlos says, "Well, it's not too late; hang up the phone and let's go with my idea. Let's just go beat the shit out of him." "No, no, no, this is the best option because I need answers," Zeke tells him.

Someone on the other end of the phone picks up and says "Thank you for calling Monument Investigations, how can I help you?" Zeke says "I'm looking for someone to track my wife and get me information on her actions when she's away from home." The receptionist says "Please hold on and I will put you through to someone that can help you in one second." "Ok thanks," Zeke replies.

The next voice Zeke hears is Mr. Stubbs. He says, "Hello and how can I help you today?" Zeke tells him "I need my wife tracked and watched in an hour or two. Can you please tell me if you can get that done for me? I think she's cheating on me and she's supposed to be going to lunch with the man in question." He further states that "Money is no object here. I just want to make sure you can get it done in the short time frame." Mr. Stubbs asks "Is the place they are meeting local or out of state?" Zeke replies with "They are local for sure. The restaurant is in downtown D.C." Mr. Stubbs explains that he can get it done but he will need a picture of the person he is to follow. Zeke asks him "Can you come to the house and pick up the pictures?" Mr. Stubbs replies with "Sure, I can stop by to get the picture. Can I also ask you to sign a contract for services while I'm there?" Zeke says "Sure you can come and don't worry about the contract I'll just pay you cash when you get here. Just let me know how much it cost and it'll be taken care of in advance. I just need to know what my wife is up to." Mr. Stubbs gets the address to the mini mansion and heads right over. Carlos and Zeke do a couple of shots while they are waiting for Mr. Stubbs to arrive.

Some time passes and as it does Zeke has found two pictures for the investigator. They are recent photos from their trip to Australia. He cannot help but think about the good times that they had while they were there. There is a knock at the door; it is Mr. Stubbs, the private investigator. Zeke answers the door and invites Mr. Stubbs into the house. "Mr. Stubbs I don't know what is going on but I want to find out. Here are two photos of my wife; here is five thousand dollars as well. I hope it'll be enough." Mr. Stubbs replies with "I am sorry. You are paying me way, way more than what I was going to charge." Zeke tells him "Well, take this money and get the job done. If I need you to watch her again, just consider yourself paid already. If not, look at it as one hell of a tip." Mr. Stubbs is not one to look a gift horse in the mouth so he agrees. Mr. Stubbs then tells Zeke "I'll follow her and find out what's going on for you. Don't worry; I'll get to the bottom of this matter for sure." Zeke says "Ok, great, here is my cell number. You can get in contact with me through this anytime of day or night." Mr. Stubbs says "Fantastic, I'll try to have an update to you as soon as lunch is over." And he heads off to the restaurant to set up surveillance on the wife.

LUNCH WITH THE OTHER GUY

The detective goes to the restaurant and sets up surveillance outside. It is a swanky place called Morton's Steak House in downtown Washington, D.C. Since he has been given five thousand in cash, he also has called in for some back up. He has arranged for two people, a man and woman that look like a couple, to go inside and sit next to the wife and her date. Mr. Stubbs has given them both hidden cameras to take pictures of the couple. A little bit before noon, Mr. Stubbs notices the wife's car pull up; however, she does not get out. He figures she is waiting for her date to arrive. A few minutes later a range rover pulls up and the gentleman throws his keys to the valet attendant. He then bounces over to the wife's car and opens her door. As she stands up she gives him an affectionate hug and a long kiss as if she has missed him forever. Mr. Stubbs is in his car getting all of this on video. All he can do is shake his head in disbelief. After he gets her out of the car and they exchange pleasantries, they head into the restaurant. Mr. Stubbs calls his team inside the restaurant and tells them to be on point because the subjects are on their way in. The advance team is inside with cameras ready. The couple, fortunately, sits a table or two away and in full view of the advance team. They quietly snap a few photos without anyone paying too much attention to what they are doing.

Although the advance team can't hear what the couple is saying, they are, however, getting invaluable information. They have watched the couple through lunch and afternoon cocktails. The couple has been holding hands since they came into the restaurant. They have fed each other as they ate their entrees. They are doing everything that couples do, except they are not really a couple. They are even snapping selfies with one another as they sit at the table. After lunch and a drink, he walks he back outside and sits her in her car. He gives her a long loving kiss as he says goodbye to her. He then gives his valet ticket to the attendant. When his car is brought around he leaves with a big smile on his face.

Meanwhile, the detective has gotten photos of his car and his tag number as well. Mr. Stubbs also took the opportunity to place a wireless tracking device inside the bumper of the Range Rover. With this done, he will know through GPS, exactly where the truck goes. Mr. Stubbs heads back to his office after the stakeout to compile and organize the information that he has gathered. After getting the information that he and his team has compiled, he calls Zeke on his cell phone. Zeke sees his phone ringing and does not want to face the truth so he lets it go to voicemail. After he sees a message has been left, he doesn't even listen to it. He just calls Mr. Stubbs back and says, "What did you find?" "Well, Mr. Hill, I would like to stop by your house and show you what I have instead of telling you over the phone," Mr. Stubbs tells him. Zeke agrees and tells the detective "I am home now please stop by when you can." Mr. Stubbs says "I will be there in twenty minutes." While Zeke waits for his arrival he is a nervous wreck. He cannot sit still; all he can do is pace the floor, back and forth. Carlos, who has been called back to the house to hear what the detective has to say, tells Zeke "why don't you just sit down. You pretty much already know what's up so it's not a surprise at this point." Zeke looks at him with anger in his eyes then says "I know, I know but what can I do? I am too nervous, pissed and hurt to sit still. I just want to hear what the guy has to say so I can figure out what I'm going to do next with my life." Carlos tells him, "just calm down and just wait to see what he has to say. You never know, you could be wrong about their meeting. I don't think you were but you could be, I'm just saying."

Mr. Stubbs rings the doorbell and Zeke hurries to answer it. He invites Mr. Stubbs in and escorts him into his office, where Carlos is already waiting. Mr. Stubbs has his laptop and proceeds to open it up. Mr. Stubbs, who has been through this type of thing before in his profession, begins to soften the blow that is ahead. Mr. Stubbs says "well, why don't you sit down so I can show you a few things. I have some video from your wife's lunch appointment. It is just video and you can judge for yourself what's going on. So, if you're ready, I will run the video." Zeke says "just play it already." Mr. Stubbs starts the video, it begins with Taylor pulling up and waiting on her date. As Zeke watches the video, Mr. Stubbs is giving a verbal play-by-play of what is going on. As if Zeke can't see it for himself. He sees the woman he loves so much hug and kiss this man with such passion. As he watches, he gets more and more upset. Surprisingly, he is taking it very good. He is controlling his emotions very well. Mr. Stubbs has also included the still photos that the advance team took while they were inside the restaurant. He sees how this other man is holding his woman's hand. He sees the photos of his wife being romantically fed by another man. As Zeke and Carlos are watching, Carlos is just sitting there speechless while shaking his head in disbelief.

Carlos looks at Zeke and says "So, how do you want me to handle this? Do you want me to go and take care of this problem now?" Zeke says "No, I have to do some thinking. I don't know what to do at this point. But what I do know is that I need more information." Zeke then looks over at Mr. Stubbs and says, "I want you to find out more information. I want to know everything. I want to know everything that is going on, no matter what the cost." Mr. Stubbs says, "Ok, now that I can do. I will put together a team and a plan to find out everything about your wife and her movements." Zeke says, "That's fine but I also want to know everything about him. I want to know why she's chosen this man. I want to know what makes him so fantastic that she feels it is ok to cheat on me." Carlos chimes in with "You know you are crazy, right? Why not just lullaby his ass and keep it moving? Why are you making this so difficult?" Zeke replies with "I have to know why; I thought she loved me. I thought and believed that we were truly best friends. There must be something that is allowing her attention to be turned to him. And I need to know what that is. So, Mr. Stubbs, I need all the information you can get me on this guy. I want his name, address, what he does, what he ate for lunch, what his mother's name is. Do you understand what I am looking for? I want it all and then some. How much will this cost me?" Mr. Stubbs leans up and says, "Well, Mr. Hill you've already paid me five thousand dollars. That should be more than enough for me to take care of everything. I will get you the information that you're requesting." Zeke turns to him and says "Look, I want total secrecy and I want to know everything. On top of that, I want to know everything like yesterday. I need this information as soon as you can get it. So here is what I propose, you go ahead and keep that five thousand to get started. When you come back with the answers to my questions I'll pay you another ten thousand dollars in cash. Look around, money is no object to me, I have everything. Well, everything except my wife's devotion. I need you to do this for me as soon as you can." Mr. Stubbs simply replies with, "Alright Mr. Hill, I'll have some answers for you soon. I promise I'll have more than enough information for you." "That's good," Zeke says. He walks over to the bar in his office and starts to pour another drink. This time he goes for Patron. I guess Zeke needs a stronger drink than he had before. Zeke turns to Carlos and says "can you please escort Mr. Stubbs out to his car? I have some thinking to do." Carlos quickly gets up and walks Mr. Stubbs out to his car. Carlos speaks with Mr. Stubbs as they walk out, "You know that is my man in there. We have been friends for years and I care about him and Taylor. I would have never believed Taylor would have cheated on him, if I didn't see the video with my own eyes. Can you please hurry and get him the information that he's seeking? He doesn't deserve to go through this type of nonsense." Mr. Stubbs just replies with "I understand, I will do my very best as fast as I can." Carlos says "Thank you and thank you for coming today. We really appreciate all of your help." "No problem that's why Mr. Hill is paying me," says Mr. Stubbs. Mr. Stubbs gets into his car and proceeds to drive away.

GET YOUR MIND OFF OF THINGS

So, as Carlos is walking back into the house he realizes he needs to get his man out of the house and get his mind off of things. With that in mind, he starts to text the crew. You know that main circle of friends that are ride or die no matter what. The ones that you have spent time with and have broken bread with. Those friends who don't care what you have or what you don't have for that matter as long as you are you. The ones you can let your hair down with. The ones that you have shared your war stories of women and life with. The ones that you sit around with, get drunk and tell lies to. Those are the friends that I am talking about, your real friends. Carlos just sends out a massive text to the crew that reads 'Guys night out, we need the collective to meet us at Stadium tonight at 9 p.m. Don't be late and bring your cash! Lol'. Carlos laughs as he hits send because he's thinking ahead. He knows that this night will end up being one to remember for sure.

Carlos goes back into the house and tells Zeke that he is taking him out to get his mind off of things. Zeke replies with "I don't want to go and all I want to do is stay here at home and wait for Taylor to get home." "Well you can get back to her later; she's working now anyway. You need to get out of the house and clear your mind. I've already texted the fellas that we are all headed to Stadium tonight and to meet us there at 9:00," Carlos says. Zeke responds with "How can you do that when I am in the middle of so much pain?" Carlos says "What better way for you to get over your pain than with models and bottles?

Don't worry about anything I'll take care of everything, it'll be so much fun." Zeke finally gives in and says "Ok." Carlos is happy about changing his best friends mind. He knows he needs to get out and have some fun at this point. Carlos says, "Well, since we are having a fun day at this point, how about we grab some cash and head up to Maryland Live? I hear that they have table games now. We need to blow off some steam anyway and what better way to do that than throwing away some hard earned cash?" Carlos can't help but laugh at the statement. Zeke replies with, "You know what? That's not a half bad idea. Let me crack the safe and grab a quick twenty thousand. That'll be ten thousand for you and ten thousand for me. All we can't do with that then screw it." Carlos is more than happy to comply. Hey, it was his idea in the first place. And not that he needs it but now Carlos gets to gamble for free today. His best friend is kicking him gambling money and that is always a plus.

The safe gets cracked and a few stacks of hundreds get thrown into a Gucci book bag for easy transport. After the bag is filled, the two men head to the garage to jump into Zeke's everyday driver, his Porsche Panorama. Before they head off to the casino, Zeke wants to let the dog, Chad, out for a quick walk. Carlos asks, "Man, why do you have a dog that's bigger than you are?" as he laughs. "Hey, you know me, I like everything big, plus I had to keep at least one dog from the old days. And this one has been hand fed and raised by Taylor and me. He is our baby so I have to keep him forever," Zeke says. Carlos replies with "Ok, but that damn dog is going to eat you out of house and home." " It is funny you say that, he has already eaten half a couch, Taylor's shoes that she always makes me replace, and scratched a hole in the damn garage door. But he's my kid and that's what kids do, they just mess up things sometimes" Zeke says as he laughs. The dog runs out of the garage and goes and does his business. He trots back in the garage and Zeke tells him, "Cage up." He immediately gets into his cage and sits down waiting for the door to close. Carlos says, "Well, at least you have this monster trained and he listens to you. I'm just glad he knows me, I'm glad I had a hand in raising him as well." Zeke chimes in with "Well, he better listen to me or he's out of here for sure." Carlos adds "I still think you have issues with some of that stuff you train him to do. You really have problems man; you need to see someone for real." Zeke replies "I know you're not talking about problems." As he laughs, he continues with "I got part of that off of one of those Silence of the Lambs movies. I just wanted to see if it would work. And it evidently does." They both break out in laughter and get ready to leave.

As they push out of the garage, Carlos says "You know I have liked this car ever since you picked it up. You need to just let me keep it for a couple of weeks." Zeke says, "Sure, man, knock yourself out. Just make sure you leave your truck at the house when you take it." Carlos says, "Great, that was easier than I thought it was going to be. You're the best and to be nice I'll even bring it back with gas in it." They both just sit there and laugh at that comment. Carlos says, "Hey, look, why don't we stop at Chili's on the way and hit the happy hour special. They have margaritas for, like, two bucks." Zeke looks at him sideways and says I have twenty thousand bucks in the trunk and you want to stop for a two dollar happy hour drink?" Carlos says emphatically "Yes I do. It's not about the money. It's just about us starting this day out right. Plus you ain't got shit else to do, so, why not? Let's just go and see if we can get one or two drinks to get the day started out right." Zeke says "Well, I guess so and you're right, what else do I have to do today? I guess two dollar drinks it is then. You are a wild boy, can't believe I'm hitting a happy hour this early in the afternoon, this is nuts." Carlos just laughs and tells him to hit the one in Greenbelt that's on the way to the casino.

When they arrive at the restaurant they head straight for the bar with no detours. They pull up some chairs and start looking at menus. The bartender comes over and asks them how they are doing and what can she get for them today. Carlos reaches into his pocket and gives her a hundred dollar bill. After she takes it, he says to her, "Bring us four margaritas and whatever food we decide to have and you can keep the rest." She asks "Are you serious? You just gave me a hundred bucks!" Carlos says "Yes, I wanted to pay you in advance to make sure we get outstanding service." The bartender says "Fantastic you'll get the best service of your lives." She puts beverage napkins down for them both and starts making the four margaritas.

Zeke says "You're always talking about me throwing money around. Look at you. I see you're getting your grown man on today." Carlos says "Well, I had to get to your level. We earn all this money and you can't take it with you. So, you might as well have some fun every now and then." "I'm really happy to hear you say that. You are turning over a new leaf I see," Zeke tells him. Carlos says "Well since I'm going to be living in America, I might as well get used to some of the customs and ways of doing things. I must say that I'm enjoying life a bit more since I started spending some of this money."

The waitress comes back with the drinks and takes their orders. They settle in and kick back a few drinks over day-to-day conversation. Carlos says "Well I've told the fellas to link up with us later, everyone is pretty much down. It's early and a couple of the guys were still trying to clear their schedules. I also called your secretary and had her hold all of your calls. I also told her to give you a call about four this afternoon and give you a call back priority list." Zeke replies with "You're always saving my life. Thanks man, I was wondering why this damn phone hasn't been ringing."

"Well that's the reason. You have enough going on right now. So, why did you agree to gambling today? I thought we were going to just hit up Stadium and relax for a bit. I know what it is, that damn Lisa isn't it? Well, I guess with Taylor doing her thing I guess you're free to do what you want. You know you are weak for that Lisa, right?" "There you go," Zeke replies. "That little Korean lady has you open and has had you open for years," Carlos replies to clear up the issue. "Well that doesn't mean I'm weak for her now. When I decided to get married, she pretty much cut me off. She said she was finished wasting time on my dumb ass. We kept in touch for a year or two after I got married but I think it was too much for her to take. We sort of lost contact. We keep in touch mainly through Facebook these days. From the pics I've seen her post she's doing well for herself." Carlos takes a good gulp from his glass and says "Now, you do know and understand she was weak for you as well? You two got on my damn nerves there for a minute," he says laughing as he takes another drink. "I was really surprised when you chose Taylor to marry instead of her." Zeke takes a minute to think to himself and says "Well it was touch and go there for a minute. I didn't know which way I would go either, both of them were fantastic women. But since Taylor was there from the beginning, I had to go in that direction. I think she understood my life better since she was there from day one. It hurt me to have to choose, but I had to in order for all of us to try and have some happiness. It gave me and Taylor a chance to make it. It also gave Lisa the opportunity to find someone that deserved all she had to give, she's a wonderful lady. I just hope if we bump into her, she speaks to me after all of these years."

Carlos sits back and looks at his drink and says "Well, the way you two were, I don't think it'll matter, but who knows. Are you sure you're not setting this thing up? You're pissed at Taylor and, yeah, she hurt you but are you sure if you see Lisa you want to throw it all away for her?" "Ahem" as Zeke clears his throat. "Well, as I see it, Taylor threw it all away. I'm just reacting to what she has begun. I can't be wrong for that." Carlos says "In Colombia, there's an old saying, something about two wrongs don't make it right. Just because she did something wrong, you should too? I know you love Taylor and maybe she just thinks you are doing something and you're really not. Maybe it's all just a big misunderstanding." Zeke says "Misunderstanding? Misunderstanding my ass! If you have a misunderstanding break a car window, pour Clorox on some clothes, shit even break my phone. You don't go get on some dick! These margaritas must be getting to me already." Carlos looks at him as he is picking up the glass again, "Well, it ain't the drinks. I just know you're weak for this woman and you have all the reason to keep it moving at this point, just be careful. I can't protect you from her." Zeke picks up his glass to toast to his man "You are the best Carlos. I'll be fine." Carlos taps glasses with his man and replies "Ok, remember I warned you, that woman really loves you."

Zeke looks at him smiling and says "Let's have some fun." Zeke motions the waitress to come to the table and she scampers over "Miss all drinks on me!" The waitress looks at him crazily, "Are you serious?". Zeke pulls out his American Express Black Card and tells her "I'll pay for all drinks and food for the next hour for everyone in here right now. This will include their present tab as well. Please feel free to tell them and spread the word. I'll take care of the tip for the wait staff as well." The waitress is shocked but is so happy. She goes back to the bar and calls the manager to inform him of what is going on. The manager then comes to the table and says "Excuse me, gentlemen, but I was just informed that you're paying for everyone's tab for the next hour, is that true?" "Yes, sir, that's correct. We have just closed a big real estate deal and we want to share our happiness with others. Call it paying it forward, if you will," Zeke tells him. The manager says "Congratulations to you, but can I ask you if I can run your card and reserve maybe five thousand dollars to cover what is sure to be a large bill?" Zeke just smiles and says "Do what you need to do, sir, we understand. As a matter of fact I'll pay for your lunch as well. You can even order something if you like." The manager replies with "That's ok. I'm fine and my staff and patrons thank you for all of your kindness today." "You're very welcome and let me know if you have any problems," Zeke tells him. The manager walks away to the cash register, he then runs the card for five thousand dollars. The transaction comes back as clean and valid. The manager then informs the bartender and wait staff that they can make announcements to the patrons. You can all of a sudden here chatter and high fives are being seen. The wait staff begin to come back to the table with thanks from the rest of the restaurant.

After about an hour or so of back and forth chitter chatter the two decide it's time to get to moving to the casino. The margaritas have set in for sure because now they are cracking jokes about a whole bunch of nothing and everything seems to be funny. Carlos asks the bartender for the final bill. She comes back over and hands him a long receipt of charges. She then tells him that once it was clear that he was paying for everything, seems like everyone started ordering a bit more food and drinks. "Here is your bill, sir, it is not quite five thousand but it is pretty close." The bill comes up to forty one hundred bucks. "Wow," Carlos says as he looks at Zeke. "You just had to come in here didn't you? Your happy hour margaritas add up quick. I think I'm going to just give the rest as a tip to the staff. They can split it up amongst themselves. What do you think?" he asks Carlos. Carlos, feeling kind of good from the drinks just laughs and says "Well, if you think they should have a good tip then, by all means, give it to them. I'm having a good day!" They finish settling up and head out to the car. Both of them have smiles on their faces. All Carlos can think is that his plan is working and that his friend and brother has forgotten his problems, if only for a little while.

KOREAN QUEEN

Zeke and Carlos have jumped back in the ride. There is just a short ride up the parkway to get to Maryland Live, the casino of choice lately. As they ease into traffic a conversation starts up. Carlos asks, "So, are you going to see her? You know you want to. No matter what I say, I know you are going to see her aren't you? What do you think she is going to say? She is probably going to slap the shit out of you." As he laughs, Zeke says, "hold up, hold up, if you give me a chance to talk, I can answer some of these questions. First, ain't nobody slapping nobody. We are friends and will always be. The fact that I will probably always love her has nothing to do with anything." Carlos just looks at him and grinning and says "You know she is probably the top pit boss or something by now. You know she has met a few ballers by now. You still think she wants you?" "Well, for us it was never really about the money. Well, she did have this thing for four thousand dollar purses but that is a whole other topic. She always had her own cash, she still spent mine but at least she had her own. She was a really good girl, she was cool. I liked her hanging around the house and her cooking was the best. I mean it was the little things, at my house on football Sunday with her awful Redskins jersey on with the little daisy duke shorts. Shit you liked that part your damn self, Carlos," as he laughs. "I mean we were just good together. When she would do her hair that would be a two hour or more adventure. But I didn't mind, it was fun for me to just sit back and watch her while she did it. I would read the paper to kill time anyway. She would be on the phone yacking to those girlfriends and texting. I always told her that if she would turn off her damn phone while she did her hair, she would be able to do it in half the time. But it is what she enjoyed doing so who am I to stop that. But, anyway, she is always going to be my baby no matter who she is with." "I see you are real confident in yourself. I just hope she don't just slap you just for the hell of doing it," Carlos chuckles as they arrive at Casino.

"So do you want to valet today or just park and walk?" Carlos asks. Zeke replies with "Well, let's park since we got the cash with us. I don't feel like any nonsense today." "Ok, cool, that works for me. I'll hit level three so we can come out right on the slots floor." The car heads up to parking level three. They park and get out. Zeke throws the Gucci backpack on and they head inside. From the instant they walk in, Carlos can tell Zeke has an eye open for Lisa. They head over to the slot machines just to have some quick fun and get warmed up. They start to play for a while but Carlos can tell Zeke is distracted and not really having fun.

"Why don't you call her and tell her that you're here? She would probably be madder if she found out you came up here and didn't at least reach out to her," Carlos says. "Well, maybe you are right. How about I just text her and say hello. If she responds I will let her know where I am. If she is on the floor right now she would not be able to answer the phone anyway." He pulls out his phone and drops her a quick text. Carlos chimes in with, "Well, I think that's a great idea. So, at least if she's not here, you can stop looking like a lost puppy," he says laughing. "Go straight to hell, Carlos, straight to fucking hell. You and your damn jokes," Zeke replies.

A few minutes pass by and then buzz buzz there is the text he has been waiting for. 'Hello and how are you?' the text reads. Zeke quickly types in a response 'Hello there sweetie, I know you're probably very busy but I wanted you to know Carlos and I are in your establishment. And if you get some time, can I see you for a moment or two?' Zeke quickly hits send and patiently waits for a response. When the reply does not come right away he looks at Carlos and asks, "Oh hell, do you think I did the wrong thing by contacting her?" "No way, good or bad you did the right thing by telling her you're here. I wonder if you have the nuts to tell her you still love her too," Carlos adds. "Well, she knows that will always be the case. Plus, she is not the type to be single forever; she probably has a man. Shit, she is so thorough she probably has a man and a dude on the side". They both just break out laughing. "Well, all jokes aside, a woman likes to hear that you love her more than anything else. You know, reassurance and you ain't been around to reassure anything since you married Taylor. So now what are you going to do? The way I see it, Taylor is doing her thing so you might as well have fun too. But because of who Lisa is, you better come clean and tell her what the deal is up front." "Wait a minute, who made you the love doctor? Who told you that you was Dr. Phil?" Zeke says as he laughs. Carlos replies while laughing too, "Well, hey, I am irresistible to the ladies you know." They both really get a good chuckle off of that one.

All of a sudden it comes, she finally replies. The text reads 'meet me at Bobby Flay's restaurant in thirty minutes. I have already reserved a table for you and Carlos. I can't wait to see him!'. "Ok so how am I supposed to take this? She says meet her at the restaurant in thirty minutes and we have a table reserved. But, wait, get this, she says that 'she can't wait' to see you. Well, damn what about me?" Carlos just smiles and says "I just told you I am irresistible to women." "Man, whatever," Zeke replies. At that point they just relax and kill some time playing slots until it's time to meet Lisa at the restaurant.

The two buddies make their way to Bobby Flay's spot. When they arrive they are greeted by the wait staff as if they know who they are "Hello and welcome to Bobby Flay's. We have your table ready for you. There is an open bottle of wine already breathing for you as well. The rest of your party will arrive shortly," the hostess says. Carlos and Zeke just look at each other as they sit down. Thank you comes from both of their mouths. Zeke with a smile on his face says, "I guess my baby has made it. She is doing big things now, and the wine is great." "Yes, seems like she's all grown up now and doing very well for herself. And how did the hostess know us? She never even said our name. I hope we're sitting in the right place. If she has set this up from two text messages I'm impressed," Carlos says. "Man, who are you telling? I'm impressed by this one my damn self," Zeke replies.

Across the room they both see her at the same time. She is walking in with two large gentlemen. She is the type of woman that is really hard to miss. She gracefully walks across the room. You can't miss the fact that she is looking oh so stunning. Long silky black hair all curled up flowing all the way down her back. Fantastic business suit with a skirt so short you can damn near catch a glimpse of her vajayjay. Just to make the look complete she has those damn red bottoms on deck, giving those calves that extra pop. She knows I have a thing for those damn shoes. Carlos looks over at Zeke and tells him, "Look, man, close your mouth and boy are you in trouble now. You got your hands full buddy."

She strides up to our table and says "Hello guys and Carlos come and give me a big ol' hug, I miss you so much." Carlos gets up to give her a big old bear hug. "And you, Mr. Hill, are you going to give an old friend a hug?" as she looks at Zeke. All Zeke can do at this point is smile from ear to ear and get up. He reaches out to hug her as if he has not seen her in years. That is because he hasn't. He has been distant since he has gotten married. He has been faithful to his wife. They embrace and just hold one another for a second or two. Zeke can see the two men that are with her looking at him strangely. Zeke says while still holding her and looking at these two middle linebackers behind her, "Baby, I miss you but can you please tell these two nice gentlemen to stop looking at me like this please." "Oh, sure, I am sorry. Zeke this is Edward and Steven. Edward and Steven this is Zeke. We are all friends here; Edward and Steven are my floor security protection detail. They make sure I'm safe and sound. You're not the only one who can walk around with security Mr. Hill," she says with a smile.

"What brings you guys out this way today? I hope you came to gamble," she adds. "Well, we're here to blow off some steam and have some fun for a little while. We have an appointment in D.C. later and just wanted to unwind for a bit first. But how have you been, dear?" Zeke asks. "Well, hold on, Edward and Steven, can you please take a seat over there and wait for me? Thanks. Well, guys I've been great just trying to work my way up in the company and not have to do it on my back, if you know what I mean. I refuse to take part in any of that nonsense. I demand and attain respect but I have earned it. I'm doing pretty well just trying to keep busy, you know. As you can see, I have a lot of responsibility now. I am in charge of the floor pit bosses and I also oversee our whale team. " Carlos asks "Whale team, what's that?" "Oh, sure, our whale team staff members are responsible for the care and support of our high rollers who come into town. Being this close to BWI, we have folks who fly in from all over the world and we have to cater to them. So, in short, we have a staff that does nothing but deal with the super rich and I supervise those fantastic people." Zeke slides in the comment of "Well, now, my baby girl has really grown up. I am so proud of you!" "Thank you daddy, I'm trying," she says as to flash back to the old days. "See, with a comment like that I'm out. I'm going to give you two a minute. I'm going to be over here at the penny slots. Let me know when you're ready to hit the craps table." Carlos gets up and walks towards the penny slots that are just outside of the restaurant. He sits at what he thinks is a good machine and places a quick hundred dollar bill into it and starts to play.

Meanwhile, back at the table Zeke picks up the bottle of wine and tries to poor some into her glass. She stops him by placing her manicured hand over the top of her glass. "See, you're trying to get me all messed up and I have to work. How have you been? And how is the software development business?" Lisa asks him inquisitively. "Well, things are great. It was rough for a minute but even in our worst year we still cleared maybe five million. But, if nothing else, it's fun and I enjoy trying to venture into new directions. So, who are you seeing these days? I don't see any rings on those fingers and I haven't seen you post any couple pictures on Facebook. So, what gives, how is your love life?" Zeke asks as he looks at her for an answer. She laughs as she inhales to give an answer. His question has her laughing so hard she has to cough a little bit. "Aaahhh excuse me, someone is being a little nosey aren't they? I mean you just show up and I am supposed to just tell you what I have going on? You are too funny. Where is your wife? Where is Taylor? Is she here with you today?" "No she is not here with me today. She is probably out with her new man," he says. "New man, what new man, and what happened to her old man, meaning you?" asks Lisa. "Well, her old man recently found out that her new man has been tapping that ass. So, the old man doesn't know exactly where he stands right now" Zeke tells her with sarcasm in his voice. "Damn, baby, as much as I want you myself, I don't want to see you hurt to have you. I'm sorry that she did this to you. Are you sure that there is really something going on? Maybe it is some type of misunderstanding." Zeke just takes a deep breath and says "No, I am sure she is up to something. Exactly what, I'm not sure. But it is what it is."

"Zeke," Lisa says "I know you and I know how you are. Don't do anything crazy to her or him. Do you hear me? You have a great life now and it is really peaceful and quiet. You and Carlos are playing golf all the time. You are hanging out with friends at pool halls. You know really peaceful, quiet and most importantly, a regular life now. Don't let this drag you down. Don't do anything stupid again; I know how you can get." "Well, for now, I just want to try and breathe and figure out what is what. Just figure out where things went wrong, et cetera. And you here looking all dynamite, you know I want you Lisa. If I had...," he says. "Oh shut up!" she says. She continues with "There is nothing wrong with the decision you made. You made what you thought, was the best decision for you. I gave you ample time to figure out what you wanted and then you chose her. Remember I was at your wedding, the hardest day in the world for me but I was there. I was there for you, just like I am going to be there for you now. Don't get it twisted, you can't have any of these cookies but I am here for you. You are my friend first and foremost and I will always love you. Do you need the keys to my place?"

Zeke just looks at her in amazement and says "And to think, some people wonder why I am sprung for you? See you are a true friend. I am going through this nonsense but you are here for me. You are again putting your feelings aside for me. I will never forget that. Thank you, but I don't need a place to crash. I will be fine as far as that goes. I would like some of you however. Did you know I was coming, why are you looking so damn tasty today?" Zeke asks her. Lisa, now blushing but still full of confidence in her game says, "Zeke, look, I am always looking good and no you can't have any. You should know how much I spend on clothes because you hated shopping with me," she says laughing. "You always wanted to either stay at home or in the food court and have me come and get you when I was ready to leave." Zeke says "Correction. I would sit in the food court and hold all the bags that you had acquired as we were walking. Someone had to stay put, I was just tired of carrying all those shopping bags as you went from store to store. So, I was being supportive and, yes, I do know and understand that you have a shopping problem." Lisa just laughs as she grabs his hand a little tighter.

Lisa then says "Well, when you figure out what you want and what you want to do with your life, get in touch. I might entertain your advances and then again I might not. I don't want you running back and forth between me and her. Been there, done that, and got the stinking T Shirt. I don't want to go through that again ever." "Well, how about just a good night together until I can figure things out," Zeke asks. She replies with "HELL NO, I don't want to get wrapped up in all the drama just because you are feeling a little lonely. I don't feel like going through all of that right now. Like I said before, figure out what you are going to do with Taylor and get back to me." Zeke looks at her and says "Damn it, woman! Why are you being so difficult?" he says laughing.

"Well, how about a bet then? If I win, you spend time with me. If you win, then I don't." Lisa rubs her chin and thinks for a minute. Then she replies with "There is nothing in it for me, seems like it is a win win for you. What do I get out of it besides a possible roll in the hay with you?" as she laughs. She has caught Zeke off guard with that one. He thinks fast on his feet and comes up with a response that may or may not help him. Zeke says "Well, how about we put some money on it. I know you are down for that." Lisa says, "Wow you are serious. I know how you are about just giving your money away. So, ok, I will take your bet but with conditions." Zeke asks, "And what are the conditions can I ask?" "Sure, you can ask. Well, I want you to pick a table, any game of your choice and put some money down as a bet. If you win, you donate your winnings to a charity of my choice. If you win, you also get to come to my house for a Korean massage. I am sure you remember those and I am sure you will not turn down my offer. It will have to be tomorrow because as you can see I am working today."

Zeke quickly replies with "Yes, I remember and, yes, I will take the bet. Carlos has all the cash and when can we make this happen? AAhhh by the way, how much do I have to put down as a bet?" Lisa just looks at him as she grabs his chin to speak directly to him. She whispers and says "Sweetie, the more you put down, the better the massage will be, but you still have to win first." Zeke's eyes brighten up and he finishes his glass of wine. He responds with "Let's go to the tables now. Let's make it happen. Let's have some fun today. Where is Carlos? He has my bag. How about something simple like rou-lette? If I bet on red or black and win, I get them cookies. And if I lose I don't. Now, if I win, your charity gets proceeds, is that correct?" "Yes, that is correct. But you have not heard all the conditions," Lisa says. "Wait there's more?" he says. "Yes, just one more little wrinkle. Now, if you lose, you take yourself home, after some fun of course, and think about what you did wrong to put her in this position. Try to take some time and think about things from the woman's point-of-view. Most women do not arbitrarily just go out and cheat. Something usually pushes them to do it. I also want you to think about if you really want to be with her. Figure out if one seemingly innocent affair is worth you letting your wife go forever. You married her and you love her. Do you re-ally want to throw all of that away? One more thing you need to do. She was able to get you away from me one time because of your history together and I can respect that. But this time with her making her little mistake if you and I get all intertwined again, I will not be so kind twice. I will fight for you until the end. So, just think about all those things if you lose. Are you accepting of all of my conditions?" she asks while looking at him deeply in his eyes.

"Yes, I am willing to accept your conditions. I can tell you are a true friend. You laid it all out on the line. On the way here, I was worried that you may have found someone else and the possibility of even seeing you today would be remote at best. I am glad all of my fears have been put to rest. I will win this bet and tomorrow will be a fabulous day for sure. Now, where is that damn Carlos? He has some cash on him, we can gamble with that. Can I still use my card and get rated for this crazy bet?" he asks. They both get up and head towards the penny slots to find Carlos. "Sure, you can use your card to get rated," she laughs. "We want you to receive all of the special benefits you deserve for being an active player here at Maryland Live," Lisa says jokingly. She then gestures for her security team to fall in behind herself and Zeke.

"There is Carlos now," Zeke says as he heads towards his friend. "Carlos, come on, we have to head over to the roulette tables. I have a bet going on with Lisa." Carlos replies with "But I am up three hundred bucks on the penny slots, no one walks away from that." "Man, just cash out. We can come back. I have a bet with Lisa and it needs to happen before she changes her mind," Zeke says.

"Oh Lord, what have you done now? Are you about to lose your shirt again? What are you two betting on?" he asks as he grabs his cash out voucher. "Well, I will give you the details later but long story short if I win, I get to go to her house and if I lose I don't get jack shit." They both look at each other and just burst into laughter. "And you took this bet? I told you that you were weak for her. This more than proves it; your nose is still open for her." Carlos laughs and then adds "No offense, Lisa, you know I love you. The boy just has no backbone when it comes to you. You two are too damn funny to me." Lisa says, "Well, it's ok. I love you too, Carlos, and I can't figure us out my damn self. I gave up trying to figure it out years ago," she laughs.

They all end up at one of the roulette wheels. Lisa motions to one of her roulette pit bosses and informs them that Zeke is one of her whales and that he is clear for any bet he would like to make. The pit boss knows with that said, the casino will cover any and all of his bets. Meanwhile, Zeke fills in Carlos about the details of the bet. After, Carlos finds out the details, all he can do is shake his head as he has a big grin on his face. He then tells Zeke, "It is your money and you can do what you want with it." They talk amongst themselves for a minute. Zeke then says, "Ok let me get ten thousand out of the bag. That should be enough for one hell of a massage. Ok I want to put ten thousand on black," and he drops the money on to the table. The dealer counts the money and then recognizes the bet. The wheel is then spun. Anticipation runs high amongst all the players because of the amount of the bet. Carlos is just shaking his head the whole time as the ball just spins around and around. Lisa has a lock of her hair in between her fingers twisting it, as she smiles at Zeke. Then there it is, the ball drops and bounces once, bounces twice, it lands on red. A big sigh comes out from everyone. Lisa says, "I'm sorry, honey, but no go. What I want you to do is call me when you're ready and you're sure that you and Taylor are done. I will not let you go again." She reaches over and gives him a soft passionate kiss on the lips. Turns and gives Carlos another big hug and tells them she has to get back to work. She struts off with her security in tow. All Zeke can see is legs and red bottoms as she sashays away.

Carlos turns to Zeke and asks, "So, now what? You done gave away half the cash? I can't believe you let her work you like that. Your just soft, the shit is just sad, Jefe`! Do you want to keep gambling or roll out?" Zeke thinks about it and says, "Well, since we are here, we might as well hit the craps table and see what we can do. We can head back to the city after that. How does that sound for a plan?" "Ok, we can do that but I have scheduled dinner for later just to let you know," Carlos replies. "Ok that's cool with me. I need a couple of hard fours in my life right now. Let's do it," Zeke says.

The two of them head over to the craps tables and just sit back and have fun. Zeke promises Carlos again that they will head back to the penny slots before heading back to D.C. Zeke decides to restrain from anymore crazy bets like he had with Lisa. He stretches out the last ten thousand or so dollars he has left. As the day progresses, Carlos, and Zeke have managed to reclaim five or six thousand dollars of the original ten thousand that he lost in the bet with Lisa. Carlos begins to look at his watch a few times and Zeke catches wind of it and inquires "So, why do you keep looking at that watch? Do you have some-where to go?" Carlos answers his question with, "I told you earlier that I had dinner planned for us and reservations have been made. I just don't want to be late. You know how I get when I am hungry." Zeke quickly says "Oh, yes I do. We can't have you hungry now can we. That just won't do, that won't do at all." As they both just laugh and Carlos rubs his gut.

DINNER PLANS GONE WILD

The two of them jump back in the whip and Carlos heads back towards D.C. Carlos tunes the radio to one of his Colombian stations from back home via satellite radio. The two of them start to chat as they head down Baltimore Washington Parkway. Zeke looks over at Carlos as he is feeling the effects of those last two drinks. He asks him "So, what do you have in mind for dinner? I have had a few drinks and I need to eat. I hope it is something good. Are we doing Colombian with, maybe, some empanadas, chunchullo, with, maybe, some sancocho? I know you have something up your sleeve because you've been looking at your watch and you never do that. It's usually me who keeps an eye on the time. So, what gives, spill it man?" Carlos just looks at him laughing and hits him with the standard "I don't know what you're talking about. We're going to eat very well, I can tell you that. If you really want to know what is on the menu I can tell you that it is American food today, for the most part anyway. There may be an international side dish or two on the menu for sure. I need to call Blanca and check in. You are not going to get me in trouble out here running the streets with you," as he laughs.

"Man, go ahead and call your wife, I know you have to handle your business. You know I respect your marriage," Zeke says. Carlos gets to digging and reaching for his phone. He finally finds it and starts to call Blanca, there is a ring or two and then "Hola, Poppi, how are you?" she asks. "I'm fine," he says. And then he continues with, "So, how are things on your end?" He is trying to speak in code and Blanca figures that out. She then decides that it is safe for her to just talk. She says "If he is there with you now just clear your throat." There is a pause and, then, Carlos coughs to clear his throat.

"Ok, Poppi, everything has been taken care of just like you wanted. I even added a few touches of my own. I am not going to be there myself, though. I know you guys need your man time. However, I have sent down my friends Rosa, Sandra, and a few others to make sure it is a professional environment. You better be glad I love you. I gave the manager your black card number and thirty thousand dollars has been deposited. I have called the caterer and although it was kind of last minute, they are going to do it for you. I made the order to feed twenty people. I didn't know how many people could fit in the VIP room and I didn't know how many people you told," she says. "Baby, you're the best. What is the name of the caterer again?" Carlos asks. "The name of the caterer is Ridgewells and don't worry, I picked a great menu for you. I am sure you will enjoy it.

Let me see, what else? Oh, yes, I also was able to get in contact with all of the people on the list and explain the circumstances. All have agreed to attend the dinner. One person said that they will be a bit late because of a previous engagement. I've also hired the security team that we always use just as a buffer for the evening. The manager has been informed of this as well and will comply fully." "Damn baby, you're on the ball today. I knew I had a winner from the moment I saw you," Carlos says. "Well, Zeke is like a brother to me, more than that really because if it were not for him, I would not have met you. So, I'm just trying to be there for him like you are, honey. You are not the only one that loves him," Blanca says confidently.

"Well, thank you baby, that means the world to me. And thank you for taking care of everything for me; I owe you big time. Things like this remind me why I love you," Carlos adds. Blanca is quick to reply with "Well, baby, I love you and that is that. There is no changing it, so whatever you need I will get done for you." "I love you, baby, you are so good to me," Carlos adds. Blanca replies with a loving, "I love you too, oh, and Carlos…" "Yes baby?" he says with a boyish grin on his face. She says "…don't let these bitches get you into any trouble. You better put a sock on the pickle if it comes to that!" "Baby,

I got you! No problem," he assures her. "Alright and I mean it too. That goes for your little friend next to you too," Blanca says with a stern voice. "Alright, baby, I got it, you won't have any problems out of me. Like I said before, I owe you big time, anything you want and it is yours. I am going to get off the phone now and thank you again my sweet." He hangs up the phone and looks at Zeke smiling. "She is the best woman ever! Damn, I love that girl," Carlos says with enthusiasm. "Alright she is the best ever but did she say what is for dinner? Come on, man, I'm hungry," Zeke says. "Oh calm down already you'll be fine, we pasted Greenbelt a little while ago and we are almost there," Carlos says.

Carlos is steadily driving. He comes down BW Parkway and takes a right onto Route 50 West / New York Ave exit towards D.C. When he ends up on New York Avenue, Zeke just looks at him and asks "Man, where are we going? You have passed twenty restaurants by now and all I want to do is eat at this point." "Calm down already, we're almost there. Trust me, you will thank me later," Carlos says to him. Carlos then makes a right off of New York Ave, then a quick left and there it is, The Stadium Club. The Stadium Club is a dream of a gentlemen's club. Zeke just laughs and says, "This is where you are bringing me for dinner? I mean, this is cool and all but I was all set for some Colombian. I didn't know what you had up your sleeve. But the food here is great". Carlos says, "Yes it is, but this is it with a special twist, you will thank me later. Speaking of thanking later, make sure you thank Blanca for helping me out. I could not have done it without her." "You know what? I will do that, I will do that for sure," Zeke says.

They pull up to valet and get out. Carlos tells the valet to put the car in the fenced back lot and he will come and get it tomorrow. He tells the valet to see the manager if he has any questions. The two of them walk in and head directly for VIP.

Carlos has put together a nice get together in just a short period of time. Carlos tells Zeke "I have spoken to JR and everything is all set up for dinner." JR is the owner of Stadium Club.

As they walk into VIP, Zeke can see his whole crew there. He can tell Carlos has put in some work to help him get his mind off of things. All of the fellas start dapping each other up and exchanging nonsense jokes as men do.

As the fellas are shooting the shit, one of the ladies comes in running while blowing a whistle. She now has everyone's attention for sure. She announces that a special dinner has been prepared by the chef and if we will all take our seats, dinner can be served. The guys start to take seats and get relaxed for a good evening with the guys.

All of sudden, the lights go out and music starts playing. The song is some old school wild house music. Zeke can tell someone has been digging in the crates. There is a line of four men dressed in tuxedos. The fellas can see them carrying something but it is in the distance. As the men come closer to the table, they finally get a glimpse of what is being carried. They are carrying a gorgeous woman from some part of Arabia. She is completely naked with assorted foods spread out on top of her body. The gentlemen gently lower her onto the table and the whistle girl returns. She blows the whistle again and the four men in tuxedo's leave in unison.

The whistle girl then takes a breath and starts to talk, "Hi my name is Seduction and I want to welcome you guys to Stadium! You are about to embark on the best night of your lives. We have an entire list of activities planned for your dinner this evening and Aisha here will just be the beginning. She is a lovely woman that hails from Cairo. Assembled on her body you will find assortments of fruits and sushi. This course is designed to wet your appetites and get you ready for an exciting evening. Also, please feel free to lick any of her juices that you desire, she will not bite you back unless you ask her to," Seduction says laughing. All of the guys begin to take samples off of Aisha's beautiful body.

About five minutes or so go by and Seduction then blows that darn whistle again and four women run in with sparklers burning in one hand and a chilled bottle of Ace of Spades in the other. Did I mention that all four women have on G strings and pasties to cover their nipples? They pour all of the fellas a glass of champagne and after they are done, they place the bottles into ice buckets as they scamper off. The fellas continue to enjoy picking the appetizers off of the naked woman. All the while they are sharing smiles and laughter. Some time passes and as the last of the appetizers are eaten off of Aisha's incredible body.

Seduction starts to blow that damn whistle again and the four ladies come running back in again. This time, they come to the table and assist Aisha off of the table. They take her and stand her next to Zeke who is sitting at the head of the table. Zeke just looks over at Carlos and smiles. Even though she is naked, the ladies then maneuver her in a way to expose all of her directly to Zeke. Then all of a sudden, Seduction blows that darn whistle again. The guys in tuxedoes come running back out with buckets of water and they soak her down from head to toe and run back off into the shadows. The ladies who picked her up off the table start to towel off every inch of her very seductively. All of the fellas are now giving high fives and cat calls.

As she is now dry Seduction blows that damn whistle again, here the guys come running back with bottles of some sort. The bottles are handed to the ladies and they run back off again. The ladies surround Aisha and they start to pour the liquid that is in the bottles onto her. Turns out the bottles contain some type of baby oil. Aisha is then sexually massaged by the four women and the guys are going nuts. Carlos is getting thanks for the invite from all angles of the table. Aisha, who has not said a word since her arrival in the room is now oiled up from head to toe. She turns to Zeke and tells him, "I am yours this evening and anything that you wish of me I will be happy to fulfill." All Zeke can do at this point is just sit there for a moment. He turns to Aisha and says "Ok, since you will do anything for me, can you do a five way kiss with the rest of the oil up team of ladies?" She replies with "Well, yes I can, we are all here for you. Anything that you wish of any of us we will be happy to provide." She gestures to the ladies and they all converge into a circle. They start the wildest five way kiss I have ever encountered. After they are done, Aisha turns back to Zeke and asks, "Is there anything else I can do for your pleasure?" She reaches for and grabs his hand as she is asking him the question. Before he can get an answer out, she shoves his hand into her soaking wet kitty kat. Zeke, Carlos, and the rest of the fellas are all stunned as they watch the scene unfold.

Jose, one of the guests screams out "This is the best dinner I have ever had!" Carlos chimes in with, "I think we are all in agreement you on that one." The fellas are very happy that they came to the get together for Zeke. Zeke then instructs Aisha to find a chair and sit by his side for the rest of the evening.

He also instructs Aisha to pick one or more of the ladies to eat or fondle with her kitty kat. He also tells her that this must go on for the rest of the evening without a break. So, if she wants to rotate the girls out, that is fine with him. Zeke tells her to relax and get comfortable because it will be a long night. She naturally complies with his demands.

Then, out of nowhere, that darn whistle blows again. All the fellas are looking around like, what does Miss Seduction have in store for us now. All of a sudden, a complete roasted pig laid out on a tray is carried into the VIP for service. Seduction says "I want you guys to eat up and enjoy. We also have a great variety of sides." She blows that whistle again and servers come running out with sides already placed on plates. They gently place a plate in front of each person at dinner. Then the chef meticulously cuts the pig into serving parts. All the guys start to dig in and enjoy. Some time passes as everyone is getting close to finishing. Seduction again blows that whistle, servers come running out to collect plates and used glasses, et cetera. After that small phase is complete, she orders the servers out.

After the servers leave she asks, "Ok, guys, are you ready to get this party started?" The natural reply and look from Zeke and everyone else is a, "Isn't it started all ready?" Seduction just laughs and says, "Ok, I hope you guys are ready!" She says it with enthusiasm as she again blows the whistle. This time, in comes running three female little people dressed in bikini bottoms only. They have trays full of shots already made and deliver each man there three shots. When every man has three shots, the little strippers inform the guys that they must toast to a great evening and drink all three shots back to back. But, before they can drink them, the ladies light them on fire. All the guys proceed to stand up like knights at the round table. They all give toasts back and forth and start to drink them down back to back. The little strippers then collect the shot glasses and run off to the back.

Then, here goes Seduction again with that damn whistle. This time the tuxedo guys come back. They deliver hookahs to every man. They are already lit and smoke is coming from them. Funny thing is, that they have all been filled with some fantastic smelling exotic loud. The guys just pick up the pipes and go to work. None of them need any instruction on how to use them.

Seduction then says over the crowd noise, "Ok, fellas, here comes all of your desires gift wrapped for you." Arabian music starts to play as seven or eight belly dancers with little to nothing on enter the room. All of ladies are of Arab decent, like, they are fresh off a plane from Abu Dhabi. These ladies are so skilled that all of the guys are mesmerized by the movement of their bodies. The belly dancers start to strip as they dance. That is only making it worse for the fellas. They are uncovering soft succulent skin all with no tattoos and no scars. Someone has taken the time to choreograph their moves. They are all moving in unison and taking clothes off in exact unison as well. None of the guys have seen anything like this before. It is one thing to watch a belly dancer; it is a whole other party to have them giving you lap dances and bouncing on tables.

More high fives are given and even more money is thrown as one of the ladies gets up on the table. She is handed an Egyptian sword of some type. She continues to dance as she places the sword on top her head. She moves ever so gracefully and fluidly all while balancing the sword on her head. She seems to move like a cobra moving to music. As she moves, making it rain is not the ideal term you would think of, more like make it hurricane or even typhoon.

Seduction again blows that damn whistle, the dancers run out and the lights go down. There is a few moments of silence as everyone is waiting to see what is next. Some type of music starts to play and the lights come up. The lighting has changed for the room. Now, everything is a rich and dark deep red. Smoke machines start to fill the room with a grey mist. Out of the shadows, a veiled covered woman starts to dance sensually. As she moves ever so gracefully to the center stage, another red light highlights another veiled covered woman from another corner. She begins her dance on the way to the center stage. When she is half way to the stage, another red light comes on in an opposite corner, bringing to life yet another veiled dancer moving her body to the engaging music.

All three of the dancers make their way to center stage, dancing seductively as if all three of their bodies are as one. Their hands are floating over each other's body touching in various places. Nipples are being gently caressed as asses are being grabbed firmly. As they dance together, one of the ladies pulls her veil off. She reveals the sexiest black woman that most of us have seen. She is of the international super model type, if you get what I am saying. Then as the men are just getting comfortable with her beauty, a second woman unveils herself. Low and behold, she is the twin of the first woman. You can start to hear the cat calls and the guys in background with "Hey, that's alright, twins." All three of the women continue to dance with one another. Then slowly and gracefully the third woman unveils herself. The third woman has revealed the third sister. Yes they are identical triplets in front of the crew. Money, again, starts to be thrown at center stage.

The triplets throw caution to the wind and start a three way kiss that sends the group into frenzy. I am not sure where the oil came from, but somehow, all three women ended up all oiled up and freaking one another. They, basically, were having a threesome in front of us. Carlos looks at Jose and says "I need to take notes. These ladies are teaching me how to eat pussy for real." Jose replies with "Yeah, I know what you mean; I don't think I brought enough money." They both break out laughing over that one. Jose continues with "I love the triplets having sex. This is like an all-out porno we are getting to watch. Plus, this is better than any porno, it is live!" Carlos says "I know I am enjoying it and I figure Zeke's mind is off of things. Looks like the triplets have pulled him up on stage. Jose, look at him now." Jose turns around and shakes his head knowing things have gotten out of control at this point.

Seduction is lurking around and there it goes again, that damn whistle. In comes every woman that has come through that evening, including a new set of five ladies never seen before. All of them are now dressed in some skimpy outfit. Seduction comes on the microphone and announces "This is now a closed door session. What that means, gentlemen, is that anything goes. I will close these doors behind me and I will open them again in two hours. If you need drinks, food or anything else please go to that small window in the back and your needs will be fulfilled. What happens in this closed door session stays in this session. I want you to enjoy yourselves and I will be back in a couple of hours." She exits the room and the door is locked behind her. The triplets continue to basically rape Zeke on the middle of the stage. He was so engaged he heard nothing about a closed door session. He is good and drunk at this point anyway.

A couple of hours go by and Seduction opens up the doors. She finds what she finds, a bunch of happy customers that have had the night of their lives. She gets on the microphone and announces "I want to thank you gentlemen for coming out and partying with us this evening. We hope you have enjoyed yourselves and will come out and enjoy our establishment again. We had each of you park in the gated parking in the rear upon your arrival so that we can provide you limousine service on the way home. You can come and retrieve your vehicles tomorrow. They will be safe here, of course. So, when you are ready, please exit out of the side door to your awaiting transportation. And remember, please come again."

After that, the guys try to get themselves together to leave. Carlos looks over at Zeke and he is slumped over in a chair. He even has two or three sets of panties either on his head or around his neck. Carlos is sure he had a blast this evening. Carlos gestures for Jose to come over to help him with Zeke. They both get an arm and they hoist him out the chair to take him to the side door. When they walk out into the fresh air Zeke starts to mumble something but no one can understand what he is saying. The door to the limo is held open by one of the guys as Zeke is, basically, poured into the back seat. After the limousines are loaded, Jose has the team head to Zeke's house to drop him off.

Jose looks over at Carlos and asks "So, what are we going to do with him? Do you want to take him upstairs into the bedroom or just throw him on the couch?" Carlos, drunk as hell himself, comes up with "How about we leave him in the garage? I know the code to get the door open. That way we won't wake up his wife and get all of us in trouble. What do you think?" "That's a great idea. We can put him in there and when he is ready, he can take himself inside," Jose replies. It is funny how the best laid drunk plans seem to be the most ingenious, but in actuality, they are crazy as hell.

About twenty minutes pass and the limos pull up outside of Zeke's house. All of the fellas jump out and act like they are helping him into the house. Someone goes and takes a piss on the neighbors bush. Zeke puts in the code on the outside of the garage and the door slides open. Jose and one of the other fellas carry Zeke to the car. He is passed out and has no clue where he is. They lay him out in the back seat and close the doors. Someone in the crew comes up with the idea to take his phone apart so that it won't wake him up in the morning. The phone is dismantled and left on the dash of the car. Rodrigo comes up with the great idea of putting the pit bull in the car with him. The guys are all drunk and are in agreement with the prank. Carlos takes Chad out of his cage and puts him in the car with Zeke. Then, he hits the close button on garage and watches the door close. He gets back in the limo as well. The guys are all laughing hysterically as they stumble back to the limos so they can be driven home as well.

I WANT TO KNOW MORE

Some hours have passed since Taylor has woken Zeke up. Zeke finally has gotten out of his car and has his orange juice trying to recover. A few more bouts with nausea and he seems to be coming around to normal. As Zeke again tries to focus on the issue at hand, he is left with what to do next. There is a knock at the door and it is Carlos. He lets Carlos into the house. He then proceeds to ask Carlos about the night before. Zeke says "Can you tell me what happened last night?" Carlos begins to laugh and says "Well, I'm not too sure myself. All I know is that we all had a great time. You, in particular, had a fantastic time. No one can deny that at all." "Alright, I believe you, but how and why did I wake up in my car with the damn dog?" Zeke asks. Carlos, again, breaks out into laughter "Oh that, well, it was not my idea but I sure didn't stop it either. You were on your ass and knocked out cold. We were all drunk our damn selves and no one felt like carrying you all the way into the house and run the risk of seeing your wife. We came to the decision that we should just leave you in the garage. You know I have the code, so, we left you there. I'm not all together sure exactly how the dog got in the car with you" he says laughing louder. Zeke replies "Do you know that damn Champ ate my car dashboard. I woke up to him licking the vomit off of my face and Taylor banging on the car window."

"So, how did that go for you? I mean, Taylor banging on the window" Carlos asks. "It went, is all I can say. My head was hurting like shit as she woke me up. I didn't know where I was or how I got there. Then there was Chad all over me. It was not good at all. She, actually, had the audacity to tell me she had spoken with her girlfriend and that she was going out tonight because I supposedly did not come home last night. She saw that I was in the garage asleep, but whatever" Zeke tells him. "Have you given anymore thought about what you are going to do with her?" asks Carlos. "Yes, I want Mr. Stubbs to keep looking into this guy and find out everything that there is to know about him. As a matter of fact, can you get him on the phone for me, please?" asks Zeke.

Carlos picks up the phone and calls Mr. Stubbs for Zeke. When he gets Mr. Stubbs on the line, he passes the phone to Zeke. "Good afternoon, Mr. Stubbs, and how are you today?" Zeke asks him. "I'm fine, just working hard on your case" Mr. Stubbs replies. "That is great news. I'm happy to hear that. Have you found out any more information about this guy yet?" Zeke asks. "Well, yes, not much but, yes, there is some" Mr. Stubbs replies. "In that case, please come to my house again. I want to hear all about it in person. I don't want to misinterpret anything" Zeke tells him. "Yes, sir, I will be right over as soon as I get my notes together" the detective replies. The two hang up the phone and the waiting begins.

"Oh, my freaking head" cries out Zeke. "I feel your pain because I'm right there with you. I made fun of you last night for passing out. However, when I finally got to the house, I ended up throwing up a couple of times before I passed out my damn self" Carlos tells him. "See, that is what you get for getting me drunk and then making fun of me. It is all good. Go ahead and get your little jokes in. You need a laugh or two anyway. That is just karma coming back on you," Zeke says laughing while holding his head. Another twenty minutes or so passes and Carlos sees Mr. Stubbs walking up the driveway. He tells Zeke that the private investigator has arrived.

The doorbell rings and Zeke goes to answer it. "Come in, Mr. Stubbs. How are you today? Can I take your coat for you?" Zeke asks. "No, I'm fine at the moment. I just want to get in here and bring you up to speed of what is going on with me and my team" he says. "In that case, come on in and sit down. Please make yourself comfortable" Zeke tells him. "So, what have you found out about this guy? Is there anything interesting thus far?" Zeke asks him. "Well, I did find out a little more information about the guy and it is a little disturbing, to say the least" Mr. Stubbs tells him. "Please go on," Zeke replies.

"I have found out that this guy has women all over the place. The worse thing is that this guy is already married. We tapped into his cell phone and he sends text messages to at least five different women all day long. I think he is, actually, juggling them and your wife is one of the pack, unknowingly. I also get the feeling that all of these women think that they are the one. Well, the main one outside of his wife. I think the women know he is married but I'm not sure if they all know about one another" Mr. Stubbs says.

"Now, that is interesting news, for sure. Can you tell me more about his wife? Do you have pictures of her, at this time" Zeke asks. "No, not at this time. I am not even sure if I have her name correct, so, I don't want to speak on her just yet. I don't want to give you bad information." Zeke sits up and replies with "Ok, I can respect that and I appreciate that as well. However, I would like a dossier on his wife prepared for me as soon as possible. I want to know everything about her just like I want to know everything about him. Please get me photos, family history, her bio, what she drives, you know, everything! I even want to know what size panties she wears. I want to know this guy Mitch's wife as intimately as he knows mine. Are you clear on what I'm asking of you?" Zeke asks the investigator. "Yes, I'm very clear, Mr. Hill. I will have all the information in your hands as fast as I can get it" Mr. Stubbs tells him.

"I need to ask another favor of you, as well" Zeke tells him. "Sure, Mr. Hill, how can I help you?" the investigator asks him. "I also want to know about all these other women. I need photos of them and information packets on them as well. I know I'm asking a lot of you and your team but, like I said before, I want to know everything. I hope that will not be a problem for you" Zeke says to him. "No, sir, I will not have a problem at all. I will get you full information packets on all of the women associated with this man Mitch" Mr. Stubbs tells him.

"There is just one more thing, Mr. Stubbs" Zeke says. "I would like for you to investigate his wife personally and allow the rest of your colleagues to watch the other people involved. By doing this, I can be reassured nothing will be missed in her investigation." Zeke leans into Mr. Stubbs and says "I am presuming correctly, aren't I?" "Yes, without a doubt, you are correct. I will find out everything there is to know about his wife and get you the information as quickly as possible. Is there anything specific you are trying to find out about his wife?" Mr. Stubbs asks. "No, nothing in particular. However, if I say 'I want to know everything about her' would that pretty much cover the bases of what I need to know?" Zeke replies. "Yes, that gives me a great idea of what you are looking for" answers Mr. Stubbs.

Funny thing is that Mr. Stubbs is getting an idea of the type of man he has been dealing with. A no nonsense individual with money and muscle around to take care of any problem that may arise. Mr. Stubbs then excuses himself to get started on the task at hand. Carlos walks him to the door and lets him out.

Carlos says "You know you look horrible. I'm glad I came over here to check on you. Zeke, you have Stubbs in motion, so, why don't you take something and go back to bed. He is not going to find out much more today anyway." "I know, I'm just pissed but, damn, my head hurts. I think I need to stop drinking. Have you heard from Jose?" Zeke asks. "Yes, I left him at his house last night. He had the little Cuban cutie waiting for him when the limo arrived there last night. I also got a text from him about an hour ago," Carlos replies. "Ok, cool, as long as the crew is locked in, I can go back to sleep. Come and wake me up tomorrow" Zeke says as he tries to laugh. He continues with "I'm going back to bed. I will get with you guys tomorrow." "Alright, I'm going to head back to the house and knock out myself, then. If you need anything, give me a shout," Carlos says. "Alright, will do," Zeke replies. He heads off to his bedroom and Carlos heads home.

THE DOWNLOAD

Four days have passed and no information has been shared thus far. Zeke's cell phone rings and it is Mr. Stubbs calling. "Hello," Zeke says as he answers. "Hello, Mr. Hill, I was wondering if you were at home and is this a good time to stop by and talk?" Mr. Stubbs asks him. "Actually, it is a great time. My business associates and I are at my home now going over some paperwork. Please, feel free to stop by" Zeke tells him. "In that case, I'll be there in twenty minutes and I'll see you soon," Mr. Stubbs says. "That would be great. I'm anxious to see what you have found out. We will be waiting" Zeke says as he hangs up the phone.

A little while later, the doorbell rings and Carlos hustles to the door to answer it. "Hello, Mr. Stubbs. Come on in. Zeke has been waiting for you to call." Carlos says with a serious tone in his voice. "Hello to you to, Sir. I have information that I'm sure he is going to want to hear about." "Great, follow me down to the office" Carlos tells him. They enter the office and Zeke is still on a call. They stand there quietly until he is able to speak to them.

Zeke ends his call and says to Mr. Stubbs, "Please, have a seat and tell me what you have found out." Mr. Stubbs opens a big notebook that he has and places it on Zeke's desk. He begins to flip pages and describes each photo. At the top of the list is Mitch's wife. "This is Mrs. Deborah Erickson, she is the woman who is married to this Mitch person. She is an international lawyer. She is the youngest of three partners that started a firm that specializes in international banking and corporate acquisitions. I'm not sure, but I think she is the majority stakeholder in the firm as well. They have offices in Washington,

D.C., Tokyo, London and Hong Kong. Rumor on the street has it that they are headed to Dubai next. The company grossed somewhere around twenty million dollars on paper last year. But with that much exposure to global markets, you have to presume that they are moving money around the world. We could only track down their U.S. earnings. Her mother's name is Jo Anne. She is a Black woman with a PhD in Colombian art history. I can't find out any information on who her father is. It is as if he never existed. She looks mixed or Creole but I can't be too sure. And, Sir, since you asked me to find out, she wears a size six panties," Mr. Stubbs tells him.

"You are very thorough, I must say. For you to find out what size panties she wears is very impressive. Looking at this binder you gave me. You have tabs down the sides, what do they represent?" Zeke asks him. Mr. Stubbs replies with "Each tab is for a different woman that he is sleeping with. All of the women, we have found out, are married. The last woman in the book is not married and he is not sleeping with her. This young woman is the intern at his job. She seems to be hot in the pants for him, if you understand what I am telling you, Mr. Hill. So, we included her too. In that binder is everything that we have on them right now. We will keep looking, of course, and update you with any future findings."

"Thank you. This is just the type of information I am looking for. Is there anything special about these women that I should know?" he asks. "No, all of them are pretty ordinary. They are all married and they all have their own careers. It seems as though this guy is just a cock hound. He wants his cake and to be able to eat it too. If the woman is not married, he does not sleep with her. I guess he feels that is a safety net or something," Mr. Stubbs tells him.

"So, all of his conquests are married? Do you know if his wife has a lover?" Zeke asks him. "We have only been monitoring her for two or three days. From what we can gather so far, she is just a regular woman who is very driven in business. She works late hours and hits the gym at the crack of dawn. We will keep watching her and keep you posted, of course," Mr. Stubbs tells him. "Yes, please keep me abreast of this woman. She is very pretty don't you think? A man would have to be a fool to cheat on a beautiful woman like this," Zeke says smiling.

CAN I RETAIN YOUR SERVICES?

For the next two and a half weeks, Mr. Stubbs periodically checks in with Zeke to feed him new information. During these updates, Zeke learns of more escapades between Mitch and his wife. He also learns more about Mitch's wife, Deborah. He then figures it is time to meet this woman. He calls his attorney and asks him to set up a meeting between himself and this Deborah Erickson. His attorney wastes no time in getting the meeting set up for the following week in her Washington, D.C., offices. After confirmation of his meeting, Zeke takes some time out to think about what he will say to Mrs. Erickson during his meeting.

There is a flip side to every coin. After the meeting is set, Deborah, who does not go into any meeting empty handed, decides to do some investigation into this man and his company. She wants to be prepared when she meets the client. She does a quick internet search with his company's name. Sure enough, information comes up also about his connection with the company. Mrs. Erickson is intrigued by what she is reading about this man and his company.

The date for the meeting quickly arrives. Zeke is dressed and in route to his 10:00 a.m. meeting with Mrs. Erickson. He wants to see her face in person. He figures he will know instantly if she is an unhappy wife. He will know instantly if she knows her man is having an affair. He arrives at her offices with his attorney in tow. The receptionist tells them to please have a seat and Mrs.

Erickson will see them shortly. Zeke then instructs his attorney that he wants to see her alone and he will be staying in the waiting area in case he is needed. The attorney obliges and takes his seat accordingly.

A few minutes pass by and the receptionist gets up to show Zeke into the office. When the door opens, Mrs. Erickson arises and says "Welcome, Mr. Hill, to our firm. Won't you please come in and have a seat. It is so nice to meet you. I have heard so much about you," she says to him. Zeke replies "It is nice to meet you as well. I'm just happy that you had time to squeeze me into your schedule. I know you're a busy woman." "Well, of course, I did. Even if I didn't, I would have made some time for you, a self made man like yourself. You purchased a struggling software development company and turned it into a diversified conglomerate. Your company has expanded not only in software development but also IT security, data management with a very large component of data storage," Mrs. Erickson tells him. "Wow, I'm impressed. You have really done your homework. The company is no big deal. We were just really lucky in a few areas. We kept the business plan really simple and worked very hard," Zeke tells her.

"That may be true and I appreciate your attempt at humility. However, your company has a real foundation and it has been very successful. Also, from what I'm hearing, there seems to be rumors you are thinking of taking the company public," Debbie tells him with a serious look on her face. Zeke replies with "Now I am very impressed. You have done more than just Google the company. But I could say the same about you. You were third in your class out of Georgetown Law. You started your own international law firm with two friends four years later. Now, you have offices in Hong Kong, Tokyo, London and Washington D.C. I'm just a small business man compared to an international business woman like you, Mrs. Erickson." "Mr. Hill, you are too kind and I see you have done your homework as well. I'll admit that I too am very impressed. Thank you for Googling me," she tells him.

Zeke cracks a big smile on his face as he says "Well, maybe a little more than that. Since you know about my company going public, I will admit that I know a few things. I know your mother has a PhD and her name is Jo Anne. You're married and your astrological sign is Leo." "Is that right? I see we both are really good at homework," she says laughing. "So, tell me, Mr. Hill, how can I be of assistance to such a resourceful man?" Debbie asks. "Well, Mrs. Erickson, I am in the middle of a small project and I am in need of outside counsel. I would like to retain your services because I feel if I do, I can save us both a great deal of money in the future," Zeke says.

"You have my attention. What do you have in mind? Please, tell me more," Mrs. Erickson says. "I tell you this in confidence, correct?" he asks. "Yes, complete. Discretion is the key to my business," Mrs. Erickson replies. "This is a delicate matter for me and I'm dealing with it as best I can. Mrs. Erickson, three weeks ago I was getting dressed and found out my wife is having an affair. I never thought she would cheat on me let alone have an ongoing relationship with another man," Zeke says. Debbie replies "I am so sorry to hear that, would you like for us to represent you?" "Yes I would but in time not right now. The thing is, Mrs. Erickson, and this may come as a shock to you, but my wife is having an affair with your husband. I'm sorry that you have to find out like this. However, I have thought about it and this is a controlled environment for you and you are on your own turf, so to speak," Zeke says.

Debbie replies "Thank you for making the best of a horrible situation. Please, give me a second," she says as she reaches for her desk phone. Mrs. Erickson picks up her desk phone and says "Adrienne, please hold all of my calls." She hangs up and gives her attention back to Mr. Hill. "Now, Mr. Hill how do you know my husband is involved? Do you have any proof that I can see?" she says. "Yes I do, actually. The thing is when I first discovered the affair, I hired a private investigator. That gentleman has investigated my wife for the last three to four weeks. She has spent the bulk of her free time in that period with your husband," Zeke tells her. "Can you tell me more, please?" Mrs. Erickson replies.

Zeke reaches into his small briefcase and pulls out his tablet. He pulls up the gallery folder and opens it. When it is finally open, he passes the device to Mrs. Erickson. Mrs. Erickson begins to scroll through the more than two hundred photos. She does not make a sound; however, tears begin to fall from her eyes. The tears fall slowly at first. The more pictures she views, the more tears begin to fall. Zeke can tell he has devastated Mrs. Erickson. "I know it is a shock and I know it is a lot to take in all at once. But this is why I am here. I want you to know about the situation but I also don't want you to tell him that you know he is having an affair" Zeke says. "Why the hell not, fuck him! I am going to whip his ass. Oh, and I am whipping your wife's ass too" Mrs. Erickson says reassuringly. Surprisingly, she is no longer crying either.

"Your husband is now exposed to you just as my wife has been exposed to me. I have looked at this situation a hundred different ways. Our best bet is to keep our silence for awhile. I actually came to you to beg for your silence and I will give you reasons why" he tells her. "Go ahead. I am listening" she says. "First of all, I know how hard it will be for you to keep quiet. I am going through it now with my wife, as you recall. I know how hard it is to have your spouse in the arms of someone else. I have known and had these photos for weeks and still I have said nothing. I know that in the end for this to be resolved peacefully and nonviolently, we are going to have to go through someone's court. She is going to have to agree on an amount of money and whatever else. The whole process will get drawn out, expensive and, at the same time, possibly air my dirty laundry. I feel you are in the same type of situation. Second, I want to continue to have them monitored so I can have enough evidence of adultery that she dare not ask for alimony or any type of settlement. Well, she might ask but, hopefully, a court will not grant her my money for sleeping with someone else. I feel the same could work for you. I mean, I have seen video and photos of your husband and his lifestyle for weeks. I am guessing he is driving a two hundred thousand dollar car because you purchased it for him. He throws money around on women like it is water. Most dentists don't do that. He is spending way outside of his earning potential. I figure that is because of you, Mrs. Erickson" Zeke says.

"It sounds like a beautiful idea. And you are right; I am the one with the money. He lives his lifestyle because of me" Debbie says. "I am so pissed right now, you have no idea. I just don't know what to do. I need to protect my money that much is true. Please, continue your investigation and I will keep my mouth shut. I want to see exactly what he is up to anyway. I have some cognac over here on the table. Do you want yours with ice or neat?" Zeke stands up and says "I'll take it with ice, thank you." Mrs. Erickson proceeds to make them both drinks. She picks up a both glasses, turns to Zeke and hands a glass to him. Zeke says "Mrs. Erickson, what shall we toast to?" "Before we toast, please call me Debbie. There is no way I can treat you like a formal client, at this point" she says. "Alright, Debbie it shall be. Debbie, please call me Zeke, all of my friends call me that. Well, amongst other things anyway," he says laughing. "Let's toast to new beginnings and new horizons" Debbie says. "Well, here's to new beginnings and new horizons," he replies as they both raise their glasses in toast.

When the toast is done, Zeke puts down his glass and says "Debbie, can I have your business card? I would like to stay in touch with you." "I thought you came here to retain my services. Didn't you need outside counsel? I will gladly take on your case. I will charge you one dollar for any and all services that you may need. Any request that you have, I will happily fulfill for you" Debbie says. "I will, certainly, take you up on your offer and, yes, I want to hire you and your firm. Here is my card and my personal cell phone number is on there too. Please, feel free to use it at anytime" Zeke says. "I have your card now so I will be calling you soon. I hope that is alright" Debbie says. "Yes that is fine, please use it anytime!" he tells her smiling. "I'm going to get out of your office now and head back to mine. It has been very nice meeting you and I'm sorry it was under these circumstances" Zeke says to her. "Well, it was very nice meeting you as well. I also wish it were under different circumstances," she replies. He turns and walks out of her office. He rejoins his attorney who has been waiting in the lobby. They enter the elevator and press the level one button. Deborah is left crying alone in her office. Her heart has truly been broken.

A week or two has gone past and nothing has been done. Zeke can tell that Debbie has not said anything because his wife is still running around all willy nilly with Mitch. Since he has met with Debbie, the happy couple has been together five times. Zeke is sitting in his home office when he gets a phone call on his cell. He answers "Hello." "Hello there and how are you? This is Debbie can you talk?". "Why hello there, yes I can talk. I am fine just sitting here doing a little paperwork. I was thinking about you yesterday, actually" he says. Debbie replies "I wanted to reach out to you and ask you if we could meet. The initial shock of this crazy situation has worn off. I want to sit down and try to get some level of clarity. I have a lot of questions and you seem to have a lot of answers." "That would be fine with me. I'm sure you have questions but I am not sure I have a lot of answers. I am still in the dark myself, pretty much" Zeke tells her.

"Can you tell me when you have time? I have so many things running through my head" she tells him. "I am free this morning, if you want to get together. Just tell me when and where and I am there" Zeke says. "Well, I don't know where you live so just give me a place and I will meet you there" Debbie replies. Zeke thinks for a minute and comes up with "How about the new harbor in Fort Washington. I will meet you at the ferris wheel, let's say at 11:00. Is that good for you?" "That is perfect. I will see you there at 11:00. Thanks for doing this for me" she tells him. "It is no problem; I think I need it as much as you do" Zeke replies.

Eleven a.m. rolls around and Zeke is standing near the rail looking at the statue of the awakening. As he glares in thought, Debbie approaches him and grabs his arm. She says "Hi." "Hello to you. I should tell you thanks for meeting me. It is a great day outside today" Zeke says. "No, I asked you to meet me so thank you for picking such a wonderful place. I know you can help me make sense of all of this. You are in the same situation, you know" Debbie tells him. "Well, I will try but I make no promises" he tells her. "Let's walk up here along the shops and act like tourists. You know, the happy couple that window shops. We can walk and talk at the same time. Is that ok?" she asks. "Yes that'll be cool, let's go." They turn and head up the incline towards the shops.

As they are walking, Debbie takes a breath and says "Can I ask you about some of the particulars? This bullshit has been on my mind since you told me and now I have questions. How did you find out about the affair?" "I was at home doing some work in my office. My laptop went dead and my wife had taken my power cord. When I went to retrieve it, her PC screen was on. There was an email account open that I didn't even know she had. I read a few of the emails and they pointed to your husband and her meeting for lunch that day. I know crazy right?" Zeke says. "That is wild for sure, purely by accident. Can you tell me how long have you known about this? You may have told me before but I don't recall" Debbie says. "Today makes it almost five weeks. It has been hard not saying anything, that is for damn sure" Zeke replies. "How long do you intend on monitoring them" she asks. "I thought about that too. I figured long enough to make sure she will not get a dime if we go to court. I mean having sex with someone is one thing but this is a full on relationship that they have going on" Zeke replies. "I know that's right!" Debbie exclaims.

Debbie takes another long breath and says "So, tell me, how did it make you feel, because right now my whole world is shattered. It seems that my whole life is a lie. I don't know what to believe. How do you bounce back from this?" "For me, I have been taking it one day at a time. I think me having them monitored has helped me. I know it sounds crazy but it is hard for me to wrap my head around this whole situation," Zeke replies. He continues with "You know, we could give them a dose of their own medicine." She shuts him down quickly and asks "Tell me this, why haven't you told your wife at this point? You have been watching them for five weeks. As an attorney, I know that you have more than enough proof, at this point, that adultery has occurred. So, what is the real reason?" she asks him. "To be truthful, having the proof is not enough for me, I need to know why. I need to know what makes your husband so special. I, like you, am at a loss. I need answers too" Zeke explains.

"I know what you mean. That is why I am here. I thought you would have more answers than I do. I think we both care more about our relationships than our partners do" Debbie says. "That is for damn sure. We are not the ones out there fucking around. I am tired of them having all the fun while we are left at home doing nothing. They get to go out and enjoy life. The shit isn't fair" Zeke tells her. "I totally agree with you. Now that I know he is screwing around, I have been taking notice of the bullshit excuses he gives me when he is going out. I have a suggestion, next time he gives me a nonsense excuse, can I text you and see if your wife has given you one? If she has, you and I should get together for coffee or something" Debbie says. "That is a great idea but I can do one better. I have them monitored twenty four hours a day anyway. When my people see them together, I will text you and let you know. Then, we will be free to meet for coffee. How does that sound" he says. "That sounds great, so, we have a deal then? We will get together when the love birds are out enjoying themselves. I love it!" Debbie says smiling.

The two of them continue to walk along the pier taking in the sites. Zeke holds her hand as they walk for another thirty minutes or so having general conversation. Debbie decides to end their time together. She turns to him and says "Thank you, again, for coming to meet me. I just don't have anyone else to talk to about this nonsense." "It wasn't a problem, after all, we are going through this together. We can be each other's support group. I just don't know what else to call it" Zeke says. "That is a good name for it since that is what we are doing. Helping one another through this crazy period in time" she replies. She continues with "I am going to head back home and try to get through the rest of this day. I know it is going to be hard but you helped me more than you know." She leans in and gives him a kiss on his cheek. Zeke is now surprised and smiling. "Thank you, I am going to head back to the office too. I have one or two things to take care of today. Please drive safe on your way back home. As a matter of fact, text me when you get there so I know you made it ok" Zeke says to her. She looks at him smiling and says "Ok, I will do that. You have a good day now." She heads off to her car and Zeke heads towards his car to leave as well.

SOMEONE HAS HAD ENOUGH

A week or so has gone by and Debbie has gone on with her life as if nothing has happened or changed. However, she has kept in touch with Zeke. They have been texting here and there to touch base. Zeke has also been sending her live updates on the happy couple. His investigation team informs him and he in turn informs Debbie.

Then, on a bright sunny Wednesday afternoon, Zeke sends Debbie a text that reads 'my wife has just checked into their hotel and your husband is now in route to your house.' Debbie reads it and replies 'Thanks, I will see how he reacts.' Ten more minutes pass by and Mitch comes bouncing into the house as if he owns the world. Debbie is now on the couch sipping a glass of wine.

"Hi dear, how are you"? He asks. "I'm fine, just flipping thru a magazine" she says. "I just came home from the gym, so, I am going to shower. The guys are playing cards tonight, so, I'm going to drop by and play a few hands" he says. "Ok, I see, but it is Wednesday isn't it?" she asks. "Yes, I know. That is what I said but you know Jeff, anytime is a good time to gamble" he replies. "Alright, dear, enjoy yourself. Oh and one more thing, if you win, can I get new boots? You know a girl likes nice things," Debbie says to him. "Sure no problem, as a matter of fact just pick out two or three of them and email them to me. I will buy them tonight when I get home" he replies. "Thank you, baby, you are the best. You have a good time tonight, alright?" she tells him.

Mitch takes that as a green light to head to the shower and get dressed. Debbie gets up and refreshes her drink. She sits back down to read her magazine. Seemingly not giving a fuck about what Mitch has on his agenda. Mitch must have taken a bird bath. He is dressed and headed back down stairs within fifteen minutes. Debbie takes notice and says "Hey, Mitch, did you even get wet? It feels like you just went upstairs five minutes ago." "I know I took a quick shower so I could hurry up and get there. You know, you have to get there early to catch the money coming through the door" Mitch replies. "Ok, I see. One more question, dear, is that the shirt I bought for you when we were in Paris that you are wearing?" Debbie asks him. "You know what, it is. I wanted something flashy tonight; at least I can look the part of a high roller. And the stuff that you get for me always looks great," he says smiling. "I see, well, you have fun and I hope you win. Dear, don't forget to buy the boots when you get home" she tells him. Mitch replies "I won't" as he scoots himself out of the door.

Debbie gets up from the couch with her wine glass in hand. She heads directly to the window and watches Mitch drive away. She can't do anything except stand there shaking her head in disbelief. As she stands there watching the car disappear she decides to sit back down on the couch and relax. While relaxing, Debbie picks up her phone and sends Zeke a text that reads 'my husband just left a few minutes ago. Can you let me know if he arrives at the hotel with your wife?' Zeke replies 'ok.'

Debbie heads upstairs with bottle and glass in hand. She begins to draw herself a hot bath. As the tub is filling up, she adds scented oils and bubbles. She gets undressed, pulls her hair up and gets into the soft bubbles. She leans her head back and closes her eyes. Thoughts of all kinds race through her head. She is just trying to find a quiet place within all the madness that is her emotions at this point. As she is trying to ease her mind, she comes to the conclusion that enough is enough. She won't just sit by and let him do this to her, all the times before she had forgiven him or looked the other way because he was a man being a man. But now he is having a relationship and that just won't do. She relaxes in the water for a little while longer. She gets out and towels off her face after she puts her bathrobe on.

She goes into the bedroom to check her phone for messages. Sure enough, there is one from Zeke that says 'he has arrived.' She sends a reply of 'thank you.' She waits for a few minutes then sends Zeke another text that reads 'can you meet me at the ferris wheel at the harbor again?' Zeke replies 'yes I can. What time is good for you?' Debbie replies 'can you meet me there in two hours?' Zeke quickly replies 'yes I can. I will see you there.' Debbie sends him another text that says 'can you do me a favor and me at the Belvedere Lobby Bar inside the Gaylord Hotel? Zeke starts to smile as he reads the text. He answers her with 'yes, I will meet you there in two hours.'

Debbie has decided to get in tune with her neglected body. She begins prep time by trying to find something stunning to wear. She can't decide what lingerie to put on. She knows the thigh high back seam stockings with the garter belt will be worn for sure. She knows she wants to wear a dress because she can be accessible. By this, I mean she can display her assets playfully without revealing too much too soon. She goes through thru outfit after outfit to find the perfect one. She knows she wants something sexy but not too casual but at the same time not to dressy. She finally has an opportunity to truly enjoy herself and she is going to take full advantage of it. Zeke has no clue that Debbie has decided to fuck the shit out of him. He is going to get the surprise of a lifetime.

She finishes getting dressed. She heads off to the hotel. Debbie wants to get there early. She wants to get a suite before Zeke arrives at the bar. She has been thinking about sex since she was in the bath. She has been having foreplay in her mind already for hours, so she is ready. All she needs now is a strong man to make her quiver. She has taken care of primping herself. She is sure that once she reveals her true intent to Zeke, he will fulfill her needs. To be truthful, this night is all about her.

As she is driving to the hotel, Debbie calls ahead and books a suite. She also asks for an upper floor and a view of the Potomac River. When she arrives, she quickly picks up her keys. While she is at the front desk, she requests two bottles of champagne to be sent up to her room. She goes upstairs to inspect her room. Upon entrance, she sees that the Gaylord has lived up to expectation because the suite is fantastic. Everything is top quality and more than acceptable. The floor to ceiling windows offer spectacular views of Washington, in the distance.

Debbie looks in the mirror to give herself that final once over and then heads downstairs to meet Zeke. When she arrives at the bar, surprisingly, she sees Zeke. Apparently, he has arrived early himself. "Hello there can I sit with you?" Debbie asks. "Yes you can, please, sit right here" Zeke tells her. She takes her seat and says to Zeke "Thank you for coming out to meet me. I really appreciate it" she says. "I am happy for the invite, actually, and I would like to say you look fantastic" he replies. "Thank you, you look very handsome too, Mr. Hill" Debbie replies. "Thanks. So, what can I order for you to drink" Zeke asks. "Well, actually, I don't want to drink now. I asked you here to see if you might be interested in coming upstairs with me. Can we have a drink together in my room?" Deborah asks him. Zeke, who is stunned by the question, wastes no time in giving his response "I think that would be an excellent idea! Are you ready to go now?" he asks. "Yes I am" she replies. Zeke quickly reaches into his pocket and leaves some money on the table to cover his bill. He escorts Debbie to the elevator. She is holding his hand the entire way up to the room.

Upon entering the room, Debbie sits Zeke down and pours them both a drink of whiskey. She gives him a glass and sits down next to him. Debbie tells him, "I am going to give you everything that dummy gets at home. Later on, I am going to ask you if you were in his place, would you sleep with all those other women. I am going to let you decide if this pussy is good enough to keep a man." Zeke takes a long look at Debbie while he takes a sip of whisky from his glass. "Well, now, I would ask what has gotten into you but that would be a dumb question. I will say that I am grateful to be here with you now and you are so beautiful. Whatever you want to experience, I would be honored to be a part of it" Zeke tells her. "All I want you to do is relax and not think about the outside world. Are you in a position to be able to turn your phone off without causing any problems" she asks him. "Yes I am. Just let me send Carlos a quick text and I will turn it off immediately" he replies. Zeke picks up his phone to text Carlos and to turn the damn thing off.

When Zeke turns back around, Debbie is standing there in a two piece all black lingerie set. She is also sporting thigh high hose with garter belt attached.

It does not hurt that she is completing the package with those darn red bottoms! Zeke's mouth won't move, he wants to speak but he can't. He gathers his composure and says "Wow, look at you. I never would have imagined such a beautiful woman existed under the clothes" Zeke says. "That is what I am here for, to surprise you. I hope you like the outfit. I was not sure if you were into this kind of thing" Debbie says. "I am a man how can I not be into it? You are so beautiful and your skin is flawless. I don't know how this night is going to end up but I want to thank you in advance for choosing me" he tells her. "No, I want to thank you for opening my eyes and helping me to see and for that, I am in your debt" she replies. "You don't owe me anything; we are in the same predicament. I only shared my knowledge of the craziness" Zeke says to her. "Whatever has put you in my path, I am thankful for, now, allow me to show you my gratitude" she replies.

She takes him and places him on the bed, sits him up as if he were going to watch TV in bed. She fluffs a couple of pillows and places behind his head and back. She then goes and gets the bottle of champagne that she has had delivered to the room before they arrived. She gives him a glass and then seductively fills it up. Debbie then reaches into her Louis Vuitton overnight bag and pulls out a wide array of candles. She places them all around the room lighting them as she goes. She reaches back into her bag and pulls out some scented oil and heads towards Zeke. She begins with taking his shoes and socks off and quickly gets them out of the way. She goes for his belt buckle and zipper as Zeke looks on smiling in amazement. She dispatches with his pants rather quickly. Zeke has to negotiate the glass of champagne as she takes off his shirt. No words are being said and Zeke is not stopping her. When she gets his shirt off, she takes a moment to look at and admire his body. She leans in and gently bites Zeke's nipple. It makes Zeke chuckle a little.

Debbie rubs her hands together and says "You are one fine specimen of a man. I can't believe she has left you all unattended. I know what my husband looks like and he doesn't look anything and I mean anything like you." She picks up the scented oil and pours some into her hands. She begins to rub his chest while he sits there sipping champagne. Slowly and seductively she then says, "Wait, let me do this right. I hate to make you put your glass down but I need you to stretch out. I want to be able to work your entire body at once" she says smiling. Zeke places the glass down and lays back. She pours oil on the length of his body. She takes care of his arms and shoulders first. She begins to do his chest. She takes her time as she gently caresses him. She can see his dick rise through his boxers. Debbie does each leg one by one. When she has finished his body, she grabs his boxers and pulls them down. She exposes his dick and looks at Zeke smiling. She gently takes his dick in her hand and begins to kiss it all up and down the shaft. She takes her tongue and swirls it in a circular motion around the head. Debbie goes for it and starts to give him the most amazing blow job. Debbie has Zeke stuck on stupid. He is grabbing the blanket like it is some type of hand rail.

Zeke then tries to sit up to speak. "Pretty lady, you are the one who deserves all of this attention. Why don't you switch places with me" he says. He pulls her up off of him not waiting for an answer. But before she can get on her back Zeke has positioned her on her knees so he can eat her pussy from behind. He pushes her head to the bed so that there is nothing but ass and pussy in the air. He begins to lick her little muffin. He can see her flinch every time his tongue touches her. He grabs her hips and pulls her pussy into him. He tries to swallow the whole thing. He sticks his tongue in between her lips as she moans in passion. He grabs both of her buttocks and squeezes them aggressively. Zeke can tell she has not had any personal attention in awhile. For some reason, Zeke can't stop eating her; it is as if he has not had a meal to eat in days. Debbie is in a state of bliss. She has a real take control man in her midst and she likes it. Zeke finally takes his head out from between her legs and sits down on the bed with his legs hanging off of the side. He turns Debbie around and tells her "Come here and sit in my lap. I want to be able to hold you and see you at the same time. " Debbie looks at him as she is still trying to catch her breath and says "Whatever you want." She sits on his lap and says to Zeke "Is this ok?" Zeke replies "You are almost there. I want you to put it in because I want to know you want me." Debbie smiles and says "Anything you say." She reaches down between her legs and grabs his dick. She places it at the edge of her pussy and slowly allows her body to slide down. She then puts her arms around his neck. He returns the favor and hugs her as well. Zeke tells her "Don't move just yet, I just want to feel you." "Anything you say," she replies.

A few moments go by and Zeke can feel Debbie's pussy throbbing on his dick. She asks him "Why don't you let me ride it like a surfboard?" "Be my guest," he replies. Debbie goes to work. Zeke can't believe how she is reacting to him. Maybe it is the excitement of having a new man between her legs. Maybe it is the revenge of her man stepping out on her. Whatever the case, she is going crazy. She is throwing it like she has animalistic tendencies. Debbie is truly enjoying herself, maybe a bit too much. While seductive and quite romantic, this love making session has a hint of all out nastiness that they both seem to be enjoying. Then, suddenly, Debbie starts thrusting faster and faster. "Give it to me" Zeke says. "YES" she replies. She moves back and forth, then forth and back. She lets out a loud scream! She shakes and quivers on top of Zeke. She squeezes him even tighter as she rubs the top of his head. She starts to kiss him on his neck and ears. Zeke has a firm hold of her. He can feel her succulent juices flowing down towards his balls.

As Debbie is trying to catch her breath Zeke whispers in her ear "I want you to keep going. I want you to cum on my dick again." "Anything you say, Zeke" she replies. She again starts to gyrate and thrust. This time even more intensely, because Zeke has grabbed a hand full of her hair that he is pulling. She throws that ass on him like she is a porn star. He can't take much more of this himself. It does not take long for Zeke to see the signs of her pending explosion. Her last orgasm was so recent it does not take long for number two to arrive but this time they both cum together. She can feel his hot semen inside of her. They both sit there and hold one another passionately breathing in motion, their bodies as one. This scene was repeated over and over for hours throughout the night.

Morning comes and Debbie wakes up and realizes where she is and what has taken place. She can't help but smile as she does not regret a moment. She feels the covers moving as she realizes Zeke is awake as well. He surprises her as he reaches over and pulls her close to him. He kisses her on the forehead and says "Good morning. Can you order room service for us? I am starving. I never was able to eat last night, you know food that is." He says this with the biggest grin on his face. "I know you must be famished. I will place an order what would you like" she asks. "You can get me anything. I am not too picky" he replies. "Alright, now that I can do, give me a minute" she tells him. Debbie calls room service and takes care of the request. She then returns herself comfortably back into Zeke's arms. Debbie can't remember the last time that she has felt this safe.

"You know you slept under me all night. I must say that I thoroughly enjoyed every minute of it too. Your skin is so soft and you smell fantastic. Can we do this again sometime soon" Zeke asks. "Indeed we can. I thought about that very thing last night. How can I see this wonderful man again, is all I could think about. Now, you tell me when will I be able to I fit into your schedule again" she asks. "Under the circumstances, you can see me whenever you want. I will make myself available to you at any time day or night," Zeke replies. "Day or night, is that a fact? You sure do say what a woman wants to hear. I am not going to lie it is working on me" she says smiling.

"It is not a game and I am serious, if you are available so am I. Most of the time our spouses will be together anyway, so, we have all the time in the world to enjoy one another's company" he tells her. "It is nice to know that you would move mountains for me. However, for now, let's just keep it light and have some fun. We both need a friend right now more than anything else. I know I do" she says. "You know, I agree with you. It is time for me to start enjoying life again and you are the perfect person to do it with" Zeke tells her. "Awe thank you, you are so sweet. I promise you we will have the best time together" Debbie tells him.

Thirty minutes passes by and breakfast arrives. The two enjoy an assortment of breakfast pastries, fruits and cheeses. After breakfast, they retire back into the bed. They decide to watch movies on television while they snuggle and enjoy the peace and quiet of the moment. "This has been a truly enjoyable get away" Debbie tells him. "I totally agree. Like you said before, I can't wait to see you again" he replies. She lays her head on his chest and they both drift off to sleep while watching TV.

Debbie and Zeke continue to carry on like this for four or five months. What began as simple get back has turned into much, much more. They attend movies, sporting events and quiet evenings alone. They also enjoy fine dining and even have attended a play or two at the Kennedy Center together. They have begun to enjoy impromptu outings with one another because they never know when the happy couple will get together, which in turn gives them an excuse to see one another. The happy couple spend so much time together that they never notice Deborah and Zeke starting to have a relationship of their own.

They have really gotten to know one another. During this time Debbie has gotten to know Zeke's two best friends, Carlos and Jose. The guys also really like her and believe that, under the circumstances, she is the perfect fit for Zeke. The guys think they would be a great couple.

———

AN EYE OPENING DINNER

Zeke calls his wonderful friend and asks "where would you like to meet for dinner?" Debbie tells him "You should choose because you always pick the best places." As she talks to him, he can hear her smile through the phone. She continues with, "Just find somewhere and then let me know later what you decide. Wherever you decide I will get dressed and meet you there by eight." He replies with "Ok, I'll figure something out and let you know. I'll even ask Carlos if he feels like getting out of the house." She then says, "Great I will see you guys later then." He agrees and they hang up the phone.

———

Unbeknownst to her, her husband Mitch has been ear hustling the whole time. He can do nothing but stand behind the door in amazement that his beautiful wife is seeing another man. He finally realizes that he has not been paying her close enough attention and that someone else has filled that void. But for now he is in his feelings and wants to know what is going on. He doesn't say anything to her about her dinner plans that he has overheard. Rather, he runs downstairs like he has been there this whole time. He has decided to follow her to her dinner date so he can find out exactly what is going on. He is shocked that his wife would cheat on him. All he can think of is his wife making love to someone else. While he is downstairs, he decides to pour himself a drink so he can think how this could have happened. He is taking a sip as his wife Debbie walks by smiling like she has hit the lottery. He is so frustrated but he does not want to say anything to her at this point and does not want to alert her to his suspicions. He wants to know who the man she is messing with is. He wants to be at that dinner tonight is all he can think to himself. Does he try to start small talk with Debbie and risk exploding before he has a chance to see who this man is? He thinks to himself. No just let it go for now and follow her later.

Meanwhile, back across town Zeke gives Carlos a shout out. Funny thing is Zeke has called as Carlos is in the kitchen digging in the fridge. Zeke asks "Do you want to grab a bite to eat this evening?" Being the size he is Carlos is always down to eat. He asks Zeke "where are we going?" "Well, I am going out with Debbie again so I am thinking somewhere romantic. Maybe that place down in Annapolis called Carrol's Creek. You know it's right on the water and they have the option of you being able to sit outside on the deck and enjoy dinner. With the weather nice again, I'm thinking it will be a good spot to just sit back and unwind." Carlos takes a second to think and says "See I'm not messing with you two again. You guys always have me being the third wheel and I am not having it this time. I'll just have Jose to come with me. We can grab a table near you guys and give you two some privacy. We'll get to eat good though, I love that place. Aaahhh and since Jose is going, you are going to have to pick up the tab," he says laughing. "I tell you, that guy has a way of putting those oysters on a half shell down. Last time we went there he ate like two dozen of them by himself. I have no idea where he puts it all and as long as you are paying, Zeke, I don't care how many he eats." They both get a good laugh out of that comment. "Go ahead and call him and see if he has time to hang out with us. I'm sure he's not going to turn down a free meal," Zeke says. "Ok, I'll call him now and see if we can get on his schedule," he says as he is laughing.

"Ok, you do that and come down to my office when you are done. I have to check on some accounts right quick. I'm getting a bunch of text messages about one of the LAN components that we service. I don't know what is going on but the alarms are going off for sure," Zeke says. "I'll be down there to give you a hand with it as soon as I check on Jose and his stomach's availability for tonight," Carlos says with a laugh coming out. After a quick call to Jose' he comes down to the office and sees Zeke in the middle of putting out fires on the computer.

"So' do you have it handled yet?" Carlos asks. "Well' almost" Zeke replies. "There was some type of virus that was stopped by the firewall. But at the same time the virus almost infiltrated the firewall in another place, hence, all the alarms going off. I think I almost have it contained; another two or three minutes and I should be fine," Zeke says. "That's great, I thought there was going to be a major problem that would cause us to miss dinner later" Carlos says. "Nope not at all. One more click and it all should be handled. That's why we build the platforms the way that we do. Have those intense security protocols to take care of virtual attacks like this on the fly. That is why people pay our company the big bucks," Zeke adds. Carlos fires back with, "I am just happy you decided to start this company and give all of us a different life. I really appreciate it too! I mean don't get me wrong there was nothing wrong with our old life. This one just makes me feel as though I am a regular person and it feels kind of good."

Carlos continues with, "So, what time are we headed to dinner? Jose said I need to come and pick him up because he is not driving to Annapolis. I tell you this guy, give him a free meal and he still won't drive. He reminds me of some of my bad dates before I met Blanca." Zeke is laughing as he says, "Tell him dinner is at eight and we are leaving from here around the seven or seven thirty time frame. Make sure you get him and be back here before that, please. I don't want to keep her waiting."

Carlos replies with "Ok but what about Taylor? Where did you tell her you were going tonight?" Zeke answers him in stern voice "Well, as much as she is with dude, I figured it wouldn't matter where I was. I haven't told her anything. Debbie and I have been seeing one another for almost five months now. To be honest with you, I'm at the point where I'm pretty much tired of lying about where I am et cetera. At first, it was cool because I was giving her what she was giving me, but now; I am doing me and enjoying it. Debbie is a great lady; she just got caught up in all of her man's nonsense." Carlos replies with, "Yes I guess you're right about that. There has been a lot of deception and craziness in this. One day it will all come to an end. Have you thought about the end game and how it will all shake out?" Zeke gives it some thought and hits Carlos with, "Well, Debbie and I actually talked about it. I told her that if she was ready to let go and leave, so was I. I explained to her that we could have a beautiful life together. I think I have convinced her that we could. I mean neither of us ever wanted to cheat, it is like we were forced into the situation, you know. So who knows how it may go, I just keep my fingers crossed that whatever way things go, Debbie will not be hurt in the end. She had nothing to do with any of this. And if it wasn't for me going after her, she wouldn't even be involved in any of this nonsense."

Carlos just looks at Zeke and says, "However it goes, you know I'm with you ride or die. So, whatever you choose, I'm with you. I love Taylor to death but since she's been playing around with dummy and for so long, I have lost a lot of respect for her. Plus, you and Debbie have so much fun together. It is hard to deny that you two don't have feelings for one another." "Carlos, I tell you my feelings for Debbie have really increased. What started out as a simple get back has turned into a caring friendship, I have to admit. Look, why don't you head to Jose's house and pick him up now. Come back to my house and all three of us can have a drink or two before we head out to dinner. Oh and when we go to dinner we are taking your Range Rover. Last time I went somewhere with you two I had to buy dinner and pay for gas," he says laughing. "Zeke, man, you are funny and you got jokes. We could have kicked you some gas money. All you had to do was ask," he says laughing. Carlos knows Zeke doesn't give a damn about the money. He is just being lazy and just doesn't want to drive. Carlos continues with, "But anyway, I'll go and get Jose so we can chill first, no problem. Do you want me to pick up anything before I head back to the house?" Zeke says, "No just bring Jose back and if the truck needs washing, please, get it done. I don't want Debbie seeing me getting out of a dirty car." "Come on man, do I ever keep my truck dirty? I'll be back in about forty five minutes. Keep yourself out of trouble and while I am gone, check on the LAN setup to make sure all of the problems are really gone." "Hey, that's a good idea. I'll do that and I'll see you guys when you get back," Zeke says.

Carlos rolls out to get Jose and to stop past his own house to change for dinner. In the meantime Zeke takes a shower and gets dressed himself. He has also sent Debbie a couple of texts to flirt with her and let her know where they are to meet. She replies to him and lets him know she is ok with meeting there. She asks Zeke what is the dress code and he lets her know it is classy casual. She is ok with that, for sure. Evidently, she has purchased some new heels that she is itching to show off to Zeke.

Some time passes and Zeke is showered, changed and is now waiting on the arrival of Carlos and Jose. He wants a drink but decides to wait for them to arrive back at his home. But just as he is thinking, where the hell is Carlos, in walks Carlos with Jose in tow. "What's going on with you Jose? How have you been and are you ready to eat?" Zeke asks him. "Hello there Zeke, I'm good and I was at home just chilling. Thanks for the invite too. The oysters on the half shell there are so fresh and juicy, I love them," Jose replies. "That's good. Make sure you order plenty of them tonight. Carlos is already making me pick up the tab but I'm making him drive. I don't know if that is a fair trade off but, oh well, let's go and have some fun," Zeke says. He continues with, "Let's go and have a drink or two before we leave. I already know she will be late anyway, you know how women are." They all laugh together from the comment as drinks are prepared. They each have a glass and toast to a great dinner and evening.

Some time passes by and the fella's load up in Carlos's Range Rover and they head to Annapolis for dinner. Meanwhile, Debbie is at home making final preparations to leave out herself. Her husband Mitch walks into the bedroom as she is slipping on her shoes and asks "So, where are you headed to this evening?" She replies with a quick, "Out with the girls for dinner and a drink." Mitch knows it's a lie and tries to figure out a way to play it. He then says "I am sort of hungry can I go with you?" Debbie gives him the standard answer of, "No, it is girl's night and you would be bored anyway. We are just having girl time to talk about men." He still knows it's a lie but decides to just let it go and back off. He responds with, "Ok, well, have fun and if you drink too much, call me and I'll come and get you." She giggles a little and tells him,

"Don't worry I'll be in good hands. Oh, and don't wait up for me; I may be a little later than usual."

With that said his mind goes into overdrive as he utters, "Ok, sweetheart, drive safe out there and don't do anything I wouldn't do." He is not trying to give her any idea that he knows what is going on as he is trying to act as if he is supportive of girl's night. He has already decided to follow her to see what is going on and who this man is. He runs downstairs and puts on his running shoes, puts the keys in his pocket and sits on couch acting like he is watching sports center on television. Debbie then comes bouncing and smiling down the stairs like a school girl going to the prom. All he can do is sit there steaming mad but cannot let her know that he knows what is really going on. She leans over and gives him a peck on the forehead and tells him, "There is food in the fridge if you get hungry." She then proceeds to head out to her car.

Debbie does not realize that Mitch is hip to her plan and is in go mode himself. As soon as she backs out of the driveway he jumps into his pickup truck and begins to follow her. He decided to drive the pickup since she would not be looking for him in it. He has caught up to her and is following her about a quarter of a mile back. She is headed to Annapolis, so, lucky for him there are not a whole lot of turns. She jumps on Route 50 and heads east towards Annapolis, never thinking to look back and see if she has been followed. I mean why would she? She and Zeke have been involved for months and, now, it is just normal routine for her to meet him. Normally, they meet when their spouses are together so neither one really has to make up an excuse.

As he follows her, he gets more and more anxious about what is going on with her. He just contemplates to himself what he is going to do to this man and his wife when he catches them together. Everything from leaving her to killing them both crosses his mind. She exits the highway and is now waiting at a stop light. He is five cars back banging on the dash out of frustration and pain. He still can't believe that his wife is out playing around with another man. He just can't fathom that someone else is tapping his wife's coochie. He thinks, "No one can put it down as good as me. Look how many women tell me I am the best lover they have ever had. I am the man," he thinks to himself.

Then the light turns green and his wife makes a left, he follows her. She then drives another quarter mile and pulls into a gated and secured parking lot. He just continues to drive not to draw attention to himself. She parks and heads towards the restaurant. As she is walking she can see Zeke sitting down on the deck, with Carlos and Jose. He can see her as well and stands up to greet her, they exchange pleasantries and she sits down. Carlos and Jose sit at a table behind them in order to give them some personal space. It's normal for Carlos and Jose to hang back from Zeke and allow him some free time with Debbie. They want him to be happy and at this point, Debbie does it for him.

Zeke tells her, "Damn, you look fabulous today and you smell even better. How long did it take you to put all of this together anyway?" She just smiles and replies with, "You say the sweetest things and it didn't take long at all. I'm a regular girl and don't need much mirror time. Also, thanks for telling me I smell good, no one has told me that in quite some time besides you." "You are very welcome and you always smell great! I am just happy I get to be around you," Zeke replies.

He continues with, "The waiter came and asked if I would like starters or wine. I explained to him that I was waiting on someone and he would have to come back later. I did have him, however, leave the wine list so that you can pick something out for us to drink. The guys ordered mixed drinks and appetizers already so we are on our own. So here is the list, please select something good." He passes her the list as he is smiling in her face. She looks over the list and finds something that she likes. "Well, Zeke how much can I spend," she asks. Carlos and Jose can't help but over hear what she asks and start chuckling to themselves. Carlos looks at Jose and says "I like this girl."

Zeke looks over at the fellas while he is shaking his head and answers with, "Sweetheart, money is no object when it comes to you. So, order anything that your heart desires." "Ok, is that a fact? Well, I found something but I would feel bad ordering it because the best year was the year that I was married," she explains. Zeke laughs again and tells her, "You can order any year or any bottle that you want. We are going to make Carlos pay for it anyway," as he looks at Carlos smiling. "Well, if Carlos is paying, I know what I want. They have Opus One from Napa Valley. I am telling you now that it is expensive and I want to make sure it's alright with you to order it. They have it listed at three hundred and fifty dollars per bottle," she says. Zeke replies back with, "Debbie, order anything you want, money is not a problem. Out of all the times that we have gone out, have I ever made you or even asked you to pay for anything?" She quickly replies with a resounding, "No you have not. Now, I do have my own money. I am nobody's gold digger that is for damn sure." Jose and Carlos just burst out laughing again as they are over hearing the conversation. They know he has a good one on his hands now for sure.

Zeke says, "Well, if the wine is that good, we better get two bottles, one for us and another one for these crazy guys behind us. Can't have them over there missing out on a good wine, they need some culture anyway," as they have a laugh together over the statement.

The waiter was kind enough to bring both in no time. The bottles are already open and breathing. One bottle is placed on the table with Zeke and Debbie and the other bottle is placed on the table with Jose and Carlos. The waiter pours wine into all four glasses and a big toast to happy times is given by Carlos. Carlos and Jose stand up to toast the happy couple. When the toast is done, they sit at their own table to mind their business and give the couple some quiet time.

———

As the happy couple are drinking and sampling some of the appetizers, Debbie's husband has finally maneuvered his pickup truck so that he can easily see the restaurant. He can see his wife sitting there with her glass of wine and a smile on her face as big as the sun. He can see the happiness just oozing out of her. The more he watches the more and more upset he gets. He can see them placing an order for dinner and he can see that a bottle of wine has been finished. He also can see a second bottle of wine get delivered to their table.

"How much can one man take," Mitch says to himself. Mitch has a range of emotions at this point. He does not know what to do. Should he just sit there and watch his beautiful wife be seduced by some strange man? Should he get out of the truck and beat the guy up? Should he just go home and call his attorney and just be done with her? He just sits in the truck thinking about all of these options. He just doesn't know what to do. Some time passes and he can see that their dinner has arrived as well. The man starts to feed his wife by hand and by fork, that is when he decides he has had enough. He has watched them for more than 45 minutes and just can't take it anymore. He decides to get out of the truck and go handle this situation. They are sitting outside under the stars and moonlight at this point so they are not hard to reach. He approaches the table and both of them can see him coming towards them. She just squeezes Zeke's hand as he approaches.

———

Mitch feeling all of himself storms up to their table and asks, "So, what is this and who the hell is this man you are with? I want some answers and I want them now, damn it!" he says with a raised voice. All Debbie can do is say "Calm down and lower your voice, we are in a public place and I am not feeling your tone." "Not feeling my tone? Well I am not feeling you sitting here with this fool while he feeds you from his fork either. How can you do this to me? Why now and what have I done to deserve this?" he asks with a puzzled look on his face.

Debbie sits up and just looks at him. She takes a minute to get her thoughts together because she is almost two bottles of wine in. She clears her throat and says "Well, honey think about it. I want you to ask yourself have you cheated on me again? You said that the last time you cheated was going to be the last time you cheated. I just wanted to show you that two can play that game. Now that you know you are not the only one who can get some outside attention, can you please leave so that I can order dessert?" He just stands there with his mouth open while Zeke refreshes Debbie's glass.

"And you," Mitch now addresses Zeke. "Stand up. I don't want to hit you while you are sitting down," Mitch barks at Zeke. Zeke looks at the table behind Mitch and gently shakes his head, to let Carlos and Jose know not to crush this man's soul and to stay seated for now. Zeke then looks at Mitch and says, "Well, I am not going to stand up. I am enjoying time with your wife and she is enjoying time with me, as you can see. Now, can you please leave so that we can get back to enjoying our dinner?" "That's it I have had it, if you don't stand up, I am going to beat you where you sit, you simple mother fucker!" Mitch screams at him.

Zeke replies with, "Mr. Erickson, you don't have a problem with sleeping with other men's wives so why are you having such a hard time because I am sleeping with yours? Furthermore, since you are sleeping with my wife, I thought it was only right that I sleep with yours. See, now what is going through your mind right now is, which one of the husbands of women that I'm fucking has found out about me?" Mitch's demeanor drastically changes quickly. Zeke continues with, "See, your problem is twofold, one; you only sleep with married women because you think it's safe and, two, you made the mistake of sleeping with my wife. You won't even sleep with the little cutie from your office, Julie I think her name is, because she is single. Shit, she has evidently been trying to give you some pussy forever. So, I'm here to let you know that sleeping with married women is not safe. I see you are all puzzled about how does he know all of this. Mr. Erickson, I'll tell you what I do know, well, at least some of it. I'll try to help you out so you can get a grasp on the serious of this situation you're in. You are now sleeping with five different women, at present time, including my wife. So, to give you even more clarity, you are sleeping with Jane, Sally, Barbara, Taylor, and Toya. All of the women I have just named are married. I will let you contact all of these women to see which one of them is my wife. Now, when you find out who is my wife, get back to me so we can talk. However, before you get back to me, make sure you ask my wife all about me. Now, normally she knows better than to spread any of my business in the streets, so, make sure you tell her that I said you are green lighted for access to me. She will know what that means. Now, if you can be so kind as to be gone from our presence that would be outstanding. And just to make sure you leave now without any drama, the two gentlemen behind you will escort you to your car." Mitch turns around and there are two brick walls standing there; he had no clue that Jose and Carlos were on guard.

Debbie turns to Mitch and says, "See, honey, I play this game way way better than you do. I will see you at home tonight when I get there." Debbie and Zeke just laugh as he walks away. "Oh, and, Mitch, one more thing," Zeke says, "under no circumstances are you to touch Debbie. If you do, the two gentlemen escorting you to your car will be over to your home to visit you personally. Do you understand me?" Zeke asks. Mitch just nods his head and walks away, looking like a dog with his tail between his legs.

As dinner progresses and another bottle of vintage Opus One is brought to the table, Zeke is just gazing into her eyes. They begin to talk some more. Debbie asks, "So, when he realizes who you are, then what?" Zeke replies with, "Oh, he will probably come to you and say, baby, I am sorry and it will never happen again. I didn't know who she was and who her husband is. He might even give you the let's just run or some other silly nonsense like that. I promise I won't hurt him unless he hurts you first. If he happens to bother you, then Carlos and Jose will have their way with him. However, the first thing he has to do is figure out which one of them hoes is my wife. We both know that is going to be a problem for him. All of his other women think that they are the only one. At this point, he knows I am no nonsense because I know too much about his world. I know who he is sleeping with and I even know his wife." Debbie replies with, "Yes, he has too many women and he won't have a clue where to start."

Zeke sits up in his chair while holding Debbie's hand and says, "We have been dating for a while now and your husband now knows about us as well. He definitely knows that we know he is fucking around. Why don't we jet out of town for a little get away? Winter has been crazy here in D.C. this year, one day it's hot and the next day it's cold. So, we have snow coming in the next two days. They are calling for blizzard like conditions. I heard Buffalo is supposed to get in the neighborhood of three feet. So, let's change our weather forecast and get the hell out of here." She thinks about it for a minute and says "You know what you're right, I do need a break let's do it. Where do you have in mind?" Zeke now smiling says, "Well, with a short notice, we better keep it in the states. So how are Vegas or New Orleans for you?" She thinks for a minute and then asks "Is Miami a possibility? My girlfriends have told me it is really nice." Zeke takes another sip from his glass and sits up in his chair and says, "You could not have picked a better place. Miami is like my second home. Hey, just in case, make sure you bring your passport and you are going to love the three zero five!" Debbie, feeling puzzled, looks at him and asks "Do I really need a passport?" Zeke just replies with, "Well, they have those party boats and we may go out on the water to gamble and drink. You need a passport for those these days." She tells him "Ok as long as I am with you I am down for anything."

Zeke then asks her "So, what time tomorrow is good for you? Well, around what time so I can get tickets." Debbie responds with, "Isn't that going to be pricey for a last minute flight? I didn't know you meant tomorrow, but ok. Call me tomorrow and let me know how much the tickets are and I'll just pay you for mine, again, I am nobody's gold digger. I may cheat on my husband because I am tired of him cheating on me, but I am no gold digger! And since I am on the topic I will say this, to be honest with you, this is the first time I have cheated on my husband. After all the mean and hurtful things he has said to me and done to me over the years, I never cheated on him. This time, I think I just had it. I have had it with strange women calling my home. I am always finding numbers and condoms in his pockets when I am doing his funky ass laundry. My girlfriends have even seen him at events or functions with women who are not me. I just had enough and after you came to me and put the evidence in my face; that was the final straw. Finally, it was just my turn to do to him what he had long been doing to me." Zeke just looks at her and says caringly, "Well hold on, I don't want you to feel down on yourself or even think about any of that nonsense right now. Just think about your brighter tomorrows. And speaking of tomorrow, you still have not told me a time that you would like to leave. And as for you being a gold digger," as Zeke is laughing, "I asked you to go out of town with me, so this time I'll take care of it. You know the next time we can go half or something." They both begin laughing together. Debbie looks at him smiling and says "You know what? You are way different than him and that is a good thing!" Zeke replies laughing "You have no idea how true that is. So, what time are you trying to go again?" Debbie nonchalantly says, "Ok, how is an 11:00 a.m. flight for you?" Zeke replies with,

"Ok, that's great. I'll pick you up at 9:30 a.m." Debbie says "That's fine with me. I do have one question. What will you tell your wife? She doesn't know about us yet. Well, she will look at it as an opportunity to spend time with your husband. If he has not told her by then, he is sure to tell her while we are gone. Snow is coming in forty eight hours and the city will be shut down and both of us will be gone. What else will they do? Plus he is in panic mode right now, so, he may end up texting or calling her anyway. If he mentions the green light thing, she will want me to go away anyway. He will be out asking questions of his boo boo's, trying to find out who I am. This will give him the opportunity to find out for sure. And when he finally does really find out, we will be on the beach sipping some drinks. So, let me get you home. We have a long day tomorrow." She looks at him and says "I feel like I have known you forever. I am taking a leap of faith that this little get away is what I need to clear my mind. I think I need this. I have not been on vacation without Mitch since before we were married. So, yes, I think this will be good for me, actually, good for us both, you and I." She leans over and gives him a kiss.

"Wow, where did that come from?" Zeke asks. "Well, I think you are the breath of fresh air that I needed," Debbie proclaims. "Hmm" Zeke mumbles to himself as he thinks of something to say as a response to that. "I totally agree with you. It is nice to have someone around that appreciates me for me," he says. "Actually, I am going to drive you home. Well, I'm not but Carlos will. We will have Jose drive your car behind us. I just don't want anything happening to you. We are both like two or three bottles of wine in at this point." "That is why you are my breath of fresh air. I think that is doable. Too bad you don't have a divider in the truck; I think I could ride it like it is a surf board right about now. Oh, Lord, I think I'm feeling this wine a little too much," she says as she is giggles. Zeke just sits there laughing and enjoying the moment of pure innocence. She is so green that you can't help but admire her. She doesn't have a dishonest bone in her body, he thinks to himself. He looks over her shoulder and motions to Carlos and Jose. "Debbie, give me your keys. I am going to have them get the cars while I take care of the check," Zeke tells her. "Here you go," she says as she hands him her keys.

"Hey, guys, we have both had too much to drink. Jose can you drive her car behind us, please; we are going to drop her off at home. Carlos can you get the car please? I will take care of the checks." "Sure thing Zeke, do you want me to take the scenic route?" he says as he laughs a bit trying to be funny. "No, man, let's get her home. We have a long day tomorrow. I will tell you all about it later," Zeke says. "Alright, baby, the fellas are going to get the cars. I have given the guy my credit card and all I have to do at this point is sign the check and we are out of here." Debbie, holding his arm says, "Thanks for a great dinner, it was very entertaining to say the least. I can't wait to leave tomorrow. We are going to have so much fun." The waiter then comes back with the receipt for signature. As Zeke is signing it he looks at her and says, "Damn it, I meant to have Carlos pay this damn check." They both just laugh at the comment. Zeke signs the check after giving a very nice tip. They head to the front of the restaurant were the guys have the cars waiting. Carlos is standing at the back door of the truck. He has the door open waiting on the happy couple to get into the back.

The cars are now loaded and they are headed back to the D.C. area. Zeke and Debbie engage in small talk on the way home. Carlos can't do anything but smile as he drives them back. He is very happy his main man has found someone to make him happy. Carlos drives quickly down the highway as Jose follows them in her car back to her house. As they get closer to the house, Debbie looks at Zeke as though she is nervous. So, naturally Zeke sees this and asks "Debbie what's wrong? Are you ok? Is Carlos driving too fast for you? I can have him slow down" "No that is not it" she says. "I am just worried what this asshole is going to say when I get there. I know it will probably be a bunch of drama." Zeke turns to her to reassure her. "I made it clear to him that he was to leave you alone. He can either listen to me or Carlos and Jose will visit him and give him something else to worry about other than you." Debbie says, "Well, I hope you're right. You did tell him and I hope he listens to you. I am in too good of a mood to be dealing with a bunch of foolishness tonight." Zeke adds, "Well, if you don't want to go home, you don't have to. Whatever you may need or want, we can just purchase down in Miami when we get there tomorrow." Debbie says "That is a sweet gesture but no, a girl wants her own things when she's on a trip. So, I will just deal with whatever he has in store for me. I know you will be picking me up in a few hours anyway. I will be fine. No need to worry about me. I don't even know why I was worried in the first place. Seems like since I have been seeing you all of my worries have gone away." She then leans over and gives him a kiss.

"Ok while you are dealing with that I am going to run to South East D.C. to catch my man Earl the barber. You know I can't go out of town without a fresh cut" Zeke says smiling. "Alright honey, don't have too much fun down there" Debbie replies.

A few more turns and they start to pull up at her house. Carlos pulls in front of the house while Jose places her car in the driveway. Carlos gets out of the car to open the door for them. Zeke gets out first and then leans in to help Debbie out of the car. When she gets out, she sees dummy in the window looking out while he holds a drink. She turns to Zeke and gives him a long passionate kiss. She knows her husband is watching so she lifts up one leg to add insult to injury. She then gives him another big hug and walks towards the house. Jose is standing there with her keys. She gives him a big hug and a kiss on the cheek and tells him thank you as she continues to walk towards the house. She gives Zeke one final wave as she enters the house and the fellas drive away.

She enters the house singing and bouncing, the effects of the wine are evident. It has not been long enough to have had sex and drive home since her husband saw her at the restaurant. So that argument is off the table at least, plus, she is not really giving a fuck anyway at this point. He storms downstairs to approach her and starts with the twenty questions. Mitch asks, "Who is that man?" Debbie replies, "That is your mistress' husband." Mitch then asks, "How long have you been seeing him?" Debbie replies, "Not as long as you have been seeing your mistress." Mitch then asks, "Are you really sleeping with him?" Debbie replies, "Are you really sleeping with your mistress?" Mitch gets a little more upset and says "Stop playing this game with me." Debbie responds, "No, you stop playing games, playa."

Mitch tries another tactic and tone of voice, "Seriously, who is this man?" Debbie then responds with, "This is the man who has opened my eyes to the person you really are. He let me see exactly how much you don't love me. He showed me how much you disrespect me and our home." Mitch just shakes his head and asks, "What is his name?" Debbie then replies, "You need to find out for yourself. That is what he told you to do right? So do it." Mitch feeling really frustrated says, "Why are you being so difficult?" "Why am I being so difficult?" she asks. "You started this in the first place by being out there cheating with these bitches." Mitch now feels his back against the wall and asks, "Are you going to keep seeing him?" Debbie just looks at him takes a breath and says, "You have some nerve. You fuck everything moving and have the audacity to be asking me fucking questions. I am tired of all your damn questions, you should have thought about that before you put your dick in all those hoes. I am going to go upstairs, light some candles and take a long hot bath, then go to bed. You can go and be on the couch or wherever you want to be but not in the bed with me. Oh, and I am going to Crystals house tomorrow for a few days. I hear that snow is coming and I don't want to be snowed in with you." Debbie heads up the stairs still talking as Mitch follows behind her trying to wait for the right moment to get a comment in.

"Furthermore, you and all of these questions are too much for me right now. I am amazed that all of a sudden you give a shit. You didn't care about me or where I was when you were out fucking your mistress so why do you care now? Wait, let me rephrase that your mistresses, that would be plural. You astound me out here going bare back with all these hoes and coming home and sticking you're nasty little dick in me. Where was the love then? You know what? I have nothing else to say. Just go downstairs so I can be alone." Mitch has no other choice but to leave at that point. He knows he has fucked up and that there is nothing he can say to change that right now. He heads downstairs to the bar to pour another drink. The night ends quietly at that point, Mitch drowning his so called sorrows in his drink while Debbie goes to sleep with happy dreams of her pending get away, with her boo Zeke.

———

TIME FOR A VACATION

As the morning sun shines through the window, Debbie's alarm goes off at seven am. She is up early to get herself together for Miami. She starts gathering up her things for the trip. She laid out most of the items needed the night before so that it would be easier to pack. Debbie heads into bathroom and brushes her teeth. After that is done, she jumps into the shower to sprinkle off. While in there, she adds a bit of shower gel to get that super nice smell all over her. When she gets out of shower and towels off she heads into the bedroom. Who else is in the bedroom but Mitch's stupid ass. Evidently, he has looked over the items she has laid out and has more questions. Mitch starts in with the questioning again "So, where are you going again? You said you were going to Crystal's house but it really doesn't look like it at all. You have so many clothes laid out here and all of them look like summer type stuff. So, what is really going on?" Debbie just looks at him and continues to get dressed. She decides she should say something and comes up with, "Did I question you all those nights you came in at 3:00 am? Did I question you when you told me you were headed to some conference only to come back with a tan? So, why are you in here questioning me now?" she asks.

Mitch is just by his wife's attitude it is like she doesn't even care anymore. When Mitch sees her coming out of the walk in closet dressed in a small linen outfit, he really loses his mind. Mitch then asks, "Ok, so you are wearing a linen outfit to Crystal's house? Is that what you want me to believe?" Debbie just looks at him in the mirror as she adjusts her skirt. She then replies with, "You know what honey? I don't even feel like lying to you because I hated it when you lied to me. So, to be honest with you, I am going on a little get away with the man you saw me with last night. I am sure you don't mind because you have spent so much time with your boo boo's and didn't give a shit about me. Don't worry, there are left overs in the fridge and extra food downstairs somewhere. Just make it work while I am gone."

Mitch is in his feelings by her candor; he then asks, "You're really going out of town with this man? You don't even know him." Debbie just smiled and says, "I thought I knew you too but I guess I was wrong. Now, can you please stop with the questions? I need to get ready to leave soon." Mitch says, "Woman you can't do this to me." Debbie responds with, "Why the hell not? You did it to me. And to add insult to injury, you did it to me over and over again. I think you kept doing it because I always let you come back. I kept telling you that I can play this game way way better than you." Mitch tries one last ditch effort, "Baby, I love you; doesn't that count for anything?" Debbie just laughs and looks at him. She takes a breath and replies, "Mitch, I love you too but I am going because I want you to feel what I felt all those times you left me home alone. As a matter of fact, I'm being picked up in an hour or so. I need to finish getting packed so I can be ready." "Are you serious? You're being picked up here?" Mitch asks. "Yes, I sure am. No need to drive my car, someone is catering to me for once, something that you know nothing about when it comes to me. Funny thing is that you treat those ratchet ass bitches better than you treat me. So, yes Mitch, my car will be arriving soon. So, can you please give me some space so that I can finish up in peace, thank you." Debbie replies. Mitch is just dumfounded at this point, he has nothing to say and just walks off. He still has no idea what to say or do to his wife.

Meanwhile, Debbie just continues to get herself ready for departure. It seems as if the clock has stopped now that she has something to do. When 9:00 a.m. arrives, she sends Zeke a text asking if 9:30 is still a good time to be ready. He responds back and tells her that he and Carlos will be leaving soon to come and pick her up. She sends him a reply that she is ready and waiting on his arrival. He lets her know that he will arrive shortly and he can't wait to see her. Debbie is happy to see those types of texts from him. She decides she needs to go out in style. She runs back upstairs and grabs her full length Chinchilla fur coat to put over her tiny outfit and open toe shoes. I am sure Zeke will get a kick out of this, she thinks to herself. She puts it on and looks in the mirror again and thinks, yeah, he will love this for sure. I look good! She takes it back off and carries it. She then heads back downstairs to wait for her ride.

Mitch is in the kitchen waiting for her ride as well. He still doesn't know what to say to Debbie. He just looks at her while she is looking out the window for the car. He is thinking to himself, how did I get myself into this mess? How am I going to get my wife back? Damn, I don't even know where she is going. He decides to chance it and ask her where she is going. The silence is broken when Mitch asks, "Can you even tell me where you're going, where you're staying, and when you are coming back?" Debbie smiling at him says, "I'm headed to Florida. I'm telling you because, at this point, I have nothing to lie to you about. And as for when I am coming back, I don't know that because I haven't been told. So, I have no idea when I am coming back and that is the truth. I am just going to stand here at the window and wait for my ride." Mitch just stands there still in disbelief that this entire episode is taking place. He then announces, "I need a drink" and goes to find another glass. Debbie just waves him away because she is not giving a shit about what he wants right now. She is too excited about her pending trip. Then, suddenly, like clockwork the car arrives exactly at 9:30 on the dot. Carlos gets out and meets her half way down the driveway. He grabs her things and she heads towards Zeke who is standing with the door open waiting for her to get in. They give each other a big hug and kiss and she jumps in. Carlos places the bags in the trunk with the others so that he can head to Reagan National Airport.

Zeke takes Debbie's hand and asks her "Are you ready for this? Did you have any problems out of your husband last night or this morning?" Debbie tells him, "Yes, I am so so ready for this trip! And, yes, he tried to play twenty questions with me, but since I had no information, it was a short conversation." "Well, what did he ask you that you couldn't answer?" Zeke asks. "He wanted to know where we were going, where I was staying, and when was I coming back. While I know we're headed to Miami, I didn't tell him, all I said to him was I was going to Florida. He saw me with my linen on and knew something was up. I couldn't tell him when I was coming back because you haven't told me," Debbie laughs. "You do have a point about that, when do you want to come back? I do have another house down that way if you want to hang out down there for awhile," Zeke says with a grin. Debbie just looks at him and says "How about we go down and enjoy ourselves and we can come back when it feels right." Zeke quickly jumps on that opportunity and says, "Ok, now that is a great idea, we can stay in Miami as long as you like. I have a boat down there as well in case you want to go splash around a bit." Debbie answers him with, "Well, I have never been on a boat. I did do a cruise once but that was like being in a big house that floats. So, yes, I want to try everything that you want to do. This is your town right? So, let's get down there so you can show me some things." Zeke replies with, "You are about to have the time of your life. I can't wait to see how you react to things," he says with devilish grin.

Some time passes and Carlos has made it to Reagan National Airport. Debbie is looking out the window and says, "Aaahh, Zeke, I think Carlos has taken a wrong turn or something because I have never been this way into National Airport. How come he did not go to the departure section on the top of the concourse like normal people do? And what is this security gate that we are going in?" she says sounding all inquisitive. Zeke looks at her and says, "Well, I have a special surprise just for you. You are a first class lady and I wanted to make sure you do this trip in a first class way. We are taking the jet down to Miami. I hope you don't mind, plus, Carlos hates flying commercial. He says the seats are too stiff and the food portions are too small. Is it ok to take the jet? I mean, I can have Carlos go back around to US Airways. I am sure we can find a flight out today." Debbie just sits there with her mouth open for a minute. When she catches herself, she reaches over and kisses Zeke again. After the kiss, Debbie says "You are full of surprises aren't you. I have never flown on a private jet but I have always wanted to." Zeke smiles at her and says, "Well, you are looking so good in this little dress with your Chinchilla coat on. I figured I better treat you like the super star that you are. I hope you like the experience." Carlos looks into the rear view mirror while laughing and says "You will love it and you will hate flying commercial forever after this."

Carlos then pulls up about fifteen feet short of the plane. He gets out and comes to the door to open it for Zeke and Debbie. They get out and head towards the plane. Debbie then asks, "What about the bags?" Zeke replies with "Carlos will take care of it. Let's get you inside and get you a mimosa or a glass of champagne to get your day started correctly." They head up the stairs of the plane. Debbie is in disbelief that all of this is happening to her. She is enjoying it but still is taken back by the whole ordeal. When they arrive inside, they are greeted by their own personal flight attendant. She takes Debbie's coat and hangs it up for her. She tells them, "Please, feel free to sit anywhere that you like." The two of them find two oversized leather lounge chairs and sit down to relax. The attendant heads towards them and asks what they would like to drink. They both say champagne and she brings them their order. While they are relaxing, Carlos is outside working with the ground crew getting the bags onto the plane. Carlos then joins them inside the plane. He heads to the back of the jet to stretch out and relax. The attendant asks Carlos what he would like to drink. Carlos replies with "Oh, just bring me a Corona for now and I'll be fine. She hurries off to get his order.

As Zeke is checking his text messages and emails, Debbie is just looking around and loving the wood grain and marble inside of the jet. She is so curious as to what is going on with Zeke. She just thinks to herself, 'should I ask him about all of this?' Zeke looks up from his phone and can see something is going on with Debbie, so, he makes and inquiry. "What's wrong, Debbie? You have a strange look on your face; did I do something wrong?" he asks her. She takes a second and figures a good way to ask and she comes up with. "OK, Zeke, I knew you were doing well in business, but private jet well? I mean you even have a flight attendant and all. How can you afford all of this? What are you, some type of secret billionaire or something? Did you hit the lottery or what?" she asks inquisitively.

"Whew, that is a lot of questions really quick," he says laughing. "Well, to be honest with you, I am not a billionaire first and foremost. I am a sound business man that loves not flying commercial. There are just too many hassles flying commercial. So, I found an affordable alternative a few years ago and have been using them ever since. What I do is purchase blocks of flying time from a company called Netjets. What that allows you to do is fly anywhere you want with a limited number of people. It is like renting a car, so to speak, but with better pricing. I purchase 30 or 40 hours at a time and use it at my leisure. Take for instance this trip to Miami, they will deduct about three hours from my total of forty hours that I have pre-paid for. It allows me to have all the comforts of jet ownership without all the problems and I love it. So, what do you think, was that a good idea for me to do?" he asks. "I think it is a great idea, actually, here I am thinking you are some secret Bill Gates or something," she says laughing. "I'm just happy you have decided to share this adventure with me," Debbie adds. He replies "I'm happy you are here with me as well. You're my breath of fresh air that I need now. I'm happy we found one another. I'm sorry that it had to be under these circumstances but I'm happy that I have found you." He then leans over and gives her a kiss.

———

Smiling at him she says, "Wow, thanks and that kiss was really nice. Can you tell me what kind of plane this is? I want to tell me girlfriends so they can be mad because they're not here with me," she says smiling. "Sure, this is a Bombardier Global 8000, it only seats fifteen passengers but for a quick flight to Miami, it's perfect. I think the cruising speed is somewhere around five hundred miles per hour, so, it will be a quick up and down going to Miami. Please feel free to walk around and take a tour. There is a bedroom back in zone four so do get any ideas. Knowing Carlos he is already back there stretched out watching tv. But take pictures and post them wherever you want. I know you're probably on Twitter and Facebook, so, feel free to post away. You can even include me in your pics if you like. However, I'm not sure you're ready to put us out there right now to the public," he says. Debbie smiles as she is blushing and asks, "Wait, there is an US?" "Well, now that dummy, meaning Mitch, knows about everything, yes, there can be an US. I was waiting on you anyway because my mind was made up about my wife months ago when I first found out about them messing around. I am so thankful for their nonsense because without it I would have never met you."

Zeke keeps melting Debbie's heart with his comments. He is not only telling her what she wants to hear, but he is also telling her the truth. He has really grown attached to Debbie. Debbie takes a deep breath and says, "Are you sure this is what you want? I mean I have grown to have feelings for you as well in a very short period of time. I don't want you to think that I am a cheater in relationships. I think I would be paranoid that you would leave me one day for not being good enough for you. While I would love to be with you too, can we just take it slow and one day at a time? I want you to get to know me better and make sure I am the one for you." Zeke just looks at her with a soft smile and says, "Sure, baby, take as long as you need. When you're ready, I will be here waiting on you. You do know and understand until you make up your mind, I will be in your face every day to remind you that I want you and that you are mine."

With that last comment she jumps out of her seat and into his and plants a big fat wet kiss on him without saying a word. "Zeke, whatever happens from here on out, just be completely honest with me. I don't want to be hurt. If I know the truth, at least I can judge for myself and determine what I am going to do," Debbie explains. Zeke replies with, "That is only fair for me to do. Can I ask a favor as well? I don't want you to think too negatively of me about my past. I'm sure your hubby will be filling you in on me soon enough. When that happens, I'm afraid you'll think I'm not good enough for you." Debbie looks at him and says, "Don't worry I won't run away from you. I'm a big girl and over the past few months, I think I have come to know the person you are. I'm sure there are things that you have done that would worry me but those things have also made you into the person that you are now. And that person is who I care about." Zeke looks at her and then hits Debbie with her own line, "Wait, you care about me?" he asks while smiling. "Yes I do! I care about you very very much, actually, and I want you in my life. However, like I said, I don't want you thinking bad of me because of the way we met and started out," Debbie says emphatically. Zeke tells her again, "You are not a cheater, you were forced into it by an asshole and so was I. We are two broken hearts that have mended one another. I'm bringing you to Miami so that I can show you how much I want to be with you. I just want you to come down here and have some fun with no pressure or thoughts of home." Debbie leans back and says, "You know what? You're right, it is time for us to have some fun. I want to enjoy Miami and enjoy you. I want to leave, no, I will leave all that mess back at home. That is where it belongs anyway. Thanks for helping me clear my head and making me feel so comfortable. It is nice to have someone like you in my life." "It is nice to have you in my life as well. I have so much planned for us; you know, Miami is like my second home. I have a bunch or surprises planned and all I want you to do is sit back and enjoy it. We are in no hurry and, at this point, you don't have any more worries," Zeke informs her.

The attendant comes back in the cabin and gives them all fruit and cheese plates. Champagne glasses have been replaced with wine glasses as the flight has been in the air an hour or so. She also informs them that they will be landing in about forty five minutes. Zeke and Debbie look in the back of the cabin and see Carlos. Poor Carlos doesn't even get to eat because he is knocked out asleep in the back. "Hey, at least he's not snoring and shaking the damn plane," Zeke says as they both get a good laugh with the attendant.

"So, is there anything special you want to do while we are down here? I made a bunch of plans on the fly last night after we decided to go. I didn't, however, consult with you and I think that was wrong," he says. Debbie just smiles as she rubs his head and says, "Baby, it is quite alright. I didn't need to be consulted. As for activities, if I can somehow swim with the dolphins, my life would be complete. I'm also sure from the way this morning has gone, anything you have planned for us will be more than acceptable to me." "Well, that's great! I cannot wait to get there so we can get started. We should be landing soon anyway. I hope you brought your bikini as well. I am sure you'll look hot in it and will turn heads everywhere we go," he says. "Yes, I brought several of them with me. I just hope that you like them. I try to keep it classy but a couple of them are a bit small." She says with that blush on her face again. Zeke is just smiling rubbing his hands together, "Yes, I'm sure you'll be just fine in them."

The pilot comes on the overhead and announces that they will be landing in about fifteen minutes and to buckle up for decent into Miami International Airport. He also announces that the temperature in Miami is a comfortable eighty five degrees with a light breeze. As the time passes, they both hold hands and look out the window. She can see how clear and pretty the water is. When she looks closer, she can spot dolphins swimming off shore in the blue water. Zeke calls out for Carlos to wake up and buckle his seat belt. The attendant has already cleared any remaining serving trays and glasses. A few more minutes pass by and they touch down onto the tarmac. The plane taxis to the private jet area. The plane rolls up to a stop and powers down. The pilot comes on overhead and lets them know they are free to exit as soon as the steps are in the locked position. He then comes into cabin and thanks them for flying Netjets.

Once the steps are locked in, they exit the plane. Debbie is surprised as Jose is there already waiting with a sedan to drive them to the hotel. Debbie runs over to him and gives him a big hug. She then asks Jose, "When did you get here?" Jose replies, "The boss had me fly down last night and prep the house since he has not been here in over five months." Debbie replies to Jose, "So, he does have a house here? And he had you fly down last night? This man is really full of surprises. I tell you." "Yes, ma'am, he is and he likes you a lot, trust me, I know," Jose replies. "Oh, you can tell, huh? How can you tell, Jose? Come on, now, you can tell me." She asks with a girlish grin still on her face. "Well, ma'am, all I can say is that you will probably see for yourself but trust me when I say, you have his eye for sure. Now, come on and get into the back of the car. I have to help Carlos with the bags," Jose replies. "Ok, Jose, I will trust you if you say he cares," Debbie says. "Ma'am, you can trust me with your life," Jose adds. He then heads to the plane to get the rest of the bags.

———

THE SOUTH BEACH LIFE

The car is now loaded and has Jose in the driver's seat and Carlos at his side, with the love birds in the back. Jose looks in the rear view mirror to ask Zeke, "Where would you like to go first, Zeke? You name it and we are there." "Well, I don't know, Debbie this is your time to have fun where would you like to go?" Debbie answers Zeke with the best answer she can think of, "How about we go to a beach and have an umbrella drink? Is that good for you guys?" Zeke laughing at this point says, "Yes, that's great for us. Jose, head to the spot in SOBE so we can freshen up a bit and maybe get those cold umbrella drinks." "Yes, sir, you got it, South Beach it is." He heads directly to Interstate 95 south. South Beach is just a few miles down the highway from the airport.

Zeke enjoys pointing out the different land marks as they head down the highway. After about fifteen minutes or so of sightseeing, they come up on A1A Collins Ave. It is the main strip of road that faces the beach. When they get there, Jose makes a right and then a quick left into the hotel. A nice hotel it is too, South Beach Marriott is as good as it gets on the strip. The valet comes down the steps to get the car. He recognizes Zeke and says, "Welcome back to the South Beach Marriott, Mr. Hill. How long will you be staying with us this time sir? We already have your normal suite available for you and your car has been readied for you as well." "Hello, Deron, and how have you been? It's good to be back. As for how long we are staying, well, that is on the lady. I think we are going to stay until she feels like leaving," Zeke replies. He just looks over at Debbie and smiles because she is all smiles at him.

Jose comes around after helping the bell captain place the bags on the cart. "Here you go, Sir, here are your room keys and everything has been taken care of. If you have any problems, let me know. I have had the captain take the bags to the room, he promised me the bags will beat you upstairs and I believe him." "Jose, I tell you what would I do without you? You are a life saver for sure. So, Debbie, shall we head upstairs? I mean, if you have a moment to go look at your room. We can go do something else if you want to, the room is not going anywhere," Zeke says. "I think we should go upstairs so I can change into some beach wear. I want to relax for a bit, like I said, and I need my umbrella drink," Debbie tells him. "Ok, great, let's head to the elevator; we can come back down in a bit," he tells her. As they walk through the lobby Debbie is amazed that all of the staff of the hotel knows Zeke by name. He seems to know all of their names as well.

When they get into the elevator, she asks him "Ok, you said this place is your second home but, wow, everyone knows you and you know everyone. How often are you down here? And how many women have you brought down here, Mr. Man?" she says with a smile. "Well, to be perfectly honest with you, I have not brought any women down here besides my wife. I really didn't get into Miami until just before we were married so she has been the only one. Either she would come with me or it would be just me and the fellas. They love it down here. They said the weather reminds them of Colombia. So, you are the first real date I have brought here. I hope you're having a good time," Zeke adds. "Sweetheart, everything is fantastic so far and I am sure everything will continue to be," Debbie adds.

As she is finishing her statement the elevator doors opens and Zeke leads her to the room. He places the key into the door and turns the handle, when he does Debbie's eyes just seem to glow, not only is this a remarkable suite but there are dozens of roses all around. Debbie asks, "Are you for real? Come on, all of this can't be for me. There is no way that I'm this lucky." Zeke responds with, "Yes it is all for you and I hope you like it. I had Jose come down last night and prepare some things for me. I hope his job is up to your liking." "Aaahhh, YES!" she quickly replies. Debbie is now looking at twelve dozen long stem roses all in their own vase. She is also looking at the words "love you" spelled out in rose pedals, on top of the all-white goose down comforter. Debbie just turns around and gives Zeke a long passionate kiss. She is speechless at this point and starts to cry. Zeke sees this and asks, "Baby, what's wrong? Are you ok? Did I do something wrong? Wait, are you allergic to roses? Please tell me what's going on. If you don't like them, I can have them removed immediately for you." "Zeke, they are beautiful and there is nothing wrong. Actually, everything is right for a change. You do things for me that I could only imagine before. I am so grateful to have you in my life and I can't imagine my life, at this point, without you in it," she says. "I tell you what; I will thank you properly later for the wonderful flower gesture because if I do it now, we won't be leaving the room today. And look at this view of the water off of the balcony; it is so clear and pretty. I just want to get changed and head down to the water with my umbrella drink."

Zeke just laughs and says, "Well, I am sure I can handle that. I will throw on some shorts and will be in the living room waiting on you. I'll call the fellas and let them know we will be coming down in five minutes or so." While she is changing in the bedroom, Zeke picks up his cell and lets Carlos and Jose know about the plan. He is sure they have been to their room and are now downstairs in the bar area waiting. He tells them to watch from the hotel outdoor bar and that they will be walking on the beach for a while and they will be ok. Carlos tells him ok and that everything else has been taken care of. Zeke tells him that is outstanding news and they will be down in a few.

Debbie finally appears looking stunning in a sexy bikini with a see through wrap on the bottom half. She has on flip flops but has heels in her Karl Marx beach bag just in case they are needed. "Damn, baby, I see you're trying to hurt them today. I'm glad you're with me and I'm glad I have the fellas because I'm going to need security with you looking like this. I'm going to need them to help me fight these dudes off of you today. Shoot, the way you look, I might need some help fighting the women off of you too. Wow, you look great!" Zeke tells her with a big grin on his face.

Zeke and Debbie head to the elevator hand-in-hand as if they have been together forever. They both reach for the down button at the same time as if their lives are in sync already. They laugh as they realize what just happened.

While they are riding the elevator down Debbie turns to Zeke and says, "I tried to hold it in but when I went to change I had to cry. I didn't want you to see me crying again but they were tears of joy. You don't know how much it meant to me to have someone get me twelve dozen roses. I wasn't going to tell you I was crying but I wanted you to know how special you made me feel today. I don't have things like that happen to me, not only with Mitch but even before him. I promise I will make it up to you later," Debbie says. "You don't have to do anything for me. I did it because I wanted to, not because I was looking for something in return. I'm just trying to show you that, at this point, I want you in my life, as a matter of fact, I need you in my life now," Zeke says. Debbie goes back to tears and hugs him and won't let go as the elevator opens and the people waiting see them in a wonderful embrace.

———

They walk through the lobby towards the back patio bar. Zeke spots Carlos and Jose and heads towards them. Debbie can see that they are having drinks already and she wants one too. Debbie goes up to Jose and gives him a big hug around his neck and gives him a kiss on the cheek. She tells him, "Jose, the flowers are wonderful. Thank you so much for getting it taken care of for Zeke, it made me feel so special. You guys are the best friends ever in life. And I see you guys have drinks. Can I get one of what you two are drinking but add one of those cute umbrellas, please?" Jose replies, "Yes ma'am we are drinking mojito's. When in Miami, you have to have one. I'll get you one now. Zeke, would you like one of these as well?" "Sure I would, but no umbrella for me, please," he says laughing. Jose hustles off to the bar to retrieve the drinks.

Carlos asks Zeke, "Since you want to relax alone, do you want us to hang around and wait or just give you time today?" "You know, I thought I was going to let you guys chill out today but then I saw her in this outfit, so, I may need you guys to help me fight these men off," Zeke says. He and Carlos just break out in laughter at the comment. Debbie chimes in with, "You guys are crazy. I'm just a regular girl. I'm no super model like the ladies I see walking around here. I see how Miami gets the reputation." Jose returns with the drinks and gives them to Zeke and Debbie. Debbie says, "Hey, guys, we are going to take a walk on the beach to get some sun. Can you guys take care of my beach bag for me while I walk with Zeke?" "Sure not a problem ma'am, whatever you need," Jose replies. "Oh, Jose, you are so sweet and thank you," Debbie adds.

Zeke and Debbie grab the drinks and head out the back patio towards the beach. She is enjoying the sun and the pure white sand. As they are walking along the shoreline with their feet in the water, Debbie asks him, "So, what are we going to do while we are here? From the looks of things so far it seems that you have some creative ideas up your sleeve. I'm up for almost anything as long as I'm with you." Zeke just smiles as he looks at her hand in his and says, "I have planned a few things but it is very fluid right now. I don't want to overwhelm you and put too much on your plate. You can tell from the hotel staff that Miami is like my second home. By me being a local, I know what places to hit and what to do. So, you tell me what would you like to do, this is as much your vacation as it is mine." Debbie thinks about it and replies, "All I wanted to do, really, is clear my mind of all that bullshit at home. I also want to relax and see some of this wonderful city." Zeke who seems to be always smiling these days says, "Well, your wish is my command. When we finish these drinks, we can go get started on some activities but I must say I am enjoying walking in the water and just holding your hand." "Aaawww, Zeke you say the sweetest things. I'm so happy that I now have you in my life and I hope I have you for good!" Debbie adds.

"When we get back to hotel, I have another surprise for you and I hope that you like it. I took the liberty of making you and I an appointment somewhere. I did tell them that you were a busy executive so the time of arrival could not be set in stone. I was assured that whenever you arrive, we would be taken care of," Zeke says. "Hey, that is fine for me, when we get back to hotel I will change and we can go wherever you want to go," Debbie says. "No, no, no, you are dressed just fine for where we're going. You don't need to change a thing," Zeke replies. "Aaahh, baby, I am in a thong bikini with basically my ass out except for this cover up, are you sure this will be appropriate," Debbie asks. "Trust me, you are fine, actually, you might have on too much to be truthful," he says while laughing. "Let's head back to the hotel and I can share my surprise with you," Zeke tells her.

As he is walking back, he sends Jose and Carlos a text message to have the second surprise ready. They have been walking for quite a while, so, it will take a hot minute to get back. However, when they do arrive back at the hotel, Jose and Carlos have ice cold bottles of Evian waiting on them. They know how hot the beach can be and it is just what the two love birds need at this time. Carlos and Jose tell Zeke that everything is ready and waiting. Zeke acknowledges their hard work with a quick thanks guys and heads towards the spa where the second surprise is waiting.

Zeke decides to let her in on the surprise a bit. He tells her, "I have taken the liberty of booking us a couples' massage therapy session. I hope you don't mind but after last night and what happened at the restaurant, I wanted to do everything I could to help you to relax. I just hope that you like it." "Well, you are full of surprises aren't you? I have, actually, never had a professional massage so this will be a nice experience for me. Do I have to take off my clothes?" "Well, for what I have ordered you might want to, but they give you a large towel to wrap up in. They will also place something over you while you are getting the massage. You will forget all about being naked once they get started. Plus, I will be right there on the table next to you so you don't have to worry about a thing. They are waiting on us to arrive in the spa area. All we have to do is get there." Debbie says, "This is sounding better and better all the time."

They get off the elevator on the second floor spa level. When they enter the spa, there is a lady holding a tray with two glasses of cold champagne for the two lovers. She says, "Good afternoon, Ms. Erickson, and Mr. Hill and welcome to a revitalizing afternoon." She continues with, "Please, follow me to the deck massage lounge." When she opens the door, Debbie's mouth hits the floor again; she cannot believe what this man has done. She now has in front of her two massage therapists dressed in all white. The room overlooks the ocean and the thirty foot sliding glass doors are opened up all the way. Naturally, you can feel the ocean breeze and more importantly hear the sounds of the waves crashing on the beach. There is soft music playing and candles lit all around the room. Even more impressive is the fact that the entire floor has been lined with rose pedals about two inches thick. There are so many pedals that the entire room smells of roses even with the sliding glass doors open.

Debbie says, "No, baby, you have to stop. This is just way too much," as the tears are now flowing again. "I don't deserve all of this. I am just a simple woman and this is just too much," Debbie reminds him. "I told you before and I am telling you now, you do deserve all of this. Someone needs to spoil you, someone like me who appreciates all that you do for them. So, let's get changed and on the table so these folks can go to work. I promise you that after it is over you will feel one hundred times better." "You know what? You're right I need to just go with it. I do deserve this nice treatment. I'm sure I will enjoy the massage. Is the changing area this way?" she asks headed to the restroom sign. "Yes just head in the back to change. Please, undress to your comfort level and we will do the rest," the masseuse instructs them.

The pair of them get undressed and put on the bathrobes that are provided. "So tell me how do I look with just a bathrobe on?" Debbie asks. "Debbie you look so tasty right now, I wish we were upstairs alone. That is how fantastic you look to me." Zeke confirms her sexiness as they both stretch out on a table for a relaxing massage. They both lay back and gaze into one another's eyes as the warm oil is poured and the pampering begins.

Zeke says, "Well, I have ordered us both deep tissue massages with warm fragranced oil. I hope you don't mind. If the therapist does it too hard, just let her know and she will adjust as needed. I have also requested that they play some Floetry as well. I thought it would bring our relaxing environment full circle." "Honey, everything is perfect. I could not ask for a better surprise than the one you are providing me with today. Everything is great from the rose pedals on the floor to the candles and music. I don't need anything else. Now, I can see how people fall asleep during their massage. These things are so relaxing and body soothing," Debbie tells him. "Yes they are" he tells her and, seemingly on cue, they both drift off to sleep at the same time.

———

About an hour or so passes and an alarm goes off ever so gently, they are both awakened at the same time. They find themselves in the room by themselves and in a peaceful state. "That was the best ever," Debbie tells him. "I am glad you enjoyed yourself. Let's get upstairs so that we can change. I think I need a bite to eat, at this point. What about you? Are you hungry?" Zeke asks. "I am hungry, I will say that, but can we eat something light now and grab a real dinner later? Now that I see how things are going down here, I want to go shopping for just the right outfit for dinner. Can I also take one of the guys with me? I would take you but then you would see what I'm buying and ruin the surprise," Debbie says. "Sure, that'll be fine, go ahead and do your shopping thing and, by all means, you can take the guys with you if you like. They will keep you out of trouble," he says laughing. "Trouble? Now, what trouble could I possibly get into?" She says with a devious smile on her face. "Oh, you could get into a lot of trouble, Miss Lady. But for now, let's go change. We can run down to the Beacon and sit on the patio for a quick bite to eat. We can do some people watching from there for sure. You can make me look good at the same time," Zeke tells her. "Oh, you're so nice, we can make each other look good," she tells him.

LUNCH AND PEOPLE WATCHING

Some time passes as they get ready for a quick lunch at the Beacon. She finally comes out of the bathroom looking fine as hell like she always does. Zeke tells her, "I see you're fitting into this Miami lifestyle pretty easily. Look at you dressed in an all white outfit. What little there is of it anyway," he says laughing. "Well, when in Miami, do as they do, plus, you told me to make you look good right? So that's what I'm trying to do," she says with an innocent grin. Debbie knows she is showing off that PHAT ass with what she has on. It is basically see through leaving little to nothing to the imagination.

Zeke calls the crew and tells them that they are headed down to the lobby. The fellas never left the bar area from their walk on the beach so they're already there patiently waiting watching soccer on tv. When Debbie walks into the bar, both of their heads turn at the same time, Carlos is bold enough to say "WOW." Zeke knows he has his hands full this afternoon. Debbie is wearing white linen daisy dukes with a shear shirt to match. Naturally, the all white high heels are also in play. She is looking stunning once again from head to toe. "Hi guys," she says. "I know the outfit is a little tight but Zeke told me to make him look good so this is what I came up with. How did I do?" she asks. Carlos and Jose just look at one another for a split second and Jose says, "Well, ma'am you look fantastic! And, yes, you are making him look good, so, your mission has been accomplished. You'll really see it for yourself in a moment when we go down Ocean Drive. Horns will be blowing all day". "See, it's not just me who thinks you're hot; everyone does," Zeke says. "Let's head down to the Beacon and grab a late lunch, Zeke says. I know Jose and Carlos love the place. They get to watch all the eye candy of south beach there," Zeke says laughing.

As they are headed to the restaurant Debbie takes the time to slip Jose a note out of the line of site of Zeke. When he opens it, he reads that he is to find a Bank of America and to keep that info from Zeke; it is a surprise. She does add in the note that he can tell Carlos. As they are walking, Jose gestures to her and says, "ma'am I'll be ready for you after lunch." Debbie just shakes her head in acknowledgement as they head down the block to the restaurant. It is just a short walk down Ocean to The Beacon Hotel. The restaurant there is called The Place. The Place is an appropriate name for it because it is the spot to be to people watch.

When they arrive, they ask the hostess for a patio seat. The four of them settle down for a fabulous lunch. Zeke arranges the seats so that he and Debbie can see the crowd clearly as they walk by. Debbie tells him, "This place looks nice, do you recommend anything to eat?" Zeke, who is a regular at The Place, tells her, "By it being lunch, you should try something light. I think you should go for the grilled mahi mahi sandwich. It's not too heavy and you'll be able to keep going, after you eat it, without a nap." Zeke tells her laughing. "Well, good, I don't need a nap now anyway. I had one about an hour ago," she tells him smiling back in his face.

Jose and Carlos being big guys they go ahead and order up real meals. Jose orders Floridian lobster tail with truffle mash and yuzu butter. Carlos orders seared duck with frisée, radicchio, endive, and pineapple star anise sauce served with fried rice. Zeke, listening to these guys order, does not want Debbie to feel bad so he orders light himself. He chooses the stuffed crab ravioli with marinara turmeric sauce.

Since they have placed their orders and there is time to kill. So naturally, people watching is next up on the menu. The four of them start to rate the passersby, each one of them assigns a number between one and five to classify attractiveness. Debbie, who was hesitant to rate people, thinking it would be rude starts to join in. She has fun with the fellas and their rating system. She realizes it is very amusing and she is not hurting anyone so why not. The fellas are having too much fun with the rating system. Jose and Carlos do most of the high rating of the women. They both can tell that Zeke is giving low scores to the passersby because he is trying to be respectful of Debbie. They both crack jokes on him because they know he is trying to be mister nice guy with Debbie around.

Lunch arrives and they all dig in and enjoy the good food and fine drinks. This is fine dining in a beach casual environment, with the diverse menu and first class service. What better way to spend the afternoon than with great friends, wonderful food and a fabulous location.

After lunch is over, Debbie asks Zeke, "Since lunch was so fabulous I can't wait for dinner. However, like I said before, I need to find something to wear tonight. These ladies down here are not going to outdo me. I saw how you guys looked at them during lunch and I see what styles the ladies are wearing down here. I need to go pick up a little something so I'm going to take Jose and Carlos with me, if that's ok." "Yes, that'll be fine. Just don't be gone too long, I'll get worried," Zeke replies. "Worried? Worried for what? I'm in good hands with Carlos and Jose, remember? They'll protect me from any and all the nonsense," she tells him laughing. Zeke says, "You know what? You're right. I don't have to worry about you. I do have to worry about my poor brothers. Please don't have them carrying too many bags," Zeke says laughing while looking at Jose. Jose just shakes his head and says, "Oh, Lord, what are we in for?" Zeke adds, "Well, I'm headed back to the hotel to rest and let this food digest, I'll be waiting on you." Debbie and the guys head off to do some shopping and Zeke heads back to hotel.

SHOPPING ADVENTURE

As Debbie and the guys leave and are walking down Ocean Drive she turns to Jose and asks, "Jose, please tell me you have found a Bank of America. I need to go there and pick up some cash out of one of my accounts." Jose replies, "Miss Debbie, you don't need any money. Anything you want, I will purchase for you. Zeke has already told me to buy whatever you pick up." "Well, Jose, this is a gift for him and while I'm sure he can afford it, I want to pay for it myself." Jose says, "Ok, I just hope I don't get into trouble over letting you buy things." Debbie replies, "You won't. I got your back just like you guys have mine." She gives him a kiss on the cheek and then hugs Carlos. Carlos then asks, "So, where is Bank of America?" Jose says, "Ok, ok, if you insist, Miss Debbie. It is two blocks over on Washington Ave. I found you a full service one so they can handle any transaction that you need. We can head over there now." "Ok, let's go and if you guys want anything let me know and I'll get it for you. You and Carlos have been so nice to me over these past few months. I think you guys deserve gifts as well. So, tell me what would you guys like?" "Miss Debbie, we don't need anything, we are fine. Carlos and I want the same thing. That is for Zeke to be happy and you are already making him very happy," Jose tells her. "Aaaawww, Jose, you're really nice and I am happy with Zeke too. I'm so pleased you guys brought me down here. I think I see the bank at the next corner; that was fast."

The walk down the street turns into comedy for the three of them. Debbie naturally notices men and some women all up in her space. She is catching them looking at her up and down. Then, she sees the looks on their faces when they see two men walking right behind her. She is tickled because she is thinking how much her life has changed in just a short period of time. Here she was this petite mixed black woman from Washington, D.C., that had a regular life, a regular career professional with a husband and supposedly good life. Now, she is in Miami with what seems to be her future man, walking down the street half dressed in heels with two Colombian body guards. 'What is this world coming to,' she thinks to herself. She cracks a smile to herself in reassurance that she has done the right thing by leaving her dumb ass husband. Oh, what a beautiful day she thinks to herself.

They walk up to Bank of America and head inside. The guys take a seat in the waiting area as Debbie fills out a withdrawal Slip and heads up to the window. Carlos and Jose and are just relaxing and flipping through magazines but they both notice the manager walk up to assist the teller with Debbie's transaction. Debbie is at the window for awhile but, finally, there is a thank you and come again. She turns around and walks up to the guys and hands Jose an envelope filled with cash. Debbie says, "Ok, guys I need to get to Mayors Jewelers on Lincoln Road. Do you know where that is located?" Carlos says, "Well, I think I do. Lincoln is at the south end of Ocean Ave. We can be there in no time. We can grab a cab down there with no problem." "Great, let's go," Debbie replies.

The three of them enjoy a nice cab ride down the beach. Mayors Jewelers is not that far. Jose asks out of curiosity, "Miss Debbie, what do you have up your sleeve? What are you going to pick up?" "Well, guys I'm going to go and get Zeke a Rolex and I wanted you two to help me pick one out that he might like. I hope you guys don't mind." "No, we don't mind at all and we are more than happy to help you," Jose says. The cab finally pulls up in front of Mayors and they get out and head inside.

Once they are inside, Debbie does not want to waste any time, she goes up to salesperson and asks, "Where are your men's Rolex watches located?" "Over this way, madam; just follow me," the clerk responds. Debbie then gestures for the guys to come on over with her. Debbie knows what she wants to get Zeke but wants the guys' approval on the purchase. She asks the clerk to pull out the Rolex Yacht Master 2 and she points to it to show the clerk which one it is. The clerk pulls it out and places it on the display cloth.

Debbie asks the guys, "So, what do you think? Is it a good choice for Zeke?" Carlos and Jose both are very impressed with her choice. They both let her know that it's an outstanding choice and that Zeke will love it. She then asks the guys "If you were buying a watch for Zeke which one would you choose?" Carlos looks down and says, "I think he would like that one." Jose chimes in and says, "Yes, that is the one I would pick for him too, I like the black face that it has." Debbie looks at them and asks, "Are you guys' sure he will like it? I don't want to get him something he is never going to wear." Carlos says, "That one is great looking and it doesn't cost a fortune like the first one you had us look at." "Ok, if you guys are sure I'm going to get it. Jose, can you please hand me that envelope that I gave you earlier? You guys have a seat and I'm going to go over here and handle this bill."

The guys go back to their seats and back to relaxing. Debbie heads over to the register to speak with the salesperson again. While she is there, she tells the salesperson that she is planning a surprise and can she have her items delivered to the hotel later in the day. The salesperson says that they are a full service jeweler and if that is what she needs it will be taken care of. The salesperson then asks Debbie, "Have you decided which watch you want today?" Debbie says whispering, "Well, yes, I need three of them, actually. I need one of the Rolex Yacht Master 2 and I need two of the Rolex GMT Master with the black face. I also want this to be a surprise so just act like I am purchasing one watch, ok?" "No problem, miss, we are here to serve you and the customer is always right." Debbie says, "Let me know the total and I'll pay it. I don't want the guys behind me to know what I am doing." The salesperson writes the total on a piece of paper and hands it to Debbie. The total is way over twenty thousand dollars. Debbie reaches in her envelope, counts out the money and hands it to the clerk. Debbie then writes the name and address of the hotel, along with her name, on the piece of paper and asks for it to be delivered there by 6:00 p.m. today. The clerk simply says "Yes ma'am." He then does some light paperwork and hands the receipt to Debbie while saying, "We will polish your watch and have it delivered to your hotel today by 6:00 p.m." Debbie winks at the salesperson and replies, "Thank you very much. You have made this a very easy transaction, thanks again." "You are very welcome, ma'am, and if we can be of service in the future, please let us know. Also, here is my card. If you have any questions or difficulties, please do not hesitate to call me." "Ok, will do but I am sure I'll have no problems," Debbie replies. Debbie turns around and heads over to the fellas.

"Ok, guys get me back to my baby; I'm missing him. The store is going to check the time and polish the watch for delivery later at the hotel. Please keep it a secret. I'm going to give it to him at dinner tonight. Also, Jose, here take the rest of this money and hold on to it for me. I think there's about fifteen thousand or so, left over. Just hold on to it for me, please." "Yes, Miss Debbie, no problem. I will leave it in our room until you ask for it." Carlos, can you get us a cab back please?" "Sure, Debbie, no problem," he says. Debbie grabs one arm of each of them and they walk out to the corner of Lincoln and Michigan to catch a cab back to the hotel. Debbie is feeling on top of the world right now. She is happy she has done something for her man. She is sure that he and the boys will love their gifts and this time the three of them will be surprised for sure.

The cab comes and they get in to head back to the hotel. While on the cab ride back, Carlos asks, "Debbie, is there anything else that we can do to make your day or evening with Zeke more special?" "Yes, Carlos, there is. Just make sure you guys are dressed for dinner. Don't look at me like that, Carlos, you two will be at the table with us tonight. No, I don't care what Zeke says, I need you two there with us, ok." Debbie tells him. "Yes, Debbie, we will be there. You are so funny to me, so small and always demanding something," he says smiling. All three of them get a laugh out of that comment, just as the cab is pulling up to the hotel.

The three of them get out of cab; Jose takes care of the bill as Carlos is ever so vigilant over Debbie. He doesn't want anything to happen to her. He knows Zeke will have his head if anything happens to Debbie. Carlos calls Zeke on his cell to let him know Debbie is about to come up the elevator to the room. He escorts her to the door and Zeke swings it open so the knock is not necessary. Debbie gives Carlos a big hug and thank you. She also tells him that she will see him at dinner. The door closes.

SHE TAKES CONTROL

At this point Debbie, basically, attacks Zeke. She throws him on the bed and starts pulling his clothes off all while kissing him seductively. After finally getting him naked she pushes him back up off of her. She says "Just wait." She gets up and goes to the refrigerator and pulls out a bottle of champagne and pours it all on him from head to toe. 'She must be feeling pretty frisky,' Zeke thinks to himself. 'I am going to fuck the shit out of him' is what Debbie is thinking to herself. She begins to lick the champagne off every inch of his body. All while making sure to play with and suck his dick to perfection, to make sure she keeps his attention. All Zeke can do is lay back and moan, you know, speechless. She lets out a small giggle because she accidently caught a glimpse of his toes wiggling and moving all about. That little sign lets her know that she is doing the right things to him. She feels confident to really let loose and truly be her. She flips him over and starts to....well you know. Zeke tries to push her off but it became too much to resist for him. She ate him well and caressed his dick at the same time. She then gently came around and sucked his dick until it was dry. Debbie leaned up on his chest kissed it and said "I need to ride him." She went back down on him again to get his dick hard as a rock again. She jumped on him and rode him. She could feel the veins of his dick inside of her. She could feel it throb inside her wet pussy.

This was the first time since their first night together five or six months ago that there was no protection, Debbie went for it. Being six months into their friendship, Debbie had often thought what it would be like to have him bareback inside of her again. She gave Zeke passion, love, eroticism, and nastiness, everything a good black man needs to keep him happy. He in turn was giving it back to her. She was definitely not getting any good sex, let alone nasty sex, at home. She was not giving any nasty sex at home either, for that matter. She was riding Zeke violently like a wild animal and she was handling it well. Right up until he started gently licking her nipples, she could not take it anymore. She erupted and let out a gigantic scream. Debbie immediately falls over on Zeke's chest giving him so many kisses he couldn't count them. She then falls asleep on top of him with his dick still sticking up in between her wet warm juicy lips. Zeke can feel Debbie's sleeping tone and decides to grab a nap too. Why move and mess up this beautiful position.

DINNER WITH SURPRISES

The phone in the hotel room rings and rings. Zeke finally hears it and realizes where he is. He is waking up inside of Debbie just like he went to sleep. She is still knocked out, Zeke realizes it has been a long day for her. Zeke goes to reach over for the phone and wakes up Debbie in the process. She goes back to kissing him while Zeke answers the phone. "Hello," Zeke says. "This is Carlos, you told me to call you at 8:00 to remind you about dinner." "Oh, that's right, thanks for the call. I'll hit you back in about thirty minutes so we can head out, ok?" Zeke says. "Ok, gotcha, boss, we will be ready. Everything has been taken care of and see you soon," Carlos says. They both hang up.

Zeke nudges her again and tells her, "Hey, we have to get up for dinner. If you don't want to go out, we can always order room service here, that would be fine with me too." "No, honey, let's get up. I want to look pretty for you for dinner. I just have to shower and get dressed right quick," Debbie replies. Zeke, thinking, he asks, "Debbie, can I ask you a question? Where are the bags from shopping? I thought you would come back with arms full." "Oh, I had Jose hold them for me in their suite. I just didn't want to clutter up our place. I had a plan for you when I came back earlier." "Wow, you bought so much stuff that it would clutter up the place?" Zeke says laughing. He doesn't give it anymore thought. Debbie runs off to shower and to get dressed. Zeke takes the time to figure out what he is going to wear.

Some time passes and Debbie comes out of dressing area. Here she is stunning again. In an all white, little to nothing, linen dress with a full length shear linen wrap. All while stepping out in Red Bottoms. All Zeke can do is look at her, legs all oiled up and looking tasty. He wants her now but knows if he takes her, dinner will be out of the question. "So, I take it this is just a little something that you just threw on?" Zeke asks. "Well, I just try to make you look good. Did I accomplish my goal?" she asks. "You certainly did and then some, I would say," Zeke replies. Debbie walks over to him and begins to adjust his shirt. "You look and smell wonderful yourself, Mr. Man," Debbie tells him as she kisses him on the neck. "You know what? Let me stop. If I keep acting like this, we are never going to make dinner," Debbie says. "You don't know how funny that is, I was just thinking the same thing. I see we both have bad intentions today," Zeke says laughing. Debbie laughing with him says, "Yes, I'm in full agreement. We better get downstairs; it is so hot in here." They both can't help but to laugh together. They grab their things and head for the lobby.

When Zeke and Debbie are on the elevator she informs Zeke that she has to stop at the front desk. He says ok and the elevator door opens. They immediately spot Carlos and Jose and head over to them. "Hey, what's up guys, are you ready? I see you already have cocktails getting the night started right," Zeke says. "Yes, we're good. We were waiting on you two. We just figured you had wardrobe stuff going on with the lady and all," Carlos says. Zeke just laughs and says "Yes, man, we did, there are clothes everywhere." "It is not," Debbie replies, as she pushes Zeke's shoulder. "Look, I need to borrow Jose for a minute. We will be right back," as she grabs Jose's hand and drags him with her. "Poor fella, I don't know what she's doing but I hope he'll be ok," Zeke says smiling. Carlos lets out a chuckle off of that one himself. Zeke picks up the glass that has been vacated by Jose and gives a toast with Carlos. "Here is to a good night!" Zeke says. "Here here!" Carlos replies.

Debbie is now at the concierge desk. "My name is Debbie Erickson. Do you have a package for me?" "Yes, Ms. Erickson, we do. We have been expecting you. Here is your package ma'am and if there is anything else, please let us know," the concierge tells her. "You don't need me to sign for it or show any ID?" she asks. "No, ma'am, you are with Zeke and we know who you are," he replies. Debbie just smiles and is once again reassured she has done the right thing. She takes the bag off of the counter thanks the concierge and gives him a generous tip. She then gives the bag to Jose and they proceed back to Zeke's location.

"Ok, guys, I'm ready to go. I had to get a little something from the desk," She says. "Hhhmm what's in the bag? Anything for me?" Zeke asks. "Maybe, but you'll have to see later when we get to dinner. Let's go. Miami is waiting on us," Debbie says with excitement. The four of them proceed down to the front of the hotel where an all black SUV is waiting for them. The driver gets out and opens the door. With fun in the air, all four get into the SUV. The driver has already been instructed to head to Prime 112.

Prime 112 is an upscale and modern steak house with a great atmosphere and great food. The staff is outstanding as well. When they arrive at the restaurant, they are given first class treatment. Valet service is on point and no waiting in line or checking to see if there is a table available. The maître d' escorts them to their table, immediately, and proceeds to pull the chair out for Debbie. After she is seated, he thanks the party for coming to Prime 112 and informs them that their server will be along momentarily.

"Gentlemen, all three of you look fantastic tonight. I must say I am the luckiest girl in here tonight." Debbie just throws it out there to loosen things up. Zeke chimes right back with, "As you know by the amount of heads that turned when you walked in, you are certainly the prettiest woman in here tonight. We are thankful to be in your presence." "Zeke is laying it on thick today," Carlos whispers to Jose. They both just laugh a little at the same time. Zeke turns to Carlos and says, "What?" "Come on, man, 'thankful to be in your presence? ' While it is certainly true and, Debbie, don't get me wrong, but Jefe', where did you get that from? It don't even sound like you." Zeke smiles and chuckles a little bit himself. "But did it sound good?" Zeke asks Carlos laughing. "Oh, yes, it sounded great and you better have meant it to, buddy," Debbie adds.

The waiter comes over and brings menus. She then asks if she can get them anything to drink at this time. Debbie turns to Zeke and asks him, "Baby, can we get champagne? I feel like a celebration tonight. Would that be ok with you?" she asks. "Of course, you can have anything that you want. Waitress, can you bring us two bottles of champagne. Just pick two good ones that you would drink yourself," Zeke says. "Yes, sir, I'll get that right away for you," she says and runs off to get the glasses and bottles together. "So, tell me, is everyone eating steak tonight since we have come here?" Debbie asks. "They do have the best steak on the beach, so, it would be a good idea. However, if you don't want steak, no one is going to be mad if you order something else," Zeke adds. "No, that's fine with me. I'm a steak and potatoes kind of girl. I'm on vacation, so, the diet is out the window anyway," she says as she is laughing.

"So, sweetness what's in the bag? Jose has been carrying this thing around since the hotel. I'm curious, at this point, about what is in it," Zeke says with enthusiasm. "Well, it is just a little something but can we wait for the champagne that we ordered to arrive?" Debbie asks him. "Sure thing, but can you give me a hint at least?" Zeke asks. Carlos and Jose just snicker to themselves. One because they know what the present is and two because Zeke is sounding like a little kid at Christmas. Some small talk continues until the champagne arrives.

Everyone is given a glass and Debbie gestures to Jose to pass her the bag. "Ok, spill it Miss Lady, what is in the bag?" Zeke asks again smiling. "Oh, be patient," Debbie says. "First, I want to say thank you to all three of you for taking me into your hearts and making me feel welcome. These last few months I have felt like I was in the shadows dating Zeke. Now, I feel that we are free to be us anywhere and everywhere. Since I am so very happy with life right now, I wanted to give you something that shows you that I care. I wanted to give you gift that will show you that I want you in my life. Now, every time you look at it, I want you to know I am thinking about you and I love you." Debbie then reaches into the bag and pulls out a big red box. Zeke is surprised and doesn't even know what it is yet. He unwraps the packaging and discovers a brand new Rolex Yacht Master 2 watch. "Wow, look at this guys! Baby, this is just way way too much. I don't need all of this; you really went out of your way on me," Zeke exclaims. "No, I did what I felt in my heart. This is what I wanted you to have, so, I got it for you. The guys helped me and I swore them to secrecy, so, please don't be mad at them for helping me," Debbie says. "No, I'm not mad at them at all. I see who their loyalty really is to now and it ain't me," he says smiling.

"You know what? I'm glad you said that. Baby, I do love you but I love Carlos and Jose too. While I was in the store I picked up you two a little something as well." She reaches back in the bag and pulls out two more boxes and gives them to the boys. Carlos and Jose tare into the packaging like they are the kids at Christmas. They finally get the boxes open and what do they find? They too have been blessed with new Rolex GMT Masters. She has gotten them the watches that they were admiring at the store. Carlos just stands up and then scoops up Debbie to give her a big hug. Without putting her down he passes her to Jose for another big hug. Jose then gently puts her down. Zeke picks up his glass and says, "Everyone, get a glass." "Here is to family and making even better and stronger bonds." They all raise a glass and toast to the well spoken verse. It was the perfect fit for the moment and gives a basic new beginnings-type of feel. It is good to see everyone smiling and enjoying themselves. The waiter comes back and Zeke proceeds to order everyone's favorite steak and sides.

Carlos and Jose are enamored with their new watches. They are impressed that Debbie was able to pull the wool not only over Zeke's eyes but their own as well. "Debbie the watches for Jose and I were a very nice gesture and what a surprise! We really appreciate you getting them for us," Carlos says. "No problem. I wanted you guys to know that I loved you too. You two are always looking out for me and taking care of Zeke. I just felt it was time for me to do something for you. I know it is not a big deal but I wanted to do it," Debbie says. "Debbie, like Carlos said we both thank you so much, they are great. You pulled a fast one asking us which one would we get if we were getting Zeke one. You used that conversation to get us a watch that we really approved of. You are a very smart woman and, again, we are very grateful," Jose adds.

Some time passes and the four of them get through dinner without too much fuss. Just drinks, laughter, and talking about the old days. "Hey, look guys why don't we hit the club after dinner for a little while. How does that sound to you guys?" Zeke asks. "Well, I want to go out with you three so let's do it," Debbie exclaims. "Alright then we will head to Liv for a little while after dinner. Carlos, can you call our folks over there and get us a table? I don't feel like all the line stuff tonight," Zeke says. "No problem, Boss. I'll make the call now. I'll be right back," Carlos says as he gets up from the table and heads to a quiet place that he can make a call. "Debbie, I will say one thing, you are certainly full of surprises. This has been a great dinner," Zeke tells her. "Hey, I had fun too but are we going to pass Carlos the check?" Debbie says jokingly. "I think that is a great idea, Debbie. As a matter of fact, I think you should order another bottle of champagne before we leave, since Carlos is paying," Jose says while laughing. "Jose you are out of control, but if you see the waiter, call him over so we can order another bottle," Zeke says laughing with Jose.

Debbie sits up and takes a breath, she knows this next question will be a winner or loser and she is nervous. "Zeke I know I want to be in your life, but I don't feel like I know you all the way. Are you ever going to show me your operation?" Debbie asks. "My operation? What do you mean my operation?" Zeke asks. "Look, I know you do software development and IT security but you walk around with Carlos and Jose so something else is going on as well. I just can't put my finger on it. If I'm being too nosey, I will just leave it alone," Debbie adds. "Well, there are some things that you don't know about me for sure. I will be more than happy to share my life with you. Are you sure we can trust you to bring you into our world?" Zeke asks. All the while Jose is just sitting there looking at Zeke wondering what he will tell her. Debbie replies, "Yes you can trust me; who am I going to tell?" "I had to ask because there is more than my life at stake. So, I have to be concerned with what and to whom you would tell my business," Zeke says. As Zeke is finishing his statement Carlos returns to the table. He informs everyone that the reservations have been made for Liv.

When Carlos is done speaking Zeke says, "Carlos we are going to show Debbie here our operation tomorrow. We are going to take her down to The Keys and really show her what is what." Carlos realizing what is going on replies with, "Boss, are you sure that is a good thing to do? I know you two are cool and all but show her the operation? Are you sure you want to do that?" Zeke says, "Yes I'm sure, we can head down tomorrow after breakfast and then she can know it all." "Ok, you're the boss. I'll call and let the crew know we are coming down. Do you want me to have the gear prepared as well?" Carlos asks. "Yes, have everything ready to go. That should open her eyes to our world for sure," Zeke replies. "Ok, guys I'm still here, can you stop talking about me like I'm not here," Debbie says laughing. "I can't wait to see this operation of yours, baby. I'm sure I'll be surprised and impressed." "Yes, I'm sure you will be surprised as well that is for damn sure," Zeke says.

"Well, folks, we are pretty much done with dinner. Carlos, we decided while you were gone that you were paying the check tonight," Zeke adds. "Wait, what? Why am I paying the bill again? You guys always stick me with the bill," he says laughing. They all just laugh with him because it has become a running joke among the four of them. Carlos goes ahead and pays the check. They proceed down to the truck to head to the club for some after dinner fun. As they jump into truck again, Jose tells the driver "Can you please head over to Liv night club? We want to have some fun." The driver replies yes and heads towards the club as soon as everyone is back in the truck.

DRINKS AND BUBBLES

So, the SUV pulls up in front of Liv. Carlos then gestures for the driver to pull around to the side of the club. They are not waiting in line anyway, they naturally have VIP service. When the driver pulls around to the side of the club, a door opens and a valet comes out to open the passenger doors. The team files out of the SUV and enters the building. They are escorted upstairs to their private skybox that has been reserved for them. From the skybox, they can see the entire club at a glance. The skyboxes are lifted fifteen feet off of the ground and are made of glass. When they enter the box, they find bottles and fruit trays waiting on them. They also have a woman there waiting to provide table service as well.

The good thing is that they have come on a great night. Some of the hottest rappers in the game are set to perform. "Hey, guys, I was just told that Fat Trel and Wale are going to perform tonight, so, we are in for a real treat," Carlos says. "Well, that explains why the crowd is so thick in here tonight. Wale is a beast on the microphone," explains Jose. "I'm sorry, baby, if I had known, I would have chosen somewhere else," Zeke says. "It is ok, baby, I like Wale. I like his music and he's from D.C., so, I'm supporting him for sure since I'm here. I am sure they both will put on a fabulous show tonight," Debbie says. "Yes, I can tell from the crowd that the energy is up and they are ready to party. All we have to do is get some party favors up here and we will be good," Zeke says. "Boss, I'm reading your mind and making a call now," Carlos says as he is dialing numbers on his phone. Carlos is calling one of his Miami folks;

he needs to get some yayo right quick for tonight. After he says a few lines in Spanish he hangs up and tells Zeke that the package will arrive soon.

"Alright everyone, it is party time; let's get these bottles popped and glasses full," Zeke says. As soon as the first bottle is popped, Super DJ Horse Raney throws on one of the hottest songs out right now. Liv has flown him down from Greensboro, North Carolina, just to spin for the evening. Horse stirs up the crowd into a frenzy! Everyone is having a blast, then, all of a sudden, the side show starts, bubbles begin to fall from the ceiling. Debbie is looking in full amazement because this club is so different from what they have at home. Debbie then grabs Zeke and asks, "Wait, am I seeing things? Is that the Mario brothers?" "You know what, it is them, I can't believe they have this in here. Look, Jose, there are Mario and Luigi of Mario Brothers fame," Zeke says. "Look over there; are those Las Vegas show girls? I am really loving this place," Zeke adds. "Honey, what is going on in here? Look over there. Is that Spiderman hanging from the ceiling? Wait, is he dancing while on the spider web?" Debbie asks. "I don't know if you call that dancing but he is trying to do something for sure. Maybe he is stuck in his own web," Jose says laughing.

Carlos' phone rings and he tells Zeke he'll be right back. He heads downstairs to meet his man. The party still rages on out of control. The bottle service lady has returned and is there pouring everyone shots just because. "Zeke, I really love this place. Can we come back again one day?" Debbie asks. "Sure we can come back as often as you want to. I like this place too, there is always something going on in here," Zeke says. Jose adds, "Hey, Debbie, that cube over there contains the guys from the Miami Heat, look." "Yes, I know. I saw those guys earlier and they look like they are having as much fun as we are. Everyone has come out to see Wale and Fat Trel; this is a fantastic turn out. The DJ is awesome. He has the whole club moving to the beat," Debbie says.

Carlos comes back upstairs into the skybox and hands Zeke a plastic bag to look at. Zeke takes a peek inside and gives it back to Carlos. "Go ahead and stretch out some lines for us. I just don't feel like doing it. And don't make one for Debbie you know she don't fuck around," Zeke says. "Ok, boss, you got it. I will make it happen," Carlos says as he sits down to break out the coke. Carlos is taking his job seriously. He is making sure that the lines are even and that no one has so much that they lose self-control in the club. Carlos takes one of the lines straight to his brain, then turns to the crew and says "Ok, fellas, come and get it." He then passes the straw to Jose. Jose is an old pro so he takes one line for each side of his nose. "Whew, I am feeling no pain now for sure!" Jose says as he passes the straw to Zeke.

Zeke just laughs at Jose as he takes a seat in front of the rows that are left. Zeke hits the left side and then the right, then leans his head back and pulls in a rush of fresh air up his nose. "Hey, you got to get everything moving into your system you know. That little rush of fresh air helps so much" he says to Jose. "Hey, baby, can I have a line or two?" asks Debbie. "Wait, you play around with this stuff?" asks Zeke. "Well, not in years but since I'm on vacation and I'm having a good time, why not? Pass the straw," Debbie says. Zeke, Carlos, and Jose all look at one another as the woman of the hour does a couple of lines. She takes them to the head like she is the old pro. The guys just smile and look at one another. Debbie finally looks up after the last line and says, "Wow that's good! Now, where is my damn drink?"

Zeke just looks at her smiling and says, "You are full of surprises today. Who knew you would even mess with coke." "Zeke, like I said before, I'm on vacation and I want and need to have some fun. I have been married to a lame ass for years with damn near no excitement. It is time for me to do me and you're just the right person to do it with. I know I'm in good hands with you guys and you would never let anything happen to me. Now, where is the bar maid, I need my glass refreshed," she says. Jose jumps up, "One bar maid at your service. Can I pour you some more Ciroc?" he asks. "You certainly can, kind sir, and I thank you," she says. Jose refills her glass and the party continues.

An hour or so passes, Fat Trel and Wale take the stage and put on an incredible show. The crowd is rocking at fever pitch. Between the two of them they put on a very nice set. After Fat Trel and Wale are done, DJ Horse jumps back on the ones and twos. He keeps the crowd moving and partying all night. Debbie is having so much fun she does not want to leave. Zeke looks down at his watch and it is somewhere after 3:00 a.m. and the club has no sign of slowing down anytime soon. Zeke looks over at Carlos and gives him the sign to get ready to roll out. Zeke then breaks the news to Debbie, who is in go mode for sure, that it is time to leave. Carlos and Jose are poised and ready to move the crowd out of their way.

Debbie asks Zeke, "Baby do you have some cash on you?" "Yes I do; what do you need?" Zeke replies. "Give me a couple of hundred please, I want to tip our waitress she was incredible tonight," Debbie replies. "Yes, she was really cool, here is four hundred bucks. Do you think that is enough?" Zeke asks. "Yes that will be enough, I just wanted to make sure we take care of her outside of the check," Debbie replies. "You are such a kind and loving person. I am happy to have you in my life," Zeke says. "Hey, I try," Debbie says smiling. "Come on, baby, follow the guys down the steps so that we can get out of here and get some sleep," Zeke tells her. "I will if you just hold my hand the whole way down," Debbie tells him. "Sure, no problem, I want to hold your hand all the time anyway," Zeke admits. They hold hands and follow Carlos and Jose out the side door and into the waiting SUV. The driver heads back to the South Beach Marriott. Once he arrives there, the crew gets out and heads upstairs to bed.

"Guys, I would say I would see you in the morning but since it's already after 3:00 a.m., you better make that lunch," Zeke says. He follows that with, "Oh yeah, Jose, is everything set for tomorrow?" "Yes, boss, we are a go for tomorrow; whatever time you wake up I am ready," Jose says. "Alright, well, I'll see you in a few hours then. You two get some rest. I know I am passing out as soon as I hit the pillow," Zeke says. Debbie then chimes in with, "I don't know how much sleep you think you're going to get but let's get on up to this room, momma got some business to take care of," she says with a smile on her face. She is feeling the effects of the alcohol for sure. Zeke just smiles and complies and heads to room still holding her hand. When they arrive to the room and go in, Debbie is already kissing him on his neck and shoulders while he is opening the door. She easily slips out of her outfit and leaves her heels on and lies on the bed seductively. Zeke looks at her with enthusiasm and says, "Baby, you look so wonderful laying there. I want you so bad just let me get in

the bathroom and take a quick shower. I was sweating so much in the club."
"Alright, baby, but please hurry back I want you to take me," Debbie says with
a passionate moan.

Zeke heads to shower for a quick rinse off. 'This damn Miami temperature
will catch up to you if you are not careful' is what he is thinking to himself.
Ten minutes later he is coming out of the bathroom and what does he find?
Debbie passed the hell out and sleeping peacefully. He just reaches down and
takes off her heels. Then he pulls the covers up on her and allows her to sleep.
He knows this crazy lifestyle filled with drinks and drugs is not her. He is
not mad that she has passed out on him. All he can think of is how peaceful
she looks while laying there dreaming. He figures it is a good time to hit the
balcony and smoke a good Cuban cigar. He pulls one of them out of his bag
and heads to the balcony and, after he lights up, he just stands there gazing at
the ocean on a moonlit night. He thinks how lucky he is to have a winner like
Debbie finally in his corner. He then looks at the Rolex that she purchased for
him. He is reminded that he has a good one in his corner.

THE OPERATION

Morning comes and the sun is peaking through the blackout curtains of the suite. Well, actually, it is late morning, the partying the night before has both of them sleeping in. Debbie comes alive first and rolls over to give Zeke a kiss on the cheek, trying not to wake him at the same time. She gets up and slips on some sweats quietly to allow Zeke to sleep. She grabs here running shoes and heads off to the beach for a quick run. Debbie does about five miles altogether and when she returns to the back of hotel, she finds Carlos and Jose having coffee and muffins. "Morning guys, what a night," she says. Carlos replies, "Yes it was a wild one for sure, we are happy you had fun. So, what do you want to do next?" "Carlos, I tell you after last night, I don't have to do anything. You guys showed me such a great time. I can't think of anything better," Debbie tells him. Jose asks, "Where is Zeke this morning?" "I left him sleeping in bed. I guess he needs some more beauty rest," Debbie says laughing. Jose says, "Ok, well, I have everything ready for you guys. I am just waiting on you two to let me know when you need it." "Wait, what do you have ready? What's going on now, Jose? Come on spill the beans already!" Debbie exclaims. "Miss Debbie, I actually thought you already knew. You know I can't tell you anything. Zeke will be mad at me. I have already said enough, you will have to wait for Zeke to tell you about whatever is going on," Jose tells her. All Carlos can do is sit back and laugh at them both. "Carlos, it's not funny. Stop laughing at me. I am just going to go wake him up and see what's going on. This suspense is killing me," Debbie tells them. She gets up from the table and marches herself upstairs to talk to Zeke. Carlos and Jose just stay at table laughing at the situation.

116

Debbie enters the suite and is surprised that Zeke is awake. "Hi honey and how did you sleep," Debbie asks. "I slept great and what about you?" he asks. "I slept wonderful and woke up in a great mood. I went down to the beach and ran about four or five miles, so I am full of energy and refreshed," Debbie tells him. "I'm happy you're in good spirits. Today is the day that we show you the operation; are you ready?" Zeke asks her. "Funny you ask that. I was just speaking with Jose and Carlos. They let it out that there is something special planned for today and would not tell me anything about it," Debbie says. "I told them both to keep their mouths shut about it that is all. It's no major secret since you're going to see for yourself anyway at this point," Zeke tells her. "Ok, well if there is not a secret, what's going on? Jose said something about having everything ready for us," Debbie says. Zeke replies with "I thought we would take a drive down to the Florida Keys and hang out for a bit if that's ok with you." "Sure, that's fine with me. I have never been there and it should be interesting. So, what is this operation all about?" Debbie asks inquisitively. "Like I said before, you will just have to see for yourself. You said Jose told you everything was ready? If that's the case, then we can get out of here anytime that you want. They're probably just waiting on us at this point," Zeke says. "If they're just waiting on us, then let me take a shower and get myself together. I want to see this so called operation for myself," Debbie says as she heads towards the shower.

Zeke picks up the phone and calls Carlos. "Hello," Carlos says. "Good morning, my friend, Debbie said she ran into you guys downstairs. She told me that Jose informed her that everything was ready for us to head to the Keys; is that true?" Zeke asks. Carlos responds with, "Yes, sir, the whip is all washed, gassed, and ready to go. The valet has put it up front and is waiting on you to arrive." "Alright, that's great. Did you guys tell her anything?" Zeke asks. "No we didn't at all. That darn Jose almost let out some but it's ok. She is still in the dark about what you really do," Carlos tells him. "Cool, well, we'll be leaving soon. What time are you two going to head down?" Zeke asks. "Well, I'm sure we will leave right after you and Debbie leave, but you'll beat us there.

There are guys at the complex and they have everything prepared on that end. They are just awaiting your arrival," Carlos tells him. "Carlos, you are the best. You take care of so much for me. All I have to do is live my life at times. Debbie and I will be leaving as soon as she gets dressed. No need to keep her waiting any longer," Zeke adds. "You know she is going to be a little mad right? You know what she thinks it is and what it actually is are two totally different things," Carlos says. "I think we'll be alright. She is really cool and will take it as more of a 'are you kidding me moment' than anything else," Zeke tells him. "Alright Zeke I hope that you're right," Carlos tells him.

Debbie comes out of dressing area looking stunning once again. "Baby I'm ready for you. What do you think?" she asks. "I think you look fabulous as always. I took the time to call Carlos and he confirmed that everything is ready. I just need to take a shower and we can roll. I'll be ready in, like, ten minutes. I don't need as much mirror time as you do." Zeke says laughing. "Well, please hurry up, the anticipation is killing me at this point," Debbie tells him. Zeke gives her a small kiss and heads off to shower to get himself in motion to leave.

Zeke is finally out of the shower and dressed. He has collected his things and is looking at Debbie. "Sweetness are you ready for this?" he asks. "Hell yes I'm ready. I'm ready to know all of you. Can we stop and grab breakfast on the way or at least some coffee?" she asks him. "Come on, baby, you know we can do whatever you want. This is our vacation so anything that you think of is ok with me," Zeke tells her. "Ok, fantastic, let's go already, grab your stuff," Debbie tells him. The two gather their things and head down to lobby. When the two arrive, naturally, Carlos and Jose are there relaxing and people watching in the lobby.

"Hey, guys, we're back," Debbie tells them. "Hello to you both and everything is ready for you. Jose made sure of it," Carlos says. "Well alright let's get it started then. We will catch up to you both when you arrive at the compound," Zeke tells them. "Ok boss see you there. But for now, let us walk you and Debbie out front," Jose says. They all begin walking and heading to the valet area of the hotel. When they arrive out front, Debbie can see a crowd has formed and is wondering what all the fuss is about. Jose and Carlos make a way for them to get to the car. Jose runs around to open the door for Debbie. Debbie takes off her sun shades to look at the car herself. "Are you serious, is this for us?" Debbie asks. "Yes, baby, it is. If it were not, Jose would not be standing there with the door open waiting for you to get in," Zeke tells her. Carlos helps Zeke into the car as Jose closes Debbie's door. "Wow, this is a really nice car. What kind of car is it anyway?" Debbie asks him. "It is a Lamborghini Gallardo LP550 but I just call it the ghost for short. I call it that because one minute you see it and the next you don't," Zeke says laughing. "So, I take it you like it," Zeke asks her. "Oh, I love it and the leather is so buttery soft. Is it new?" she asks. "No, it's not new. I have had it for a couple of years now. It is a 2013 but she still gets it done," Zeke tells her. "Oh, yeah, I can tell she gets it done alright. I bet you can't keep women out of this seat, Mister Man," she says laughing.

Zeke looks over at her, smiles and hits the start button, the ghost then roars to life. Debbie can feel the horses and power underneath of her bottom. He drops the parking break, taps the right hand paddle and gives her some gas. The ghost slides out into the sunshine and instantly starts to gain attention. Zeke heads for Interstate 95 north so he can get on exit 1A headed towards Key West. While he is breezing through South Beach, Debbie can't believe how many people are looking at them. She takes the time after a while to start waving at people as she passes them.

Zeke finally makes it to the highway and he punches it a little. Debbie is forced back into her seat and the smile on her face gets even bigger. "Oh, this is great. I love it. What is that you are doing when you hit those little things by your hands, Debbie asks him. "Those little things are called paddles and you change the gears by touching the paddle on the left or right," he tells her. After about twenty minutes or so, Debbie gets up the nerve to ask a question. "Zeke, you said I can do anything right?" she asks him. "Yes this is your vacation too so you can do anything that you want," he tells her. "Ok, well I want to drive. This is too nice of a car for me not to try it out. I want to feel the power myself," Debbie tells him anxiously. "Oh, you want to feel the power do you? Well, that's fine with me just let me drive a little further. I want to get off of Don Shula Expressway and onto Route 1 South. When I get there, you can have it. Is that ok with you?" Zeke asks her. "Sweetie, that would be great! I am in no rush but I do want to drive for sure," Debbie says. Another ten minutes goes by and Zeke takes the exit for Route 1 South and pulls over to switch seats with Debbie.

Debbie jumps behind the wheel and buckles up. "Ok, sweetness, a Lambo is different than most cars. You have driving options on this car. Do you want to use the paddles or just let the car do it in automatic?" Zeke asks her. "I want the whole experience so I want to use the paddles. Will it be hard to figure out? I do know how to drive a stick," Debbie says. "If you already know how to drive a stick, it will be easy for you. It's the same type of feel with no clutch, so, it's really easy. All you have to do is just listen to the car and everything will be fine," Zeke says. "Alright, listen to the car; that I can do. So what do I do first?" Debbie asks. "First, I want you to calm down. This is a lot of power to handle. Second, put your foot on the brake and push the red button to start her up," Zeke tells her. Debbie follows directions and the ghost is back to life once again. "Next, I want you to drop the parking brake and hold the brake. Now listen, tap the right handle to move gears up and left hand paddle to downshift. Tap the right hand paddle twice to get it to go into neutral and, lastly, be careful. I don't want you hurt." Zeke tells her. Debbie again follows directions and is now rolling. Zeke then tells her, "Seems like you have the hang of it go ahead and give her some gas." Debbie follows his direction and that snaps Zeke's head back in the seat. "This is great!" Debbie says screaming. "How fast can I go?" Debbie asks him. "You can drive as fast as you want as long as you know you are paying for any tickets you get," Zeke says laughing. "We have about another one hundred and twenty miles before we get down to the operation, so you can take your time," Zeke tells her. "Well, since I'm paying my own tickets, I want to see what this puppy can do." With that statement, Debbie steps on the gas and taps the paddle get's the ghost into sixth gear. All Zeke can do is sit back and smile, he loves a take charge woman. Debbie zips through the little bit of traffic going south with no problem.

She seems to be handling the ghost with no worries. The conversation and vibe are so cool that time breezes by like it never existed. Zeke looks up and there is the Welcome to Key West sign. Zeke looks down at his watch. They have made the last leg of the trip in just under an hour. Zeke looks at Debbie and says "You know you have a problem right?" "Problem? What problem could I possibly have today?" Debbie says smiling. "You, my friend, have a lead foot problem. We were about a hundred and twenty miles out of Key West and we made it here in a little bit under an hour! That means you were going a hundred miles an hour plus the whole trip," Zeke tells her. "Well, I beg to differ. You told me that if I got a ticket I would have to pay for it myself. So, since I didn't get a ticket I have no problem," Debbie says laughing.

"Yeah, you didn't get a ticket but you still have a lead foot," Zeke says to her. "Baby, when will I get to drive one of these beautiful machines again like this on the wide open road? I had to take advantage of my opportunity so I let the ghost stretch her legs a bit. I know I feel a whole hell of a lot better right now. Actually, I think my pussy is wet after driving her. As a matter of fact, I'm sure my pussy is wet. That was so much fun! I can't wait to do it again one day," Debbie tells him. Zeke laughing says, "Oh, so your pussy is wet? Well, if that is the case, you just keep right on driving to my house. But you have to slow down, this is a residential district," he says laughing."

"So, you have a house down here too?" Debbie asks him. "Yes, I thought I told you that already," Zeke replies. I have a small home over on North Roosevelt Boulevard. I am sure you'll like it. My house down here can get a little busy at times, but right now it should be nice and peaceful," Zeke says. "Well, from what I can see so far, this place is beautiful and I can't see why you would ever want to leave," Debbie tells him. "Yes, it's great here and I do enjoy it. Baby, look, the next street is Northside Drive. Make a right there and it'll run into my street. My house will be on the right," Zeke tells her. Debbie makes the right and realizes that there is only one house on the street. "Wow, this is your house? I thought the house in D.C. was nice but damn. What is it that you do again?" Debbie says laughing as she pulls into the driveway. As she is pulling up, she realizes why they call it the compound. The place is a humongous estate with water views all around.

When they get out of the car, a nice looking Hispanic woman comes out of the house to greet them. "Hello and how are you doing today?" she asks. "I'm fine and how are you?" Debbie replies. Zeke takes the opportunity to introduce the two ladies. "Debbie this is Yelina, Yelina this is Debbie. Yelina is our house mother. She takes care of the house and all of the team while we are here in the Keys. Yelina, how are you doing today?" Zeke asks. "I'm fine my boy, no worries here. I'm surprised to see you. I didn't think I would see you again for a while," Yelina says. "Well, you know how I am sometimes, my schedule gets adjusted on the fly," Zeke says laughing. "Yes, Zeke, it sure does, sometimes it changes more than even I can keep up with. Carlos called and said you guys didn't eat breakfast, so, I have prepared a little something for you inside," she tells them. "Thanks Yelina I really appreciate you thinking about us," Zeke replies.

"Ms. Debbie, I have everything ready for you as well. You can find your things laid out on the bed in Zeke's room," Yelina says. "My things? What do you mean my things, Yelina?" Debbie says puzzled. "I got a call from Zeke to get you clothes, bathing suits, shoes and whatever else you might need to stay here for a few days," Yelina tells her. "Wow! Yelina, all that was not necessary, but that you very much. And Zeke you are incredible; you are always thinking about me. Thank you both for taking care of me. Zeke, you are really going to spoil me," Debbie tells him. "You are very welcome and I don't have a problem doing it. You, actually, deserve to be treated like a queen. Come on in the house and let's get some of Yelina's good cooking," Zeke tells her. They all proceed into the house.

Debbie's eyes begin to open up wide as she looks around the inside of the house. There is a Mediterranean feel going on inside and she loves it. "Wow, the house is great! I love all the art work and the furnishings are fabulous. You do have good taste I must say," Debbie says. "Hey, thanks I just added this and that over the course of time. Now that I am down here more and more, I have been adding more and more as I have the time," Zeke tells her proudly. "You two get in here and put something on your stomachs. Knowing Zeke you have a long day ahead of you," Yelina tells them.

They head into the open kitchen area to find a nice selection of Cuban breakfast favorites. Yelina has prepared Cuban French toast with fruit salsa, pork and plantain Cuban breakfast hash, breakfast tortillas, and Cuban eggs. "OMG, Yelina, you have gone above and beyond anything that I could possibly imagine. Thank you so much, everything looks wonderful," Debbie tells her.

"Yes, Yelina, everything looks outstanding and I am sure it tastes even better," Zeke says.

"Thank you both, it was no trouble really. Plus, that greedy Jose called me and asked me to make extra because they are on their way down too. I take it you guys are headed over to the warehouse sometime today?" Yelina asks. "Yes we are, I guess it was not hard to figure out," Zeke tells her. "I wanted to bring Debbie down so that she can get to see and understand all aspects of me." "Taking you down there will show you that for sure. Those guys spend all of their time down there. It is a wonderful place to find out exactly who he is," she tells Debbie.

"Now, Zeke, don't you guys get to playing around down there and get this beautiful lady hurt. She is way too pretty to get all wrapped up in your little toys and what not," Yelina tells him. "Yelina, she will be fine, you are just too overprotective," he says laughing. "Well, I'm just saying don't let anything happen to this little angel. Carlos already told me that she is part of the family now. Now, whatever you guys don't eat, just leave it out. Carlos and Jose are on the way and they will finish up whatever is left for sure," Yelina tells them. "Ok, no problem and you're right, they'll finish it up don't worry," Zeke says. Yelina heads off to another part of the house to do some work.

"Alright, Zeke, we are here now so spill it, what is going on down here in the Keys that has everyone so on edge? I mean even Yelina is warning me. Well she warned you but still," Debbie says. "Well, Debbie, it's not what you think, trust me. I know it sounds a little wild but it is not the case at all. I use to have a wild life but now I work, of course, but most of it is fun. After we finish breakfast, I'll take you to another part of the house and you can see for yourself. How is that?" Zeke asks. "That would be great. I don't care what it is I just want to know at this point. The curiosity is killing me," Debbie says laughing. "I'm sorry I didn't tell you before now. It is hard being who I am at this point. You don't know if people like you for who you are or for what you have attained in one way or another. You have more than proven that you want me for me so I have no problem sharing anything with you at this point. Like I said, let's finish breakfast and I will show you it all," Zeke tells her. "Ok, baby," Debbie replies.

As they finish breakfast and Zeke is wiping off the counters, Debbie says, "I still cannot believe I am in Florida, let alone in the Keys, with you. I have had an amazing couple of days and I want to thank you again for bringing me." "Sweetie, no problem, I am just happy you are here. Now that breakfast is over, let's go to the other wing of the house so I can show you all my secrets," he says laughing. He grabs her hand and leads the way there. Debbie enjoys the open air of the house. Tropical breezes flow throughout the home, there is a courtyard as well as backyard access to the beach. Debbie loves the courtyard; it even has a couple of peacocks walking around in it.

Zeke takes Debbie through a set of nice French style doors that enter into a great room. It seems to be some trophy or award room. She can see pictures, trophies and plaques all over the place. Zeke turns to her and says, "Well, baby, this is me. I am a professional powerboat racer now. I know it is a surprise and nothing like you thought it would be but it is who I am." Debbie just looks at him with a surprised look on her face. Debbie then says "Why did you lead me on? This is not what I had in my head when you told me about the Florida Keys compound," Debbie says. "Baby, I didn't say anything about the compound, you just assumed. Now, I did know that your assumption was wrong and yes I could have changed your thought process but I figured it would be better to have shown you this way. I'm sorry if I did not tell you the whole truth earlier," Zeke tells her. "So, can I look around? There is a lot to see in here," Debbie asks him. "Yes, you can look around. Please feel free to look around at your leisure. I guess it is only right since I have kept you in the dark so long."

"Yes, you kept me in the dark far too long on this one. So, how long have you been racing boats and what got you into the sport?" Debbie asks him. "Well, after my retirement from my other business, I found that I needed something to do. I had always liked Florida and it just seemed like a natural fit. Now, when the guys and I first started, it was just to have some fun. We went out and raced a V bottom boat that I already owned. It was nothing special just your standard thirty or so footer but as time progressed; I converted over to more power and some sponsorship. Now, years later we are at the point we are now. So, it has been a good run for sure. The guys and I usually spend a few months a year down here in Florida racing and come home to Maryland in the off season. It has become our lives, pretty much. We have fun all summer and go back and enjoy the winter season as well. People say we are crazy for heading back to D.C. with all the snow and bad weather but, hey, I love it there and it is home," Zeke tells her.

She replies with "Have you thought about moving down here full time or you enjoy the off season away from the beach?" Zeke tells her, "Well, I used to like to go home during the winter because I would be missing my wife but now all of that has changed, so, I have no idea what I am going to do next off season. I guess I will discuss it with the guys and get their take on it and see what they want to do. What would you like for me to do? I mean the way things are going, looks like you're going to be in my life."

Debbie just starts blushing and tries to catch her breath. She then turns to him and asks, "Am I in your life now? Do you really want me around all the time? I know you said you do but are you sure? If it were up to me, there would be no separation, I would be more than happy to come down and be with you and the guys all summer long if I would not be in the way. " "Be in the way?" he asks. "How is that even possible? I want you in my life and in my world. Anytime you are around is a true blessing. I would be honored to have you around me all summer long," he tells her. "I want to be around you, you know that already, so, we can make it happen for sure, if that is what we decide. I, like you, have nothing back at home to worry about or concern myself with anymore," Debbie tells him. "I knew we would get along great from the first moment I talked to you. You are the best and if that is what you want, then that is what you shall have. You can give it more thought when you get back home and I am happy that you are really becoming part of me," Zeke tells her.

Zeke then adds, "I also have more to show you now that the secret is out. I will wait for Carlos and Jose to finish with breakfast and then we can head over to the warehouse. I am sure you will get a kick out of it." "Hey, that should be fun. One question, however, what does a girl wear to a warehouse?" Debbie asks while laughing. "Well, sweetie, naturally you can wear whatever you want because whatever you wear you will be beautiful," Zeke tells her. "We can take the boat out so you can get on the water. Therefore, you might want to wear something that you do not mind getting wet. We can even go shopping while we are out," Zeke tells her. Debbie replies with "I get to go for a ride, really? Now you're just really trying to make a girl feel special," she tells him. Zeke just breaks out in laughter as he says, "Ok, Miss Special, let's get you changed so that when Carlos and Jose are done, we can head right over." "That will be fine, you know how I like to play dress up," she says smiling. The two of them head over to the bungalow on the back of the property so that they can get changed. Zeke sends a quick text to Carlos so that he knows they will be heading to take the boat out after breakfast.

THE WAREHOUSE

About an hour passes and Zeke and Debbie head back over to the main house to find the fella's in order to go to warehouse. When they enter the house from court yard, Zeke sees Yelina. He says to her, "Yelina, can you have the bungalow prepared by the time we get back from the warehouse? There is no rush. We are taking the boat out for some fun and site seeing." Yelina says, "Of course I can Zeke, is there anything else you would like prepared upon your return?" Zeke says, "Just make it extra special for this extra special lady right here," he says as he is looking into Debbie's eyes. Yelina smiles as she sees how happy Debbie makes him. Yelina then says, "Zeke, I will make sure everything is super extra special for you and Ms. Debbie, don't worry about a thing." "Alright Yelina, I really appreciate this," Zeke tells her. Zeke grabs Debbie's hand and heads out to the garage where he is sure the guys are waiting for them. And sure enough as soon as he walks out into the courtyard, he can see that the boys are ready to go.

"Hello, guys, are we ready to head over to the garage?" Zeke asks. "Yes we are ready, we have been waiting for you two to arrive," Carlos tells him. They all jump into the Porsche Cayenne to head out. "Debbie, you are going to love the boat and the water," Jose tells her. "Yes, I'm sure I'll get a kick out of it for sure. I have been wondering what the secret is and now that I know, I want to take full advantage of it," Debbie says to him. "I can't wait to get out on the water with you guys." "Carlos and Jose, I want you guys to pull out the thirty two foot V bottom when we get there. No need to bring out The Queen B for a quick run around the Keys," he says laughing. Carlos says, "Ok, we'll get it done. We have been up in D.C. so long that it will be good to get out on the water again. I was actually hoping you wanted to bring the Queen out. I have not heard her engines in a minute and that is a beautiful sound." Zeke replies with, "Yes I know, but we did so much to get her ready for off season storage and we have another month or so before the season starts. So, let's just leave her in place for now." "Ok, boss, whatever you want," Carlos tells him.

The warehouse is just a few minutes' drive down the coast. Jose pulls up to a massive all white warehouse and honks the horn. Someone starts to pull open the doors and they drive in and park. "Alright, sweetie, we are here; this is our home away from home. This is where the guys and I spend most of our time. If you are ever looking for me, this is where I am when I am not out on the water," he tells Debbie. Debbie replies with, "This place is huge! I had no idea the size of your operation. Everything is spotless and very well maintained, from what I can see. Plus, the guy that opened the door had on all white overalls, so, this place is really clean," she says smiling. "Well, we do what we can. This is a multimillion dollar operation so we treat it as such," Zeke tells her. "Well, come on let me show you around." He anxiously grabs Debbie's hand to give her the tour.

"While I am showing you around, the guys will get the V bottom in the water so we can go and hit a few waves," Zeke adds. "This is some place you have and look at this tremendous boat! Everything here is just so big," Debbie tells him. "I am just amazed at this side of you. I never would have guessed that this is what you do. It seems like this place and this racing thing is really your passion," Debbie says to him. "Well, when we first started, it was just us going out and having fun on the weekends. Over time, it has morphed into much more than they or I could have ever imagined. I mean, now we have this beautiful place. We have sponsorship and the team actually makes money," he says laughing.

"Now, it was not always that way, everyone has to start small, pay their dues, and struggle. However, after we figured out what we were doing and decided to take it seriously, we never looked back. The best part is that we all love what we do. All three of us get to participate in racing the boat and that is very rewarding in itself. It is me as the driver, Carlos on the throttles, and Jose doing the navigation. It is just not me getting all the press and stuff because driving a super boat is truly a team effort. " Debbie replies with "I am very impressed by everything. Again, I can't put into words how surprised I am that you and the guys are into boat racing. I never would have had a clue if you didn't tell me. This place is awesome and it looks so professional. I have seen behind the scenes of a NASCAR garage and I think you guys are right up there with them looking at all the stuff you have in here." "Hey, we try to compete as best we can. That is all we can do. Come on, let's go out back to the dock. I am sure the guys have the princess in the water by now," Zeke tells her as he ushers her out the back door.

"Hey, look honey, they do have the boat in the water. These guys really look after you," she says with anticipation. "Ok, boss, she is all gassed up and ready to run. Do you want me to go with you guys?" Carlos asks. "No, we will be fine. I want to show Debbie some of the small islands and maybe grab some fresh drinks on the other side of the peninsula," Zeke tells Carlos. "Jose, can you please push us away from the dock and cast the bow line for me please." Zeke tells Jose as the happy couple boards the boat and takes their seats. "Sure, no problem, boss," Jose says. He springs into action to get the vessel away from the dock and pointed into the right direction. Carlos asks "How long will you be gone?" Zeke replies with "A couple of hours or so, not too long." Zeke sits Debbie down in the adjoining captains' chair. He goes back to the steering wheel and hits a button, the engines come to life. He looks over at Debbie with a 'are you ready look'. Debbie just shakes her head yes and he throws the throttles forward and they take off. Zeke leans into her and says "Are you ok and am I going too fast?" She responds with "I'm fine, I just don't want to lose my shades." Zeke just laughs and heads offshore a bit.

Zeke tells her, "The farther we go out, the calmer the water will be but I have a spot for us to go to if you don't mind a quick stop." "Baby, as long as I am with you we can go anywhere," Debbie replies. "Ok, great, I want to head over to the Green Parrot Bar and have a cocktail or two. We can pull the boat up out back and just go in and relax," Zeke tells her. "What kind of place is it and am I dressed ok?" Debbie asks. "Yes, baby, you're dressed just fine, probably over dressed, actually," Zeke says laughing. "The bar is just a local spot that has good food and cold drinks. I think it has grown in popularity with tourists over the years but to us, it is our local watering hole, so to speak," he says. "Well, that sounds wonderful I can't wait to get there," Debbie says. "We can even do some shopping and site seeing while we are there," he tells her. "Shopping? Oh, I am in love with this place already," Debbie says with a girlish smile on her face. Zeke steers the boat towards the bar and hits the throttles again. Debbie's hair is blowing in the wind as she takes in the beautiful sunshine.

About ten or fifteen minutes pass by and Zeke backs out of the throttles. The dock where he will be tying up the boat is slowly approaching. Plus, he did not want to create a big wake while pulling into the dock and disturbing the other boaters. He pulls the boat up and kills the engines while Debbie unbuckles her seat belt. Zeke jumps out to tie the boat off. After doing so he turns to grab Debbie's hand to help her out of the boat. They both walk up the dock holding hands and smiling.

Debbie attempts to get her hair coordinated after having it blowing in fifty mile an hour winds. Zeke says "There are a few neighborhood shops to stroll through. Do you want to do that first or do you want to grab a drink first?" he asks while looking at Debbie. "Well, if you are going to give a woman an option, let's shop and then grab a drink. You know a woman always wants to shop," Debbie says smiling. "Ok, great, let's go find some deals then. Make sure you haggle with these shop owners too. The price is the tourist price and I am sure you can beat them down a bit," Zeke tells her. "Now that, I can do for sure! There is nothing better than a sale!" Debbie tells him. The two of them head off for a shopping adventure.

Meanwhile, back at the house, Carlos's phone gets to ringing. He picks it up and says "Hello." The voice on the other end says, "Hello, Carlos, and how have you been?" Carlos stunned takes a moment to reply, "Hello, Sir, I am doing alright and how are you today?" "I'm fine, how are things down there in the Keys?" the voice asks. "Things are great and we are ok. Actually Don Jorge, Zeke is out on the water with his new girlfriend right now. Zeke seems very happy," Carlos says. "Well, that's good for him. I was wondering why he was not answering my phone calls and now I know," the voice says. "Yes, Sir, he cannot answer. He left his cell phone in the warehouse where we store the boats. He did not want to take a chance of getting his phone wet while he was out on the water," Carlos tells him. "Ok, I understand that and no problem. Please have him call his Uncle when he gets back," the voice says. "Yes, Sir, as soon as I see him, I will make him pick up the phone and call you Don Jorge," Carlos says nervously. "Carlos, this is an important phone call. Make sure he gets the message and make sure he calls me back today. I am putting you in charge of him calling me back today, no excuses," the voice says. "Yes, Don Jorge, he will call back today as soon as I see him," Carlos says reassuringly. "I will be waiting on that call, do you understand?" the voice says. "Yes, Sir, I fully understand," Carlos says. The voice hangs up. Carlos takes a moment to look at the phone trying to figure out what that phone call was all about. He is puzzled because he has not heard the Don's voice in years. He is afraid for Zeke because he has no idea why the Don is looking for him.

Back in Key West, the shopping is going great. Debbie is in her element, she has been browsing and picking up little items as she goes along. She and Zeke both have a couple of bags at this point. Being down in Key West has also opened Debbie's eyes to something else. Debbie is also amazed that people are coming up to Zeke for autographs and to take selfies with him. She finds it very comforting that people look up to him. It is just another validation that she has made the right decision in dating Zeke.

Debbie looks at Zeke smiling as the last fan leaves. As they keep walking and shopping she says, "You could have told me that you have fans and that you are so popular." "Come on, now, you know me, I am a low key guy and I am not into all that super star stuff," Zeke tells her. "I know that dealing with the supporters, or fans as you call them, is part of the business. It gets our sport more into the mainstream; after all, without any fans, we would not have a sport. Plus, I don't mind meeting people and allowing them to get to know me. I don't want to be considered some stuck on himself professional that is unapproachable. You know I am a nice guy," Zeke says to her as he is grinning. "Yes, baby, you are just a regular guy," Debbie tells him laughing. "Come on, Mr. Regular Guy, can we go and get those drinks now?" she says to him. Zeke smiles at her and says "Sure, baby, let's go and you have been making me laugh all day. Thanks for making sure I stay grounded and humble. I think we need two mojito's to cool us down now." The two of them lazily head over to The Green Parrot and pull up two chairs at the bar.

After ordering a couple of drinks, Zeke looks at her and says, "I know I am supposed to be humble and all of that but can you look to your left on the wall please." Debbie turns her head to look and on the wall is a picture of Zeke and the guys in front of their boat. "Baby, that is great you are a real celebrity. I am so proud of you," Debbie tells him. "Hey, thanks and I appreciate that. You see, when we go home to D.C., we don't get all of this attention. You know, it is a political town and boats and racing is the furthest thing from anyone in that areas mind. So, when we are at home, we can walk around and no one knows us. That is why the guys and I, actually, go there in the off season. It keeps us grounded and it is nice to get away from all the hustle and bustle that professional racing brings. In D.C., there are no fans so we can go to the grocery store in relative peace and obscurity," he tells her. "From what I seen today walking with you, that down time is probably good for you. I felt like a movie star today myself. People wanted to take pictures of me just because I am with you. I just can't imagine how that would be everyday and everywhere I go. I am not going to end up on TMZ or anything like that am I?" Debbie asks him jokingly. Zeke just breaks out in laughter and says, "Sweetheart, you have to do something interesting to get on TMZ. We are just regular people living boring lives. We just happen to race boats too. I don't think you have to worry about being on tv". "Well, that's good because I just got off that darn boat and I know my hair is all messed up. I can't be shown on TMZ with bad hair that is a no-no for sure," Debbie says laughing. "See, that is why I love you, dear, you keep things one hundred, as the kids say today," Zeke says to her.

"I think we should order a couple more drinks; what do think?' he asks her. "Sure, I could do with another one. Plus, I'm on vacation so why not," Debbie says laughing. Zeke motions over to the bartender to bring another round. When the drinks arrive, the two of them converse and do some people watching. Debbie is now up walking around and looking at the décor of the Green Parrot. It is truly an eclectic place with pictures and old memorabilia all around. The kind of place one would imagine of Key West. Just really laid back and inviting.

Zeke grabs Debbie's hand as she finishes the last of her appetizer and asks her, "So, are you ready to head back to the house?" "I'm ready if you are and as long as you promise me that we can come back here more often. I simply love this place," she says to him. Zeke replies "Yes, of course we can come back. I mean, this is our regular watering hole, so, you will be back for sure. I mean, if you chose to keep me in your life, that is." He says smiling from ear to ear. "But I want to get back and see what Yelina has in store for us upon our return. I am sure she has something remarkable up her sleeve," Zeke tells her. "Ok, well, let's get out of here and get back to Yelina then. Now you have me all excited as well. This trip has been so full of surprises," she tells him. The two of them finish up and head back to the boat for the trip home. The two of them walk holding hands without a care in the world.

YOU HAVE A PHONE CALL

Zeke helps Debbie back into the boat. He also helps her put her seat belt on. He fires up the engines and heads for home. The two hold hands as the wind whips past them. Debbie is smiling as droplets of water cascade off of her from the spray from the salt water waves. It is a short hop back to the compound so Zeke is relaxed as he heads back home. About fifteen minutes or so pass and he makes it back to the compound.

As Zeke is pulling up he can see Carlos standing on the dock with a worried look on his face. He is also sweating profusely and it doesn't look like it is from the Florida sun. As he pulls up to the dock Zeke throws Carlos a line to tie off the boat. Zeke asks, "Carlos, you don't look good what's wrong?" Carlos responds, "Sir your Uncle has been trying to call you. He called me on my phone when he couldn't reach you. He said it is very important that you call him right away. He didn't say what it is about but he wants you to call him as soon as you can. I promised him that I would make sure you call." "Thanks for letting me know. I wonder what he wants. It has been so long since I talked to him; I hope everything is alright. Can you make sure the bags get to the house? I need to go inside and get my phone," Zeke tells him. "Come on, baby, let's go inside and see what the hell is going on. I hope everything is ok with the family. It is so unlike my Uncle to call me out of the blue. Then, to make sure Carlos gives me the message is super strange," he tells Debbie.

Zeke heads to the work bench where he left his phone. He looks at the call history and sure enough his Uncle has been trying to reach him. He takes a deep breath and calls his Uncle not knowing how this call will go. The phone rings in his ear a few times and then his Uncle answers. "Hello, my boy, how are you?" his Uncle asks. "I am wonderful, Uncle, how are you? I have not spoken with you in so long, I hope everything is alright," Zeke says. "Yes, my boy, everything is fine. I just called to let you know I am going to Cuba later today. I am going to celebrate my birthday tomorrow and since I have not seen you in forever, I want you to come," his Uncle tells him.

"Well, Uncle, I am on vacation with my girlfriend and I am not sure that she wants to go to Cuba," Zeke says to him. "My son, it's my birthday and I want you there, don't break an old man's heart," his Uncle says. His Uncle continues with, "Plus, you are in the Keys now anyway and you were in Miami yesterday. The least you can do is come and see your family. And since I know you're not going to tell me no, please make sure you bring your girlfriend as well. I want to meet her. I have heard such good things about her," his Uncle tells him. "You've heard good things about her? How's that, Uncle?" Zeke asks. "Carlos told me that you were happy and have a new girlfriend. Plus, I was getting reports from my people in Miami. They said you were back in town with a beautiful model type woman on your arm. My son, you are not the only one with friends in Miami," his Uncle tells him. Zeke replies with "Uncle, you're always keeping your ear to the ground. You're in Columbia and I am not even going to ask why you are getting reports from Miami," Zeke says laughing. "I am who I am and I like a lot of information. What is that saying the young Americans say, 'I know people'," the Don says laughing.

"Uncle, you are too funny, where should we meet you in Cuba," Zeke asks. "Meet me at the number two location inside the Havana Port. The one with the big house, do you remember where it is?" Don Jorge asks. "Yes, Uncle, I remember, how could I ever forget? I have such fond memories of that place," Zeke tells him. "Ok good I will see you tomorrow morning then. Please bring Carlos and Jose with you as well. You will be staying overnight, just to let you know. I also want to talk a little business with you while you're there, so, don't be in a rush," his Uncle tells him. "Business, Uncle? You know I'm retired," Zeke says. "Yes, I know, but I want to put a bug in your ear about an opportunity that might present itself," his Uncle tells him.

Then, without skipping a beat, Zeke starts to speak to his Uncle in Spanish. Debbie is amazed because she has been dating him for months and he never uttered a word in Spanish. He never let her know that he spoke Spanish. 'Where did he learn to speak Spanish so fluently,' she thinks to herself. After a little more back and forth, Zeke starts speaking English again. "Uncle, I cannot wait to see you tomorrow it has been such a long time," Zeke tells him. "Alright, my son, I will see you tomorrow. I will also make sure I have some cigars waiting for you and the boys when you get there. I know how you love those," his Uncle tells him. "Alright, Uncle, I'll see you tomorrow then," Zeke says as he is hanging up the phone.

Zeke now looks at Debbie and says, "Sweetheart, remember when I told you to bring your passport with you? Well, I hope that you did because it looks like we are headed to Cuba tomorrow for an overnight visit. My Uncle is having a birthday party tomorrow and he has invited us over to celebrate with him. I hope that's ok with you." "Ok with me? Yes, that's ok with me. When you said he invited US, does that mean he knows about me? Have you told him about me?" Debbie asks him. "I had not spoken with him in a while, so, I had not had a chance to tell him yet." Zeke says tells her. "You are so sweet to take me. I would love to go and have fun at a party and in Cuba, of all places. How many times will a girl get the chance to do that? How could I say no? Are you sure it is going to be ok with your Uncle if I tag along with you?" Debbie asks him. "Sure and he asked specifically for me to bring you, he wants to meet you. Carlos has told him about you, so, you're fine," he tells her reassuringly.

"There is one problem; the guys are not going to like this. They will like the adventure but they are not going to like prepping the boat to make the trip," he says laughing. "Normally, I would help out but I am here with you so my work load will be at a minimum," he says laughing. "Aaahhhh, honey, did you say something about riding in a boat to Cuba? I know that's not what I heard you referring to," Debbie says with a concerned look on her face. Zeke breaks out in even more laughter. "Yes, we are taking the boat to Cuba. It won't take that long. We are taking the Queen B, Pegasus down there. You'll be fine, remember this is what I do. I race offshore for a living," he tells her as he grabs her hand. "Ok, if you say so, but I am worried. We could just catch a plane or something couldn't we? And why does it have to be such a little boat, doesn't Carnival cruise line go there?" Debbie asks nervously. Zeke looks at her with the confidence of a professional and says "You are my family and I would not let anything happen to you." Debbie's heart melts and she reaches out and hugs him tightly.

Zeke tells her as he brushes the hair out of her face, "Let's go give the bad news to the guys. And you have to pack a bag. Plus, I want to see what Yelina has up her sleeve for today. That's why we were headed back anyway." "Alright, and wow what a day. I go from a quick boat ride for some site seeing to taking a boat to Cuba. I'll say one thing, you are not boring," Debbie tells him. Zeke laughing says "Well, I try to keep things interesting. So, do you want to break the news to the guys or shall I? I know that they will take it a whole lot better coming from you rather than from me," he says chuckling. "If you want me to, I will. But I think you should do it, after all, it was your phone call that started all of this," Debbie replies. "Alright, fine, I'll be the bad guy but someone is about to be in their feelings. But on the flip side, I know that they want to get out on the water just as bad as I do. So, it's a love hate thing, right now the boat is in off season status. You know, fluids drained and all that kind of stuff. They have to get the boat from mothballs to ready to run to Cuba in maybe ten or twelve hours. I am very confident they can get it done. Watch their faces when I tell them, this will be funny," he says.

The two of them walk back into the house. Zeke says "Hello guys. Well, as you know I got a call from my Uncle. He has informed me that he is having a birthday party tomorrow and that we are all invited. The only bad part is the location of the party." Carlos says "Zeke, now you know we don't mind catching a flight to Columbia. That has never been a problem for us." Zeke smiles and says "See, that's the problem. The party is in Cuba and we are taking Pegasus. So, you know what that means. She has to be race ready by in the morning." Carlos and Jose just look at one another and shake their heads in disbelief and a bit of regret. Jose decides to speak up, "Ok, boss, we will get it done. She will be ready." Carlos still shaking his head, "Wow, prep the boat there goes my easy afternoon. But I am with Jose, we will have her ready." Carlos and Jose head off to the warehouse so that they can start the massive project in getting Pegasus ready to run.

FREE TIME

"Now that I have broken the bad news to the guys, you and I have some free time until tomorrow. What would you like to do?" he asks her. "Anything as long as I am relaxing. You know I have had a busy morning," she replies. "Well, let's check with Yelina to see what she has prepared for us. I am sure it's something fantastic," Zeke tells her. The two head off to find Yelina and see what she has in store for them. They locate her headed back from the beach bungalow. Yelina tells them, "The place is ready for you to relax. All you have to do is enjoy yourselves. I want you two to be happy." "Thank you, Yelina, you are so kind," Debbie says. "Yes, Yelina, you have always taken such good care of me. I really appreciate it." Zeke tells her. "You are very welcome, now, you two love birds head on down, the place is waiting for you to enjoy." They continue to the bungalow as Yelina heads back to the main house.

When they arrive at the bungalow and enter, they can see that Yelina has gone above and beyond for them. There is cut up mango and strawberries chilling on ice. Yelina has placed fresh cut flowers everywhere and the windows are open allowing the tropical ocean breeze to flow through the entire place. Debbie's mouth just opens and she gasps for air as she walks into an oversized master bathroom. "I am done, I have truly found heaven," she says. "This tub is ridiculous and Yelina is great. It is already filled with bubbles and I can see the steam from the hot water. I'm getting in," Debbie says. Debbie immediately starts to get undressed and gets herself carefully in the bath. Zeke was watching her as she was undressing. He heads into the other room and comes back with a bottle of champagne, two glasses and a bowl of fruit. He gets undressed and gets into the tub as well.

Zeke gives Debbie a glass and fills it with bubbly. He then pours some over her head and as it streams down her face he leans over and gives her a kiss. They both look at each other after the kiss and smile. "You are kind and so beautiful inside and out. You make me want to be a better man. It's very nice to have someone in your corner that you truly feel loves you," Zeke says to her as he gazes into her eyes. "I feel that you are the man for me. I don't want anyone else. You have opened my eyes to what love really is and I love it! If you want me I am yours," she tells him. "Yes! Yes, I want you forever. I never thought I would be on the market again, let alone find the perfect person for me. The almighty has blessed me more than you can ever imagine," Zeke says with serious look on his face.

"Well, please allow me to continue your blessing. I'll just get on top of you like this," Debbie says and she gets into his lap and straddles him. "How about I put this monster right here inside of me," she tells him as she reaches for his dick down in the hot soapy water. "I hope that's ok with you," she says as she gets his dick inside of her. "I hope you don't mind me taking what I want right now. Give it to me baby" Debbie tells him. "No, I don't mind at all. And if you want this dick come and get it," Zeke replies as he tries to shove it in further. He doesn't care because at this point he has two hands full of nice juicy ass to enjoy.

Debbie just rides him and grabs hold of Zeke tightly. One scream after another, one moan after another, their bodies working in unison looking for a common but separate goal to cum together as one. Debbie reaches over and grabs a hand full of fruit and shoves it into Zeke's mouth only to kiss him and try to take it all back. This is love making, this is passion at its highest level. Two people sharing themselves and being as one. A couple being as one in mind, body, and spirit all while in love. After a half hour or so of gyrations, hair pulling and intense thrusting, there it is an explosion of passion. They both get an incredible orgasm. She can feel all of his dick inside of her. She screams, "I can feel it in my stomach." "Damn it, I want you to feel it in your throat," Zeke says as he tries to push it in even further. He tries to push it threw her stomach towards her throat. He can feel the wetness of her pussy being released as it slides down his dick. He can feel the muscles of her pussy pulse and throb on his dick. She tells him don't move as she gently kisses him on his neck. He holds her with tenderness after an intense session. After a few moments he reaches over and grabs the champagne bottle then pours the rest over her head to cool her off. "Thanks, baby, that felt wonderful," Debbie says as she is still on his lap smiling in his face. "No, thank you, you attacked me, remember," Zeke says smiling. "Oh, that's right I did. Whoops, my fault," she says playfully.

When they decide to get out off the bathtub, Zeke heads to the kitchen. When he gets there he finds an envelope taped to the refrigerator. He pulls it off and opens it. When he reads it he just starts to shake his head and smile. He heads back into the bedroom and says to Debbie, "You are not going to believe this. I just found this note taped to the fridge and it reads. 'Hello guys, I figured you would end up in the kitchen at some point. I hope you like how I set up the place for you. I also have had the staff bring up the horses from the stable. They are saddled and ready for you out back. With all my love, Yelina'. Can you believe she did that for us?" Debbie replies "Remind me to give Yelina a tip. First, the place is set up fantastically. Now, horses walking on the beach. She is helping you get points romantically," Debbie says laughing. Zeke replies "But is it working?" "Oh, it is working alright. Let's get dressed and ride the horses in the water," she says. "Hey, sounds like fun to me. Let's do it," Zeke replies.

The pair of lovers get dressed and walk out back. The horses are ready and waiting just as Yelina had written about. Zeke helps Debbie onto her horse and then mounts his own. They take the horses to the surf. They gently ride along the edge of the breaking waves. They hold hands as they calmly stroll along the beach enjoying the setting sun and gentle breezes.

IS EVERYONE STRAPPED IN?

The next morning Yelina has prepared a fabulous breakfast. Carlos and Jose have eaten and have headed down to the warehouse early. "Good morning love birds and how are you?" Yelina asks the happy couple as they stroll into the kitchen. "Good morning, Yelina, we are great! Thank you so much for everything that you did for us yesterday," Zeke says. "Yes, Yelina, thank you so much. We found the note on the refrigerator and the walk on the beach with the horses was out of this world," Debbie adds. "That was not a problem for me. I wanted to do it for you both. Now, you guys need to eat up, you have a big trip ahead of you. Zeke, Carlos wanted me to tell you that they are down at the warehouse waiting on you two to arrive. He said to let you know that Pegasus is primed and in the water," Yelina says. "Thank you, Yelina, we are going to head down after we grab some of your delicious food this morning," Zeke tells her. "Alright, well, help yourselves. Everything is all here for you. I am going to straighten up a few things," Yelina tells them as she heads off to get back to her housework. The two of them sit down and have breakfast. They smile and grin in each other's face the whole time. After they finish, Zeke goes to grab their bags so that they can head down to the warehouse.

When they arrive at the warehouse, Zeke heads straight for the dock. He has not seen Pegasus in the water in almost six months, seems like this off season has been a really long one. "Hello team, how is everyone doing. For those of you who don't know her, this is Debbie my new girlfriend," Zeke tells them as Debbie waves hello to everyone. Looks like we are preparing early for the Key West World Championships," he says jokingly. "Look at today's trip as a way to shake the cobwebs off of Pegasus. We can use this little trip to get her dialed in correctly so we won't have any problems later on," Zeke tells the crew. "The engines can push up to two hundred miles per hour but we are going to keep it in the neighborhood of one hundred and twenty miles per hour for this early season shake out run. We just want to get the bugs out and don't really want to break anything. Is everyone good with that?" Zeke asks. Heads shake in agreement all around.

"Come on, baby, let me introduce you to another part of the family," Zeke takes Debbie's hand as he is showing her around the boat. "Baby, this is Pegasus. She is fifty feet long, eleven feet wide and weighs about eighty five hundred pounds. With her catamaran type body, her top speed is somewhere around two hundred and fifteen miles per hour. She is built of carbon fiber, steel and fiberglass and has twin turbine engines. I can put five hundred gallons of gas in her and she will run all day for me," Zeke tells her. "Will it get me to Cuba and back in one piece?" Debbie asks. "Yes she will," Zeke answers her confidently. "The trip won't take that long, so, you'll be ok. We will be on and off the water in ninety minutes or less, depending on how fast you want to go," Zeke says laughing. "Well, I want to get there, so, whatever speed gets me there, that is what I want," Debbie replies to him. "Ok, I see. Well, we'll figure it out as we go. Let's go get into our racing suits so we can leave. The two of them head back to the warehouse to get changed. Carlos has already started moving the bags for the trip. He and Jose are dressed and ready to roll.

Zeke and Debbie hurry and get changed. As they head back down to the dock, Zeke can see that Debbie is still a little bit nervous, or shall I say apprehensive, about the trip. He grabs her hand and says "Baby, everything will be alright." "You can say that but I am walking with a fire proof suit on that will float in case of emergency. I also have to wear this damn helmet and mess up my hair," Debbie replies. "I know you're worried but everything will be fine. The suit and helmet are for safety purposes that's all. Once we get you all strapped in you will feel much better. Plus, the suit hooks into an on board air conditioning system and keeps you cool during the trip," he tells her. "Ok, I love you, baby, and I know you would not allow anything to happen to me," she says to him. "No, baby, I wouldn't, so, let's get on and get out of here. The sooner we leave the sooner we can get there and start celebrating with my Uncle," Zeke tells her as they arrive at the boat. Jose reaches down and grabs her hand to assist her up on the boat.

Jose guides her to her seat and sits her down. Jose tells her, "Ms. Debbie, this lady comes with what we call shockwave seats. The seats slide up and down with the rise and fall of the boat. They are built and designed to lighten the impact from pounding on the waves as we are running. They kind of make you feel like you are floating. I need you to keep your feet on the stirrups so that you stay in the rhythm of the seat." "Alright, will do, no problem. I am too scared to move anything anyway," she says to him. "One more thing, Ms. Debbie, the helmet you are wearing has a built in communication system. You will be able to hear and talk to us and we can do the same to you. If you need anything, just say something, ok? Zeke will activate your helmet as soon as they are done with the pre-checklist" he says to her. "I have you all plugged into the communication system and ventilation lines now," he says as he taps the top of her helmet. Jose then goes and takes his seat in his navigator position. Carlos and Zeke are already strapped in and going through pre-trip checklist.

Zeke hits a button and pipes in all communication lines. "Baby, are you ok back there? Zeke asks. "Yes, I'm fine. Just waiting at this point," she replies. "Alright, I am about to start the engines and it will be a little loud. You will still be able to hear me though, so, don't worry," Zeke tells her. Zeke then hits a switch and the engines come to life. All the guys are happy and you can hear comments of approval from all three of them. Carlos says "It sure is nice to hear her purr." Jose replies with, "Yes, it sure is, sounds like music doesn't it?" Zeke gives Carlos the signal to give her some throttle. The boat heads slowly out to deep water. On lookers can hear her engines as the rpm's start to rise. About a half mile away from the dock Zeke comes over the loud speaker and asks "Is everyone all strapped in?" Zeke hearing yes from everyone in his headphones looks over at Carlos and tells him to hit it. The boat's back end digs down hard into the water and the engines begin to howl with power. Before too long she is cruising at eighty miles per hour.

Zeke comes back over the speaker, "How are you doing back there, baby? We are at eighty miles per hour. If you're ok, can I push it up to maybe one hundred miles per hour? We are only ninety miles from hour destination so we'll be there in less than an hour," Zeke asks her through the communication device. Debbie responds with "It's not as bad as I thought it would be. This is actually pretty fun. Can you take her up to one hundred and twenty like you were talking about earlier?" "Your wish is my command, Miss Lady. Carlos, you heard the lady, take us to one hundred and twenty please," Zeke tells him. Carlos drops the throttles down a little bit more and they easily make it to their new cruising speed. Zeke is driving well, Jose has them on course, and Carlos has the throttles locked down and in position. They will be in Cuba in no time.

SEEING OLD FRIENDS

The time passes quickly. They make it across the ocean waters to Cuba with no problems. Jose has set a course through St. Nichols Channel and then through the Port of Havana. Carlos backs the throttles down to about thirty miles per hour and then after a few minutes, he drops it even a little further. "Hey guys, do you hear all of that noise? What is going on?" Debbie asks. "Well, sweetheart, that is all love you are hearing from the other boats as we pass them. How often do they get to see a craft like Pegasus? They are just showing us love by blowing horns and sounding their whistles and bells," Zeke tells her. "Alright, now that I can understand, look at you an international ambassador. That is why I love you," she says.

"Aaahh come on you two Jose and I have to listen to this stuff too," Carlos says laughing. Jose chimes in with, "Yeah, get a room already". They all bust out in laughter. Debbie says "Come on, guys, don't tease him. You guys know I am a woman and I like to show affection. He just gets caught up in it." "You tell them, baby," Zeke says. Jose comes over the headphones "In three hundred yards, sweep to port eighty degrees and pull back on the engines. We are almost there." Immediately, being the professionals that they are, they go from joking to concentrated and focused. Zeke looks at his gages and makes the turn. Carlos pulls the throttles back to a slow crawl at fifteen miles per hour. Zeke says "Jose, you can kill the gps, if you want to. I know the way from here. Carlos, reach up and open the hatches. Let's get some air in here."

Zeke sees the house in the distance. It brings back fond memories of the old days. He pulls up slowly to the dock. There are guys on the dock to assist

Jose, who is now standing on the bow, to pull her in slowly. They make it to the dock and get tied off. Zeke and Jose then start the process of shutting down the turbines. "Ok, sweetie, we made it. You are officially in Cuba," Zeke tells her. "That was a blast and I am happy to be here. Where can I get a drink?" Debbie asks him jokingly. "I will be sure to work that out for you very shortly. Let's get off of this machine and into the house," Zeke tells her. "Ok, I am down for that," she replies. They get off the boat and stand on the dock. "Carlos, can you bring our bags up to the house so that we can change and get out of these racing suits please?" Zeke asks. "Yes, sure, right away. You go ahead up and we will be right behind you," Carlos replies. "Ok great!" is Zeke's response.

Zeke takes Debbie's hand and walks with her closely up to the main house. He sees many people that he knows. Zeke says hello to a few and also shakes a few hands. Then, an old face catches his eye and he heads in that direction. "Hola, Senorita Lopez," Zeke says. The old lady looks up and an amazing smile comes over her face. She, then, takes a deep breath and says "Well, am I seeing a ghost? Is this my boy before me? El Diablo Negro come here and give me a hug!" They embrace in a long and loving hug. "How have you been, my boy? Have you been eating, you look so thin," she says. "I'm ok and I have been doing well. And to answer your question, yes I have been eating. My girlfriend here makes sure of it. She takes very good care of me," Zeke tells her. "Yes, the Lord is good. He has blessed you with such a beautiful angel. Come here my child what is your name?" she asks Debbie as she reaches out for her hand. "My name is Debbie and it is a pleasure to meet you," she replies. "I can see the love in your eyes for Zeke and we only just met. I want you to take good care of him because he is so special to me," Senorita Lopez tells her. "I will and I try very hard every day to make him happy," Debbie tells her. "That is wonderful, my dear. I am so happy to hear you speak that way. I love a girl with an honest heart," Senorita Lopez tells her. "That means you love me because that is all that I have for this man," Debbie replies.

Zeke asks "Senorita Lopez, can we please use one of the bedrooms upstairs to change out of these hot suits?" "Yes you can and I can do even better than that. You can go up to your old room. Your Uncle told me you were coming and I have had it prepared for you. You can shower and freshen up a bit as well. You can't ask this angel to meet your Uncle in a racing outfit. I will have someone bring up more fresh towels and the bed is already turned down for you in case you need a quick rest." "Thank you Senorita Lopez," Debbie says as she reaches down and gives her a hug. "Yes, thank you so much for your wonderful hospitality," Zeke says. "We are going to head upstairs now and get this plan into motion because these suits are hot," he adds. Zeke and Debbie head upstairs to relax for a bit and change. Zeke sends a quick text to Carlos to let him know where to bring the bags.

About fifteen or so minutes pass by and there is a gentle knock on the door. Zeke opens it and sees Carlos standing there with the bags. "Come on in, buddy, I was afraid you didn't remember where the room was," Zeke says to him. "I am sorry it took so long. I kept running into people I have not seen in a long time and, naturally, they wanted to talk," Carlos replies. "Yes, I know how that can be. The same thing happened to us. No worries, you're here now. Thanks for the bags and you should ask Senorita Lopez which room you and Jose can use for the evening," Zeke tells him as he takes the bags away from him. "Alright, I'll go down and ask her now. Jose should be finished with securing the boat at this point. Do you want us to meet you in the galleria with the party folks?" Carlos asks him. "Well, this place is like home to us and nothing is going to happen. Take your time. But, yes, come down and meet us in the courtyard where everyone is," Zeke replies. Zeke closes the door as Carlos heads off to find Jose and their room.

Zeke calls out "Honey the bags are here, we can change now." Debbie yells from the shower, "That's good, baby. Why don't you come and get into the shower with me so I can cool you off." Zeke laughing says "If I come in the shower with you, the last thing I'm going to be is getting cooled off." Debbie replies with "Well, don't ever say I didn't ask to wash your back." "It's not my back that I'm worried about," Zeke says laughing. "Ha, ha, ha, very funny, Mr. Man," Debbie replies. Debbie continues to shower without the assistance of Zeke while he goes through his bag and tries to figure out what to wear.

Debbie finally comes out of the shower. She looks at Zeke and asks "Are you nervous yet about seeing your Uncle since it has been so long since you last seen him?" She continues to dry her hair wrapped in nothing but a towel. "No, not at all, I actually miss him a lot. He is a really smart guy and I have learned a lot from him over the years. He actually is more like a father to me more than anything else. He has definitely guided me into being the man I am today," Zeke tells her. "It will be good to catch up and talk to him about old times," Zeke tells her. She replies, "That's good. It is obvious he wants to see you since he invited you down here. I can see it in your face that you actually miss him. See, it will be fun for everyone". "Yes, I think it will be. It's good to see so many faces from the old days. I just want to give the old man a big bear hug. I have not seen him in maybe three years. Sure, we talk on the phone here and there but it is not the same as being there you know," he tells her. "Well, I'll get my ass in gear and get dressed. I don't want to keep you away from him any longer than necessary," she says with a seductive look on her face.

BARTENDER GIVE ME A DRINK PLEASE

Some time passes, of course, as Zeke is left waiting for Debbie to get ready. He just flips through his phone to catch up on email to pass the time. All of a sudden he hears "I'm ready" from out of the bathroom. "That's great baby. I'm sure you look wonderful," Zeke replies to the voice. Debbie walks out in the sexiest all yellow maxi dress, no bra and if she has on panties Zeke can't tell. "Damn baby we're only going to a birthday party," he says with a grin on his face from ear to ear. "No, sweetheart, we are going to your Uncle's birthday party. There is a difference! Plus, I wanted to look extra nice for you. These folks have not seen you in years and I want to make sure I do my part to make you look good," Debbie says emphatically. "Well, if you're trying to make me look good then mission accomplished!" he tells her.

"I think we need to head downstairs to party if you're ready," Zeke says. "Yes, I'm ready. Just let me check the mirror one more time to make sure everything is in place," Debbie replies. After looking in the mirror and touching her hair one last time, she announces "Ok, now I'm ready," as she looks at Zeke. "Don't look at me like that. I am serious. I am ready this time," she says jokingly. She grabs a small tube of lipstick and throws it in her purse. "Come on, baby, are you ready? Why are you just sitting there looking at me? See, I know what's on your mind and I know that look. NO, you cannot have any of these cookies right now so stop looking at me like that," Debbie says with her baby doll voice. "Alright, alright, no cookies now but as soon as we get back up here I am taking what is mine!" Zeke replies. Debbie just smiles and says "Ok, take all you want. I won't be mad." The two of them head down the hallway towards the stairs. Once at the top of the stairs, Zeke grabs her hand for the gentle decent down to the lower level.

As the two of them walk through the crowd towards the bar area, they can smell a mixture of lovely flavors in the air. He also keeps bumping into old friends and comrades. As he shakes one hand after another he can see Carlos and Jose in the distance, so, he heads in their direction. Once he and Debbie arrive, Carlos asks, "Boss have you seen your Uncle yet because he is asking for you?" "No, not yet but I have an eye out for him," Zeke replies. "Do you know what direction he is in now?" Zeke asks. "Yes, he is about thirty yards to your right, so, get yourself ready," Carlos says to him. One more hand shake and Zeke grabs Debbie's hand to head over to see his Uncle. Wading through the crowd as he walks is making Carlos and Jose more nervous as they follow Zeke and Debbie towards his Uncle.

Zeke finally reaches his Uncle but his back is turned to him as he walks up on him. "Uncle," Zeke says. His Uncle turns around and says "Well, hello my boy, and how are you? Give your Uncle a hug," as he reaches out for him. They give each other a big bear hug, Debbie is speechless when she realizes who Zeke's Uncle is but she does not say a word. "And who is the beautiful young lady that you have here with you?" his Uncle asks him. "This is Debbie and she is my everything," Zeke says proudly. "Debbie this is my Uncle, Don Jorge, he has helped turn me into the man that I am today" Zeke says as introduces the two of them. "Hello, Miss Debbie, and it is a pleasure to meet you my dear," Don Jorge says. "Yes, it is a pleasure to meet you as well. Zeke has told me such wonderful things about you," Debbie replies. "Well, I hope he was being truthful and none of it bothered you in any way," Don Jorge tells her. "No, nothing like that at all. He just said how wonderful you are as a person and that he is the man he is today because of you," Debbie tells him. "Well, in that case, it was all true," Don Jorge says smiling.

"Why don't we all head inside so that we can talk. It is so noisy out here," Don Jorge tells them. He then turns and heads towards the house. As they are walking towards the house Debbie pulls on Zeke's hand to get his attention.

"Baby, I will be right behind you. I'm going to grab a quick drink and I'll be right in," Debbie says to him. "Ok, dear, just make it a quick one, Don Jorge does not like to be kept waiting and I do believe he wants to speak with you more," Zeke replies. "Alright, I'll make it a little drink then," she says smiling. The rest of the entourage heads to the house as Debbie heads to the bar.

When Debbie arrives at the bar she says "Bartender give me a drink, please, and make it a double. As a matter of fact, make it a double Patron on ice." "Yes ma'am, coming right up," the bartender replies. Debbie has been thrown for a loop today. She can't believe that Don Jorge is her new man's Uncle. That's not all, Don Jorge is not only the head of one of the biggest drug cartels in the world but, in fact, he is also Debbie's father. Yes, Debbie's father is Zeke's Uncle. She's racking her brain as to why her father didn't say anything when he saw her. She was surprised to see him but it didn't look like he was surprised to see her. Debbie throws the double down her throat and slams the glass on the bar. She then gestures to the bartender to give her another one. Another double is poured and placed on the bar in front of Debbie. She takes that one to the head as quickly as she took the first. Debbie just stands there looking in the mirror behind the bar. She asks herself 'how did this happen and what am I going to do now?' She takes a few minutes to get her thoughts together and then heads back to the house. If there is one thing she knows about her father, he does not like to be kept waiting.

Debbie enters the back of the house. She can see Zeke and her dad sitting down talking and laughing. 'I wonder if they are talking about me', she thinks to herself. 'I wonder if my dad set all this up from the beginning', she continues to have crazy questions run through her head. Zeke motions to her to come over and join them. She complies and heads over and stands next to Zeke with her hand on his shoulder. "Baby, I was just telling my Uncle about the crazy situation that brought us together. I have also been telling him how you and I have fallen head over heels in love with one another," Zeke says to her. "That's wonderful, baby, and how does Don Jorge feel about you and I being together?" she asks. "Well, he can tell you for himself. Don Jorge, please tell her how you feel," Zeke insists. "I am so very pleased you two have found one another and that you make one another happy," the Don says. He adds

"So when are the babies going to be on the way?" With that question, Debbie is amazed, 'can he really be giving his blessing to our relationship?' she asks herself. Zeke replies to the Don "When she is ready, I am ready. I want to have one right now, seeing that I have this beautiful woman by my side. She is my world now and I can't see anything better than having a beautiful child with her." "Awe, baby, you are so sweet," Debbie tells him. "I would love to have all of the babies that you want. At this point, I can't see anything or anyone else in my life but you," Debbie tells Zeke. "It's really nice to see a young couple in love. Sometimes I forget what real love is all about; thank you so much for reminding me," Don Jorge tells them.

"Why don't we take a selfie. It would be good to capture this moment," Debbie says. "Baby, please don't impose, Don Jorge is not one to take pictures and all that kind of stuff," Zeke replies. Don Jorge smiles and adds, "No, Diablo Negro, it is quite alright, we can take some if she wants. This is a special moment for us all. Why don't we take a few of them? Someone go and get us glasses of champagne so we can toast to this beautiful occasion," he orders. One of the servers immediately runs off and gets chilled glasses and two cold bottles of libation. Zeke is stunned by the Don's willingness to take the picture.

"My grandchildren tell me about this selfie thing but I'm not sure how to do it. They call me old and tell me I'm behind the times," the Don says laughing. "Tio <Spanish for uncle> you're not old; you are wise beyond our years. They are but children and do not know what they speak," Zeke tells him. "I'm with him, Don Jorge, you're the world's blessing, the keeper of strength, and balance. I'm sure your grandchildren love you just for who you are and that is the best love anyone could ever have," Debbie adds. "I know they are but babes and know not what they say, but at the same time they speak the truth. I take it all in fun at this point. I have no problem with them. For example, I have to sit down with them when I get back. For some crazy reason they want me to sit in a chair while they dump buckets of ice water on my head. I don't get it but the things you do for your kids I tell you," he says laughing and hugging the both of them at the same time.

Upon the waiter's return, glasses are dispersed among the group. "I want to make a toast. Does everyone have a glass?" Zeke asks. "Alright, here's to the best family a man can have. All of you mean so much to me. I'm just happy my old family has accepted my new family with open arms and open heart." Glasses are raised and tapped together over and over. Don Jorge clears his throat and asks, "Can I make a toast? I would like to toast to family as well. I want to bless this happy couple and wish them nothing but peace and happiness. I want you to get married and have many babies. I could not hope for a better woman for you, Zeke, than Miss Debbie here. I have only just met her but I can already tell she makes you happy. I have a feeling she will cherish you forever. I want you to respect her and keep her safe forever in return. So, please, take a drink to the happy couple." He raises his glass and everyone follows suit. Glasses are again raised and tapped together over and over. Debbie leans in and gives Zeke a big kiss and the on lookers clap in approval.

"Now everyone, fill your glasses we have some pictures to take," Don Jorge announces. Glasses are again filled and smiles are all around. Debbie pulls out her phone and gives it to one of the servers. He begins to take photos of the group one after another. When he stops, Don tells him to take a few more. The group of people that is gathered realizes what is going on and takes advantage of this rare opportunity. Everyone wants their picture taken with him. "Ok guys, all of you can take a picture with me today but I need one picture with the happy couple. Then you can take as many individual pictures as you want with the birthday boy," the Don says. Zeke and Debbie take their places on either side of the Don and pose for the picture. As they are posing Debbie turns to Don Jorge and kisses him on his cheek and flash, the camera snaps the photo. What a classic photo! The man who takes no pictures is actually allowing a woman he doesn't even know to have her way with him. Zeke is thoroughly impressed with the poise and grace Debbie has exhibited this evening, the ease at the way she works a room, miss social butterfly, if you will. 'She has stolen the Don's heart,' Zeke thinks to himself.

"Has everyone gotten the photo that they needed? I want to make sure everyone has a picture with me. It is my birthday and I want everyone to have memories of this joyous day," Don Jorge says. Hearing the fact that everyone has an individual photo, the Don continues "I want to remember this night as well. At first, I took a group photo with just five or six people, now I want a photo with everyone in this room. So, yes, family, friends, waiters, waitresses, security come now everyone, gather around." Carlos and Jose are dumb founded considering their history with the Don but even they jump into place. Everyone in the room quickly complies with the Don's wishes, people move in around The Don. Don then tells everyone, "Big happy smiling faces everyone. This is a joyous day." The photos are taken and everyone applauds at the culmination of the photo shoot.

THE REASON I WANTED TO SEE YOU

As the crowd disperses from around the Don he pulls on Zeke's arm to whisper something in his ear. The Don tells him, "Let's find a quiet place to talk, shall we?" "Yes, sir, we should. Let me have Carlos and Jose stay with Debbie as we step out for a minute," Zeke replies. Zeke then turns to Carlos and tells him "You and Jose stay with Debbie. Don Jorge wants to speak with me." The Don motions to one of his security team to find a room to talk. The two men and Don Jorge's collective team of bodyguards stroll out of the room.

They end up in one of the offices down the hall. "Come and sit down, my boy. I have not seen you in so very long. I think I have seen you maybe twice since your retirement," Don Jorge says to him. "Yes, sir, that's true and it's all my fault. I have been busy with getting the company up and running. Then, as you know, I fell in love with boat racing and have not looked back," Zeke replies. "Yes, I know you have and I have left you alone. I see you on television, it makes me so proud. And now you have this beautiful woman in your life. I am so happy for you," Don Jorge tells him. The Don continues with "However, you know what type of life I have, what I do, and who I am." Zeke speaks right up, "Yes, sir, I do know who and what you are. I was a part of your life for so long, of course, I know." "Well, when I found out you were in Miami, I wanted you to come to the party so I could talk to you about the old days. I want to know, can you do an old man a favor for his birthday and for old time's sake?" Don Jorge asks him. Zeke tells him without hesitation "Yes, sir, anything you want I will try my best to make it happen for you Uncle." "I am happy to hear you say that because I know I said when you retired I would not ask you to do anymore collection or distribution jobs for me. But I have a special case and it needs your special talents and creativity," Don Jorge tells him. "Again, Don Jorge, retirement or no retirement whatever you need just ask and I am there for you," Zeke replies.

"My boy, that is why I love you so much; you have always been focused on the business," the Don says smiling. He continues with "I have, what I thought was a business partner, in the Midwest, outside of Chicago. I need you to do some collection for me. I will pay you twenty percent, instead of my normal ten percent finder's fee." "No problem, sir, he will be pushing up daisy's by sun down tomorrow," Zeke says with confidence. Don Jorge smiling says "While I would love to kill him myself for the disrespect, I don't want to at this time. He has a nice thing going on and I want to keep the money coming in. He is just being an ass now and doesn't want to pay, talking about he can get his product from anyone. Well, he can but not with my money. Long story short, we fronted him a lot of product to lock down a few markets all at once. He gets himself on top and now he wants to say fuck me and he don't need me. My boy, you know me, and that just ain't going to do! On top of that, he doesn't want to pay me my cash. So, he has a learning lesson coming for sure." "Don Jorge, don't worry, I will give him a learning lesson he will never forget. How much does he owe, anyway, so that there are no mistakes?" Zeke asks. "At last count, he owes the house forty million dollars and I cannot have that. With that kind of money out there, people are going to start thinking I am soft. His problem is that he knows I am in Columbia. I guess he thinks I can't reach out and touch that ass. My issue is that I have just been busy with other things and didn't have time to deal with him," the Don tells him. "No problem, sir, I will handle it and for twenty percent, he will get a true understanding of who he is dealing with for sure," Zeke says confidently.

"Now, Diablo Negro, I want you to be creative in your scare tactics because I want to keep making money without having to visit his ass again." "No problem. I will think of something that will get his attention for a long time. You won't have any other problems out of him," Zeke reassures the Don. "Thank you so much for taking care of this for me. I am so glad you took me up on my invite to come down" Don Jorge tells him. "I am happy myself, Uncle. I will get out of here at first light to take care of the issue for you," Zeke tells him.

"First light will be good and I'm sure you will do things right. Now look, before you go, I want to get to know this Deborah a bit better. Can you find her and tell her I want to speak with her alone please?" Don Jorge says. Zeke looks at him with a puzzled look on his face. "Don't worry, my boy, I won't tell her anything crazy. I just want to thank her for taking such good care of you," the Don quickly replies. "Yes, sir, I will find her now for you. I left her outside with Carlos and Jose," Zeke replies. "Alright, my boy, oh, and while I am thinking about it, that thing with Carlos and Jose so many moons ago," Don Jorge says. "Yes, Uncle, I remember," Zeke replies. "You were right and I was wrong. Thanks for making me change my mind about those two," the Don says while reminiscing about the old days. "If you say so Uncle, I can tell you are in a good mood today. I'll go and get Debbie for you now," Zeke says as he exits the room.

A little while later there is a knock at the door. One of Don Jorge's men answers it and it is Debbie with Jose in tow. As they enter the room, Don Jorge decides to speak, "Ok, all of you get out. I want to speak to Deborah alone." Following the boss' orders everyone vacates the room, including Jose. He takes a position outside of the door along with Don Jorge's guards. "Are we alone?' Debbie asks. "Yes, my child, we are alone and no one can hear us," Don Jorge says. "In that case, DADDY it is so good to see you," Debbie says as she gives him a big hug and kisses his face over and over. The Don replies "Hello, my dear, I have not seen you in such a long time. Step back and let me look at you for a minute. You are truly a site for sore eyes" he says as he extends his arms to get a better view of his child.

"Daddy, did you set all of this up? I know it's your birthday. I mailed you a card and a gift before I left on vacation. And how in the world do you know Zeke? Daddy, did you put him up to this?" Debbie seems to fire a million questions all at one time. "Well, just sit down and I'll tell you how I know him. And to answer your question, no I did not set all of this up. I did set up the part about you coming to Cuba, however. I used my birthday as an excuse to get you and Zeke down here," The Don explains. "Ok, daddy, I'm listening. What the hell is going on?" she replies.

"Well, the only thing I'm guilty of is being overprotective of my daughter. While you have been in America, I have had private security teams watching you and making sure you have been safe," the Don explains. "Daddy, you have been having me followed again haven't you?" Debbie states with a bit of an attitude. "No, baby, not followed as much as having someone keep an eye on you here and there. I love you and I would never let anything happen to you," he says with the care of a father. "I see, so, keep explaining; I still want to know everything," she tells her father. "When the people I have looking after you said you had found a new friend I was happy for you. You know how I hate that husband of yours. I also had them watching him and the reports I was getting were disturbing to say the least. As long as he didn't put his hands on you I stayed out of it. Now, when I got the report that you had hopped a private jet to Florida with the new guy and what looked to be body guards. I wanted to know who this man was. That is when they sent me his photo and low and behold it was El Diablo Negro. They had told me his government last name before but I didn't put two and two together. The day I met him I named him El Diablo Negro, The Black Devil," he tells his daughter.

"Well, daddy, why do you call him that? How did he get that name?" she asks. "I named him that because that man's reputation for torture and pain is something close to mythical. He was so proficient at it during collection procedures that the word spread around the world about his brutality. People feared him and knew that he was not to be played with. Therefore, making me even more powerful because everyone knew he worked for me. I had to give him a name that people could remember and fear all at the same time. It came to a point that if someone owed the conglomerate money, all I would have to do is say 'I will send Diablo Negro to see you' and all of a sudden there would be no more debt. So, do you understand the name a little better now?" her father asks her. "Yes, daddy, I get it. You have always taught me that business comes first and whatever it takes to succeed is a priority," Debbie tells her father.

Don Jorge continues with "There is another reason I consider him my son. That is the man who did incredible things to save your brother's life when he was in America," her father tells her. "Wait daddy, that is the American who saved Victor's life in the shoot out? I can remember the stories he used to tell about it," Debbie replies. "Yes, sweetheart, that is him and from that day, I have welcomed him into our family. Why do you think I am so happy today? My daughter could not have chosen a better man. He is like a son to me and I know he will take care of you. I know his character and his heart," the Don tells her.

"Daddy, did you tell him who I am to you?" she asks. "No I did not. Actually, when I saw the pictures of you two in Miami, I knew he didn't know you were my child. If he did, he would not have approached you or dated you in any way. That is also why I decided I needed to get you down here and see you both under the disguise of a birthday party," her father tells her. "Daddy, can you please not tell him? I will let him know in my own good time. Please daddy," Debbie says. "But, sweetheart, I was going to tell him later tonight. However, you are my child and more importantly you are grown. You can make your own choices. With that said, I will honor your wishes because you two make one another happy and I am giving you my blessing," her father says proudly. "Oh, daddy, you are so sweet and I love you so much. I promise I will tell him when the time is right. If I tell him now, he might get scared and run off," Debbie says laughing. "Yes I am sure he would," her father replies. They embrace in a loving hug.

THE ORDER IS GIVEN

When Zeke walks back into the party, he pulls Carlos to the side to talk to him. "We have been given a task by the Don. Do me a favor and find a cell phone. Make a call to the team back home. Tell them we have a hop to take. Inform them that I want them to get on the ground tonight and have things in motion for our arrival tomorrow," Zeke tells him as he hands him a piece of folded up paper. "Wow, after all this time we are getting back to work? This is going to be fun. I kind of miss our old life," Carlos says to him. "Yes, I miss it too sometimes I have to admit. Look, the Don wants some special therapy done on this one. Tell the crew that we are doing box lunches on this one and to keep the chicken in the box until we get there," Zeke tells him. "Hey, I love chicken dinners, this guy must have pissed the Don off something bad," Carlos says laughing.

"Well, you know how the Don is about his money. Playing with his money is fuck up number one, in his book," Zeke replies. "Oh boy, do I know all about that, even when the mistake is not yours he takes it really, really personal," Carlos says as he remembers his own situation with the Don. Zeke replies "Yes, he takes it extremely personal."

Now, look, after we get back to Florida; have a jet waiting for us to take us out west. I don't have time to do it myself. We are leaving at first light so you can party all night. Just be ready in the morning." "No worries, boss, we will have everything ready to roll when you want to leave. Since plans have changed, I will forgo the party and prep for the hop. I will inform Jose of the plans as soon as he gets back with Debbie," Carlos tells him. "Ok, that will be fine and make sure you guys go out and check on Pegasus before you go to bed tonight. Make sure she is all locked down and gassed up for our early departure tomorrow. As a matter of fact, assign two armed guards to protect her tonight," Zeke tells him. "Again, no worries, boss, we got you. I will go and get her prepped now. I will also have the jet waiting," Carlos says reassuringly.

Into the room walk Debbie and Jose. Debbie is smiling from ear to ear after her meeting with Don Jorge. "Hi honey, did you miss me?" she asks. "Of course I did sweetheart, anytime you're not with me I miss you," Zeke tells her with his manly charm. "You are so sweet. You always know what to say," Debbie replies. "Baby, that Don Jorge is something else. You know he has a lot of love and respect for you," Debbie says. "Yes, dear, I know and like I said before, I have the same love and respect for him. He has changed my life in so many ways I can never thank him enough," Zeke tells her. "Why didn't you tell me you were a super hero? Well, I knew you were my super hero but you didn't tell me you go around saving everyone's life. Don Jorge was kind enough to tell me that you saved his son's life many years ago. Why didn't you tell me you did something like that?" Debbie asks him. "Dear, it is not something I just talk about and it was no big deal. I was just in the right place at the wrong time. I'm glad I was there because that situation has changed my life for the better as well as his son's life. One day we can sit down and I will tell you everything about that particular incident," Zeke tells her. "I hope it's one day soon, I would really love to get to know that side of you," Debbie replies.

"No problem, one day I will. But let's put all that aside right now. We need to get our party on because we have to head back to Florida early in the morning," Zeke tells her. "Why do we have to go back so early? Can't we stay for awhile and do some sightseeing and shopping? So far, I am loving Cuba and its' wonderful people," Debbie explains. "I would love to stay for awhile myself but the Don has asked me for a favor and it requires I be in the Midwest sometime tomorrow. It's just one of those things that has to be taken care of as soon as possible. Plus, I promised the Don that I would deal with it tomorrow. Now that you have met The Don, I'm sure you have gotten the message that he is not to be played with and missing an appointment is out of the question," Zeke says to her. "Yes, I definitely get that impression of Don Jorge, he seems to be a no nonsense kind of person. But when I just met with him, he was so kind and sweet. I guess he treated me that way because I know you," Debbie says smiling as she leans over and kisses him. Laughter just comes out of Zeke as he says "Well, I think he just likes you better than he likes me."

We have to get out of here in the morning so let's get a couple of drinks and just enjoy the party." "I can use a drink for sure but I have a question. Are you taking me with you to the Midwest? You know I want to go with you," she says to him. "I was actually going to leave you in the Keys to relax at the house. There is no need for you to get all wrapped up in this. I want you to just stay at the house and get some sun," Zeke tells her. "No, I'm not staying at the house. I want to go with you. I want to know and be a part of everything that is you. I want to go and help you take care of Don Jorge's business," Debbie says in a demanding tone. Zeke takes a second to think and then looks at Jose. Jose just shrugs his shoulders as if to say 'what do you want me to say.' Zeke then says "Ok, you can go with us but I don't want it to come back and haunt me later." Debbie replies with "Thanks and you won't have any regrets, trust me. I'm more than a pretty face. I thought you knew that by now," she tells him. "Oh, I know that for sure. I'm just afraid that you'll think of me differently and I don't want to lose you," he tells her. "That is the last thing you have to worry about. I'm going nowhere without you," she tells him confidently. "Bartender, where are the drinks?" Zeke asks as he wants to change subject and enjoy the night. "Everyone drink up. We have a long day tomorrow," he announces. Everyone grabs a drink and continues to enjoy the evening.

Carlos comes over to Zeke and gives him an update. "Zeke, I have just gotten off the phone with the crew back in the States and they fully understand what needs to be done. I have been told that they will be wheels up for the Midwest in ninety minutes or so. The team will be waiting for our arrival and I informed them that you required box lunches as well," Carlos tells him. "That's good news; I know it came as a shock to them that we were getting back to work," Zeke replies. "Yes, it caught them by surprise but the enthusiasm on the other end of the phone was intense. I sent all pertinent details in an encrypted email to one of the back door accounts. I have confirmation it has been received," Carlos says. "Good job, Carlos, that's why you are my man.

You always take care of the small details," Zeke tells him reassuringly. They all continue to party until around midnight. As they are heading back to their rooms, everyone is in agreement that it has been a remarkable evening.

DAWN COMES

As dawn comes Zeke is slowly awakened by what he thinks is a dream. But, no, it is not a dream it is actually happening. He is awakened by Debbie's succulent lips giving him an incredible blow job. He wipes the sleep out of his eyes after a long night of drinking. His eyes finally focus into view and he looks down at a smiling Debbie as she is licking his dick up and down. Debbie takes a pause and says "morning." Then quickly goes back to her up and down pattern of licks and strokes. "Good morning to you too, baby," he says as he grabs the back of her head and directs her mouth further down on his dick so she can continue with enthusiasm. "Thanks for the morning wake up. I don't know what has gotten into you this morning but I ain't complaining," Zeke adds.

Debbie takes the dick out of her mouth and clears her throat a little bit and says "You see, I wanted breakfast in bed this morning and I figured this was the best and fastest way to get it. I didn't think you would have a problem with it. Plus, you were asleep and I didn't want to be selfish and wake you up, just to ask for permission. Far be it from me to interrupt a man's sleep," she says with a soft giggle at the end. "No, I don't have a problem with it at all. Actually, can we put that on the menu more often? Your soft lips are a way better wake up than any alarm clock I have ever owned," Zeke tells her. "Oh, you can have it every day if that's what you want. I need my sausage and juice in the morning. I can't think of a better way to start my day," she says as she is feeling all of her womanhood.

"I see where your head is at today. This is going to be a great day; I can feel it already," he says. Debbie takes a break from sucking his dick and says "Yes, I can feel it already too, why don't you give me that nut already." She says as she goes back to sucking and jerking his dick simultaneously. "I'm trying to give it to you," he replies and he grabs the back of her head again and starts thrusting back and forth in her mouth. He thrusts deeper and deeper and then suddenly he tenses his body as an explosion occurs. Debbie takes in all of his hot juice and swallows in one big gulp. She takes a quick glance at Zeke then she goes back to sucking harder and harder in attempt to pull even more sperm out of his soul. There is none left to retrieve so there is none left to swallow. Debbie leans up and kisses him on the forehead and says "Thanks for breakfast, baby." She then scoots out of bed and heads for the shower bouncing and humming a tune. Zeke yells out "No, thank you for breakfast baby! I really appreciate it!" "You are oh so welcome, baby," she replies.

"Now that I'm awake, we need to get down to the boat for the run home. It is going to be a long day and we need to get things moving," Zeke tells her. "No problem, just let me take a quick shower so I can at least feel like a woman before I get into that big ole racing suit," she tells Zeke. A smile comes over his face and he tells her "You know what? Take all the time you need I am in no rush."

Zeke reaches for his phone to text Carlos and Jose telling them to wake up. Carlos responds back to him with a text saying, 'We are at the dock and the boat is ready. When you arrive, we can leave'. That is even better news than Zeke could have hoped for. He sends his a reply of 'Ok, be there in thirty minutes. Have the engines warm'.

Zeke then walks into the bathroom where Debbie is showering. He opens up the see through glass shower door and says "Hey, sweetness, I'm going to have to change my statement. I just heard from Carlos and he says that Pegasus is prepped and ready to go. I told him that we would be down in thirty minutes. I just wanted you to know and I hope it's alright." She looks at him and smiles, "Yes, baby, it's just fine." She gives him a kiss and asks "Do you want to get in with me since you're here?" "That's a good idea but please remember we have to be on the dock in thirty minutes," he tells her. She just smiles and says "Oh, that's plenty of time. Now, get in here so I can give you a shower." "Sometimes you are so demanding," he says as he places himself under the streaming water to get wet. And so the bathing process begins.

Thirty minutes later, the happy and smiling couple, are walking down the dock towards the boat. Carlos reaches into his pocket and pulls out five hundred bucks and gives it to Jose. He has lost a bet they had on if the two love birds would be on time. Surprisingly, they are. Jose has racing suits ready and turbines are running. "Hello guys," Debbie says. "Good morning, I have your suit ready for you right here," Jose tells her. "That's great. Let me hurry and get into it so we can get out of here. I'm sure I'm the one that has held you guys up this long. I'm sorry guys," she replies. "No, ma'am, you are fine. We are sure it was that strange guy you're hanging out with that caused the problem," Carlos says laughing. "Sure, blame everything on me why don't you? I could blame you for my lateness because of all those extra shots last night," he laughs as he replies to Carlos' comment.

"Let me get this suit on so we can get out of here. Baby, how is it going? Do you need some help with that?" "No, I'm good. I'm almost done, actually," she replies. "Alright, as soon as you're done, let me know so I can get you strapped into your seat. We're going to open her up on the way back and I don't want you bouncing around," Zeke tells her. "Wow, sounds like fun. I hope my stomach is ready," she replies. "I'm sure you'll be fine. Now, come on and let me get you all strapped in," he tells her. He then turns to Jose and says, "Jose, plot us a quick course back to the Keys, please. We will have a jet waiting for us at Marathon Airport. It is the start of a long day, so, tighten up and get ready for it everyone." Zeke continues to get Debbie strapped into her cockpit. When he finishes with her, he goes to his seat and gets himself all strapped in as well.

Carlos unties the last stern line and pushes the boat away from the dock. As he brings himself in through the door and locks it behind him, Zeke tells him "See, I am not the only one dragging this morning. You look like you're moving pretty slow yourself, Carlos." Carlos smiles and replies with "Since we are laying blame, I blame Jose. It's all his fault," Carlos says laughing. "Wait, wait how is this all my fault? Now I have to take the blame?" Jose says laughing,

"You men are just too much. We all know where the blame lies," Debbie says with a smile as chuckles fill the air.

Zeke comes on the intercom and says "Alright beautiful people, Cuba was nice but let's get out of here. Jose, get that course dialed into the PC and also aligned with the GPS. Carlos, bring up the throttles for me but not too much. Let's pull out slowly so we can allow folks to take pictures and stuff." "Yes, boss, the course is hot and active. As soon as you clear the harbor, turn left a hundred and twenty degrees and let her fly. There will be nothing in front of us as I look on radar," Jose tells him. "We are running about fifteen miles an hour and will be clear of the harbor in about ten minutes," Carlos says. "Alright, then, you all know the drill. Let's do some system checks before we get out here on the ocean," Zeke announces. The crew goes through their normal check lists of to do's before launch. Everything from oil pressure to blade speed of the turbines is checked one last time.

"Hey guys, can everyone hear me?" Zeke asks. One-by-one everyone says yes they can hear. "Just so you know and that so we are all on the same page, we are running flat out back to the States and with that we might draw some attention. That's why I had everyone bring their passports with them. But, hopefully, it won't come to that. If the Coast Guard jumps on us, we are going to slow all the way down to, say, the crawl speed we are running now. That way they can see Pegasus with her colors and racing gear. Most of the guys stationed out of Miami know who we are but we don't want any problems either. If they board us and get to asking twenty questions, we were out training yesterday and ran into problems with our starboard turbine so we pulled into Havana to get off the water for the night. I just want everyone on the same page if it comes down to that. I doubt it will but want to be ready just in case." "Baby, you're not going to let them shoot at us are you?" Debbie asks. "No way, Debbie, it's just a formality for them. If they catch something running at the coast at two hundred miles per hour or so, it's going to peak their interest for sure. Something like that does not happen too often so they have to check it out. We'll be fine," Zeke answers her.

"Alright, Carlos, after this last boat up here on the left, let's push the throttles down and stretch out her legs a bit," Zeke says through the intercom. About three hundred or so yards passes by them and Carlos eases down the throttles. The engines start to hum a little louder as the four of them are pushed back into their seats. Zeke keeps his eyes out on the water in front of him. Carlos and Jose both check the gauges to make sure Pegasus is running correctly and not too rich. Jose looks down at his radar and sees nothing but open water for the next fifty or so miles.

Jose tells Carlos through the headsets "You are free and clear for the next fifty miles. You can go ahead and let her run." "Alright, baby, hold on tight, ok?" Zeke says to Debbie. "Carlos, you heard the man, go ahead and push them throttles a little further down. Bring the power up to eighty five percent and make sure you trim out the tabs to stabilize us. With that we should be back in the States in no time," Zeke tells the crew. The crew then settles in for a quick relaxing trip home.

After running flat out for sixty minutes or so, they come into Florida coastal waters. Zeke tells Carlos to back the throttles down since they are pretty much almost home. Pegasus takes a few more turns up the canal and pulls back into the compound's back dock. There is a maintenance crew standing on the dock waiting for their arrival. They pull the boat up and it is tied off by the maintenance crew. There is also a Mercedes Benz S500 with a driver waiting to take them to Marathon Airport. This has also turned into a business trip and the team needs to stay focused.

The team gathers their things and heads to the awaiting car. They jump in and the car takes off for the airport. "I sure wish we had time to get some of Yelina's cooking," Jose says. "Yes, I'd like some myself but we don't have time," Carlos adds. "Speaking of time, did you have time to speak to any of the guys on the progress of the operation?" Zeke asks. "Yes, I spoke to ground control early this morning before sunrise. They informed me that the box lunches were prepared and awaiting your arrival. I didn't want to wake you just to tell you that so I waited. I hope I was right in doing so," Carlos says.

"No, that's fine. I just didn't want to have to go there and have to do any leg work. I'm on vacation, as you know," Zeke says with a small laugh. "Yes, you're on vacation, Mr. Man, and don't forget it. You still owe me some quality time when we get back," Debbie tells him. "Yes, baby, I know this is just a small distraction and will be taken care of rather quickly, I hope," Zeke tells her. "If all goes well, we will be wheels up and headed back about two hours after we have landed and you can go right back to working on your tan," Zeke tells her confidently. "Alright, I'm going to hold you to that. You know a girl needs her sun time," Debbie says smiling.

About fifteen minutes pass by and they have arrived at the airport. The Mercedes pulls up to the side of the plane. The driver gets out and opens Zeke's door. Zeke and Debbie get out and head directly into the awaiting jet. Carlos, Jose and the driver handle the bags that are in the trunk. The plane is quickly loaded and the door is closed by the flight crew. This time the wonderful people at Netjets have provided an Embraer Phenom 300 that seats eight people comfortably. The pilot comes over the loud speaker and announces, "Good morning and thanks for flying with us today. We will be traveling at around four hundred and fifty miles per hour and with clear skies we should be landing in Chicago's O'Hare airport in a little bit over three hours. Your hostess today will be Ashley and she will take care of anything that you need. Please make sure your seatbelts are fastened; we will be taking off in three minutes or so." Everyone buckles their seatbelts and prepares for liftoff. The jet taxis to the end of the runway and proceeds to take off.

EXACTLY WHO ARE YOU?

As they are ascending to get to their cruising altitude Zeke holds Debbie's hand and asks her "So, dear, are you still interested in a normal and regular guy like me?" "Yes I am, even more so now that I have been on super boats to Cuba and now I am racing to Chicago," she replies. "Ok, I was just checking. I know my life can be a bit abnormal at times and I didn't know if I had scared you off," he says with a smile. "I'm not scared off but I am curious about some things. So, do I get to ask you some questions? I mean, you don't have to answer them. I know you are a private person," Debbie says to him. "You know what? You are right. I am a private person but since I hope to be with you forever, you should be able to ask me anything, so, go right ahead and ask away," Zeke tells her. "Now, if any of these questions get too personal, you don't have to answer. I want to make that clear," she says. "No, I'm fine. Ask away but can I get a drink first?" he says as he calls out for Ashley the hostess.

"Yes, sir, how can I help you?" the flight attendant asks. "Can you bring everyone a glass of champagne, please, and the big guys in the back, can you please bring them some food to snack on. It has been a long morning for them," Zeke tells her. "Yes, sir, right away. Would turkey club sandwiches be ok for them?" the attendant asks. "Yes that'll be just fine and add a couple of beers for them as well, please," Zeke says.

"Now that the drinks are out of the way, Miss Lady, what questions can I answer for you?" Zeke asks Debbie. "Ok, to start, how in the hell do you know Don Jorge? I mean, he is the head of a drug cartel for God's sake," she says. "Well, that is a long story, baby," he says. "The pilot said we have over three hours together, so, I have no place to be but here next to you," Debbie replies quickly. "Alright, well, about fifteen or so years ago, I was working in Baltimore as a night auditor at this hotel near the baseball stadium. I was in the hotel nightly by myself from 11:00 p.m. to 7:00 a.m. I had this guy and four of his friends check in one night and I could tell they were some serious men. I continued to see them in and out of the hotel for the next four nights. I would speak to them as they entered and exited so they knew who I was. You know, the front desk guy," Zeke tells her.

He continues with "Well, about 4:00 a.m. on the fifth night, I heard gun shots in the back of the hotel. So I grabbed my Glock and went out back to see what was going on. There was a man with an AK-47 shooting at them. There were bodies everywhere as a shootout was taking place. When I went out there, I found the guy from hotel and one of his partners shot and pinned down behind a minivan. I guess I was feeling like a super hero. I went out the other door and I shot the guy with the AK in the head. After shooting him, I thought to myself 'now what the fuck am I going to do?' I then went back over to the guys from hotel. They both were shot up bad and the other guys with them were already dead. I knew I needed to get the fuck out of there because Baltimore's finest would lock me up for sure if they catch me with this Glock no matter what took place. The minivan was still running so I somehow got the man and his friend into the minivan and took them to my house. My days of slinging rocks in South East D.C. had taught me that I could not take them to a hospital, there would be too many questions. So, I took them to my house to have Taylor work on them discretely. Taylor, my wife, was my girlfriend at the time and she was living with me. She was in medical school at John Hopkins. She was also working part time as a nurse at Saint Agnes Hospital, so she had some medical training. After getting both of them out of the minivan and onto my living room floor, she went to work. She somehow stopped their bleeding and stabilized them. She kept begging me to take them to hospital but I kept saying no," Zeke tells her.

"Wow that is crazy! What happened next?" Debbie asked. Zeke tells her "When I took them out of the minivan, I noticed there was a box or something covered up in the back of the minivan. I pulled the tarp off and what did I find,

I found what looked to be like two hundred kilos of cocaine. 'Oh shit' is all I could say to myself; first I caught a body and now this. I knew I needed to get back around the corner to finish my shift and deal with the feds that were sure to be at the job by now. I covered the drugs back up and locked the minivan up and took Taylor's little VW back to the job. Sure enough, when I got back to work, the feds were everywhere. So I parked across the street and went into the hotel through a side door. When I got to the lobby, the cops got to playing twenty questions with me. Luckily, I washed the blood off and changed my clothes before I came back. They were asking me where I was and all of this stuff. I told them I was scared and had run upstairs to hide in one of the rooms. It took me a few hours to deal with all of that nonsense."

"That is intense for sure. Then what did you do?" Debbie asks. Zeke continues with "Well, about three days passed and the big guy wakes up in my living room with IV's and stuff stuck in his arm talking about where am I? He notices that it is me, the front desk guy, and asks me where is his boss? I tell him that he is upstairs in my bed trying to recover. He rushes upstairs to check on him. He then immediately asks me for a phone after seeing his boss in really bad shape. He makes a call and about an hour or so later there are three all black SUVs' in my drive way with men pouring out of them. They rush into the house and take the two men away. As they are leaving one guy asks me what happened and I explained it to him. He then asked me where the van was and I tell him that it is out back locked up in my storage shed. When he heard that, he was amazed and sent some guys to my back yard to retrieve the minivan. He then drops about five grand in my hand. The three SUVs' and the minivan roll out as if they were never even there."

"See, I knew you were a good guy. A super hero even," Debbie says smiling. Zeke replies telling her "I don't know about all of that. I was actually pretty damn scared to be truthful." He continues with "I had taken a few days off, telling the owners that I was emotionally shaken after the shoot out. Five grand wouldn't last forever so, yeah, I went back to work as if nothing happened at all. Nothing happened for about two or three weeks and then one night the guy walks into the lobby with a crew of other dudes. He came to shake my hand and thank me for saving his life. He also said he wanted to talk to me. We sat down in the lobby for a conversation. During that conversation, he asked me why I stepped in and why didn't I turn him over to a hospital or the police. I had to explain that one of the bodies left outside that night, I was responsible for and that I didn't need any more drama than I already had. He asked me did I look in the minivan and I told him yes I did. He asked me why didn't I just take the product and run, saying it was enough to start a new life. I explained to him that at one time, I was in the game and I knew from experience that you don't just take that much product without someone coming to look for it and I didn't want any trouble coming my way.

He said that he liked me, my honesty and my work ethic and how would I like to come and work for him. I knew, at the time, that I should have said no but I had a girlfriend in medical school and I was making seven dollars an hour. So, with that, I said fuck it and told him that I would work for him. He asked for my number and told me that someone would be back in contact with me in a few days. He also told me he wanted me to keep working for now but I definitely was on his team. He handed me another ten thousand in cash as good faith money. I thought of it more as a signing bonus. He, again, thanked me and then he left.

A couple of weeks went by and this guy shows up at my house. He knocks on the door and when I answer it, he asks if my name is Zeke. I tell him yes and he hands me a cell phone. 'Hello Zeke this is Victor again and the man in front of you will explain to you what I want you to do. Is that ok for you?' Victor asked me. I tell him yes. He asks me 'do I understand fully' and I say yes. Victor then hung up the phone. The guy begins to tell me what I need to do. I had been instructed to drive this minivan to Richmond, drop it off and then get a rental car and come back. I ask is that all I have to do and the guy says yes. I take on the task nervously but with enthusiasm. Upon return from Richmond, the same guy shows up at my house and gives me a backpack with thirty thousand dollars in it. I knew from that point, I was connected with the right people.

After that first mission, things went on like that for about a year. Then, I was asked to do collections instead of deliveries. I liked this part more because it was less risk and the reward was five percent of whatever

I collected. It goes without being said that I was an excellent collector. It is actually pretty easy to do when you have the green light from your boss to say fuck the money and just kill the motherfucker because he was playing with the boss' money in the first place. They had me flying all over the country and Canada doing the collections. I was amazed at the size and scale of the operation as a whole.

The collections went on for about a year and, then, one day Victor calls me and asks me 'do I have plans for tomorrow morning?'. I told him no I was free and he said 'well, good, there will be a plane ticket waiting for you at US Airways ticket counter and that the flight leaves at 10:00 a.m.'. I told him ok I would be there. When I asked him where I was headed this time, he just said 'you will find out when you get the ticket but be sure to bring your passport'. That was strange because usually he would tell me at least what airport I was flying into. But, oh well, I was on money so I did what I was told. I made it to the counter the next morning only to find out I was headed to Bogota, Columbia. 'Oh, damn, I am about to be killed' is all I could think of. Talking about a nervous six hour flight but I had no choice. If I didn't go, I would be found, questioned and probably killed anyway, so, might as well get the inevitable over with. That flight changed my life. When I landed, two men met me and escorted me to an awaiting limo. Victor was inside the limo and I had not seen him since he last was at my job so many years before. He reached out and hugged me like he was generally happy to see me.

That ride to the main house was interesting. He told me I was brought to Bogota to meet his father. My name kept coming up as someone who could get things done properly. It seems that his father was impressed with my performance and my attention to detail when I carried out his orders. He told me his father was entertained by the way I handled certain individuals. These individuals were those who did not cooperate with the terms and conditions of the contract that they had with Don Jorge. When people needed to be put down, the Don always wanted to send a message. He left it up to me to use my creativity to make sure that message hit home. The funny thing is that until this point, I had been working for the man and never met him. I was a bit nervous, to say the least.

I must admit that when the car first pulled into the compound, I was a bit awe struck. I had never seen such luxury and expensive things. It, basically, was a mega mansion in the middle of maybe two hundred acres of manicured lawn and trees. Also came with armed guards everywhere. This was some old Scarface type shit to me, you know. We were escorted into a back office where the Don was supervising the beating of two men. We didn't say a word; we just looked on as he was chastising them for their shortage of money that was collected from someone that owed the Don. It seems as though these two men were responsible for collecting two million dollars and they were one hundred thousand short and the Don wanted his money. He told them that the beating would continue until he received his money.

The Don turns and gives us his attention. "Hello there, is this the man I have heard so much about? Is this the man that saved my son's life? Come here my boy and let me shake your hand. I want to thank you for getting my boy back to me. You will never know how much that has meant to me," the Don said. I told him "Saving your son was just me being at work at the right time. It is an honor to finally meet you. Thank you for changing my life. Things are great for me and my family. You made that happen for me." He told me "No, you made it happen. When my son was shot, he was doing the job that you have taken over. He was a collector at the time and the guy he was dealing with thought he could just take the product that my son showed him. You even took out the guy with the machine gun that had them pinned down. So, I owe you everything. You will now be recognized as one of my sons for saving my son's life. Everything they have is now yours."

I thought about what he said for a minute and thought how to respond. I came up with something, like, "Thank you so much for such a great honor. I really appreciate it but it is not necessary when you have put me in a position to do so much for so many. I would like to ask one small favor in order to make doing collection and business, in general, easier." The Don said "Sure, anything, what would you like, my son?" "Don Jorge, you know how hard it is to find good people. I want to expand operations and I need people I can trust. I am due two million dollars for my last collection and I would like you to keep it in exchange for the lives of the two men over there. The two million is more than enough to cover their debt. I am sure their loyalty to me for this small gesture from you will pay dividends for both of us for years to come," I told him. He looked at me and then looked at them and said "You would give up two million dollars for these worthless pieces of shit, for what? You already see that they are thieves and if they will steal from me, they damn sure will steal from you. How about I just kill these two, like I planned on doing, and assign you two more guys. That would make me feel a whole lot better. Even better you can choose any two of my men that you want." "Don Jorge, Sir, with all due respect and with your blessing of course. I would like to take these two under my wing and see what we can make out of them. I have been where they are and sometimes you don't count the money you weigh it. Now, in this extreme heat, the digital scales we use can be off a little bit. Please give me these two and let me bring them to the U.S. We will make money for you, I promise. Can you see a way to release them to me? I will be responsible for them," I explained to him. "

"These two are damn near dead with broken bones and all. You don't want these two," Don Jorge says. "Yes I do, they will become my right and left hands. If they don't speak English, I will teach them. I know two million is nothing to you but please take it, Don Jorge," I begged him. "Fine, you can have them. Someone cut these fools down and get them taken to the hospital," Don Jorge commands. He continues with "You two assholes were food for my hogs this evening. If El Diablo Negro comes and tells me that you two are screwing up, I will have you right back in here in front of me again." He spits on the both of them one last time and motions for them to be taken away.

Only thing I could think of is, where did the name come from? At that point, I had been around Columbian's for three years so I could speak Spanish. I knew he called me The Black Devil. I was just happy to get the two men released and who cares what he called me. Plus, the name stuck and pretty much that is the name that people know me by or El Diablo for short. It was well worth the two million bucks. Those two men are the two men on the back of this plane right now. Yes, it was Carlos and Jose. They have been with me, pretty much, constantly for the last fifteen years or so. I think it was a great move and it has paid off in so many ways. We have watched each other's back ever since day one.

Also, from that day one, Don Jorge has kept his word and treated me as a son. I know he loves me as one of his own. After being in the game for over ten years, I flew to Columbia on a visit and sat down with Don Jorge and Victor. I asked him for permission to leave the organization. I explained to him that while I loved and respected everything that we had been building together, I needed to get out for me. He, naturally, asked me why and I explained to him that I had never pursued this life and that I had stumbled into it. I told him if he remembered I was working a regular job and ended up saving Victor's life. I asked him if I could go and pursue some of my other dreams. Reluctantly, he said yes. After all, I had moved tons of cocaine for him over the years and brought in millions if not billions of dollars. He told me I was one of his children and he had to let me go and be the person I was supposed to be. That was major because in that particular lifestyle, normally, once you are in, you are in. There is no getting out. He also let me take Carlos and Jose with me because they also deserved a new life with me. When I first flew there to ask him about the departure, I will admit that I was scared. I was his best earner in the States and did hits for him all around the world. I was afraid he would, actually, kill me and my team because I knew where all the bodies were buried, so-to-speak.

But as you can see, things have worked out great. I got out and purchased a software development firm. So, I have a real job," Zeke says laughing. He continues with, "I have the race team that really takes up all of my time. Carlos and Jose love the racing life because they get to be on television and have groupies. Oh, how they love the groupies." Debbie replies "And you, you can't tell me you don't like the groupies. I saw you in the Keys when we went out for lunch. How they hug up on you and beg to take pictures with you." "Who me? No, I'm not into groupies that much. Maybe at first, but I got past that really quickly. Now, I am more concerned with trying to win and be competitive. I must say, the last two years, the guys have bought into it more and more. This team puts in a lot of hours trying to be in a position to win. I can't be more proud of them.

I know that was a lot to take in all at once. I hope that I have not scared you off by being truthful and telling you the whole story. I just wanted you to know everything, since you asked me. I know that transparency means a great deal to you. So, tell me, have I scared you off? Do you still want me in your life now that you know all there is to know about me?" Zeke asks. Debbie holds his face in her hands and says "Baby, I want you more now than ever. It is so refreshing to have someone who is honest with me. You don't know how much it means to me that you were able to open up and tell me everything there is to know. You gave me the opportunity to choose for myself if I still want to be with you. You didn't lie or hold anything back. I know with everything that is good in me, that I want to be with you. You are the man I have been waiting for my entire life. I can't even see myself with anyone else in my life, at this point. You are perfect for me. As long as you want me, I will want you and, hopefully, that is forever." Zeke leans back in his seat looking at Debbie smiling. He clears his throat and says, "Sweetheart, you are the one for me. I don't need anyone else in my life either. We will be together forever. One day we will be married with children running around everywhere. I say all that to say I love you." He leans over and kisses her long and passionately.

"This has been one interesting flight, I tell you that," Debbie says as she motions for the hostess to refresh her glass. She continues with "It has been very eye opening in deed. I am so happy right now. I feel as though everything is starting to fall into place for me. I know you and I have become closer because of it. I am in a very good place, that is for sure." "I am happy about things myself. It is good to know that you are sticking with me after all the clarity of today. I just hope that we can get through the rest of today with no drama but I have a feeling that is not going to happen. So, with that said, I am just going to enjoy the moment and try never to forget how I am feeling right now sitting here with you," Zeke says. "I feel the same way, baby, I really do. I would not want to be with anyone but you and those two crazy guys in the back too," Debbie tells him. Zeke turns his seat and sees that both Carlos and Jose have eaten and they both are knocked out asleep. "They didn't hear you; they are asleep," he says laughing. "Typical for the both of them, eat then pass out," he adds. The two of them just laugh as they look for more champagne to drink.

LET THE FUN BEGIN

Some time passes as Debbie has had time to allow all that Zeke has told her to sync in. She seems to be ok with everything that Zeke has said. Zeke is just in a state of bliss as he leans back watching television on the plane. The pilot comes over the intercom and announces that they will be starting their decent and will be landing in fifteen minutes or so. Zeke throws one of the pillows towards the back and it catches Jose squarely in the chest. He wakes up startled but he wakes up nonetheless. Zeke tells him with a raised voice "Come on sleepy head wake up and nudge that other guy next to you too." Jose replies "Yes, boss," as he stretches and wakes up Carlos at the same time.

"Ok guys, we will be landing in fifteen minutes. Carlos, did you arrange for transportation for us?" Zeke asks. Carlos replies, "Yes, we have a van waiting for us on the tarmac as soon as the jet arrives, we can step into it. One of the guys from home is driving it for us." "I'm glad that is taken care of, you know how I hate waiting" Zeke says. Carlos replies "No need to worry it is all taken care of. The guys told me that they acquired a quiet farm house on the outskirts of the city and that the package is awaiting our arrival." "That's good, no time for nonsense and it is nice and quiet. Maybe they even have some pigs there that we can play with," Zeke adds. With that comment, Debbie just looks at him for a moment and says "Baby, I love you but I am not playing with any pigs. They stink and they kind of scare me." Zeke looks at her smiling and says "Well, no worries, you will not be the one playing with the pigs, just wait and see."

The team prepares themselves for landing. The jet gently slows down its speed and lowers its altitude. The pilot comes on the intercom again and gives the local Chicago weather report. He also thanks the team for flying with Netjets. The plane circles O'Hare airport and then is cleared for landing. The plane touches down and taxis over to the executive airport hanger where the van is waiting to take them to the next location. The door opens and the steps fold down to allow the passengers to exit. Zeke and Debbie get off the plane first. They are then followed by Carlos and Jose carrying what little baggage there is. They all jump into the van and start the journey to the farm house.

The man driving the van tells Zeke, "We are headed to a secluded spot in Arlington Heights, which is about twenty miles outside of Chicago. We will be there in no time and the place has all the privacy that you require." Zeke replies "You guys did good to get out here and secure the package and the location on short notice like this. I owe the whole go team big time. I know you all were enjoying your regular lives relaxing. Then, for me to call on short notice and you guys get it done so quickly, is impressive." "To tell you the truth, when we got the call, we all jumped at the chance for some action. All of us have been transitioning into regular lives, so, some excitement is just the break we need. I know you all have had a long flight. Just relax and we will be there soon," the driver tells them. The group settles in for a short ride and has light conversation as they go.

The driver takes Interstate 90 out of Chicago and makes good time to Arlington Heights. Sure enough, it took him about twenty minutes, or so, to get to the farm. The van takes a left off of the main road and onto a long dirt road. As Jose is looking out of the window, he says, "Where in the hell are we this time?" Carlos answers him with "Oh, don't worry about it. You know all of these places look the same after a while." "You know what? You're right. They do all look the same but am I the only one looking forward to this? It has been so long since we had any enjoyment like this," Jose says. "I'm with you on that one. It's good to get my feet wet again. I miss the life," Carlos says.

Zeke then turns to Debbie and says "Alright, dear, we are almost at the point of no return. One last time, are you sure you want to be a part of all this nonsense? It's not too late to back out." Debbie just looks at him and says "No, dear, I don't want to back out. I want to know all there is to know about you and your world. I am down for you and whatever that may bring." Zeke, looking at her smiling, says "I am very happy to hear you say that but at any-time if you get to feeling sick or uncomfortable, please feel free to leave. We all have been there and we will understand." Debbie responds with "I think I'll be fine and don't worry about me. I'm a big girl and I know what I'm doing." "I hope you're right because don't look now, but we are here," Zeke says as the van pulls up to the farm house. They all exit the van and head over to the barn area where the package and the rest of the go team are waiting.

"Hey, what's up fellas? I have not seen all of you together since that night we were all at the Stadium Club in D.C. a few months ago. How is everyone doing?" Zeke asks the team. Rodrigo, who is a crazy Columbian from the early days, answers for the team, "We are all good and it is good to see you again. We were talking earlier about how surprised we were to get the call for this hop. When is the last time that we all took a hop together? It's like a family reunion for us and, to be truthful, we all admitted that we sort of missed it. You know, the action." Zeke replies with "We were saying the same thing on the plane. How regular life is cool but we miss our old antics. See how great minds think alike," Zeke says laughing. "Yes, I guess they do," Rodrigo says with a smile on his face.

Zeke then says "Since the team is all back together, let's have some fun. Where is the package? Also, is the extraction team in place yet?" "The package is in the hog pens and yes the back up team is in place. But who is this pretty lady that you have with you," Rodrigo asks him. Zeke smiles and turns to Debbie, "Everyone, this is Debbie and she is my lady now. You all were there so you know what went down with Taylor. This wonderful lady has replaced her in my life and in my heart. So, please treat her with respect and, overall, just be nice to her. She is new to this life and we don't want to run her away." Debbie smiles and says "Hello everyone, it is nice to meet everyone. I know I just met all of you but he has told me so much about you that I feel as though I already know you." She is greeted by the guys and welcomed into the crew.

Zeke takes off his coat and says "Alright, I'm ready, take me to the pack-age." Zeke follows Rodrigo to the hog pens where he finds two large footlock-ers with holes in both of them. The footlockers have been left overnight inside of hog pens to help get the occupants attention. Zeke gives the command

"Someone please take them out of there so I can talk to them." The cases are brought out of the mud and onto the dry ground of the barn. Jose and Rodrigo hustle to open the cases. Each one of the cases contains one adult man.

The footlockers are so small the men could barely fit in them. To get them inside, the team had to force the men in and then sit on the cases, in order to get them closed, like an overstuffed piece of luggage. As they are opened up, the men try to move their bodies but they are a bit stiff and it is hard to move. They have, after all, been in a very small place for more than twelve hours, so, it may be a bit hard to move. Carlos says "Come on, guys, get them out and sit them at this small table over here." The two men are lifted out of the footlockers and slowly unbent. They are then dragged over to the table and sat into the chairs facing Zeke.

"You guys can take these bags off of their heads now," Zeke orders. Jose snatches the hoods off of both men. When the hoods come off, it is obvious they have been beaten over and over. Their faces are swollen. They have dried up blood on their faces and clothes. Zeke says "You guys can take them out of the chains as well. I'm not really worried about them running anywhere." Jose and Rodrigo go to work on freeing the men from their chains. A few minutes later they are free and sitting in front of Zeke at the table. "I need someone to get me some bottled water for these guys too." Zeke tells the crew. Someone from the team comes and places the water on the table in front of Zeke.

Zeke then directs his focus to the two idiots in front of him. Zeke asks the two men "Do you know who I am and why I am here?" They both struggle to speak and say no. "Here, you guys try to drink some water. You can hardly talk and you seem like you need it," Zeke tells them as he places a bottle in front of both of them. The two men take advantage of the opportunity and begin to drink the water as if they have been in a desert for weeks. I guess being chained and locked inside of a box can make you a bit thirsty.

"Alright, all the water is gone now. Since you say you don't know who I am, let me tell you. My name is El Diablo Negro and I have been sent to talk to you by Don Jorge. He has informed me that you two have been playing with his money and treating him like a step child. He tells me that when he reaches out to you by phone, you choose not to answer him. So, before I get too involved, you two do recognize the name Don Jorge, correct?" The two men shake their heads yes. "Well, good, I just want to make sure I have the right people in front of me," Zeke tells them with a quiet authority about him.

"Now, Mr. Robert Harris and Mr. Edward Waters, I am positive that I have the right people. I have all of your information right here in front of me. As I understand it, Bob, you are the main guy and, Ed, you are the second in command. What you two have just experienced overnight is what we refer to as having a box lunch. You were placed in a small box like you were a sandwich in a lunch box. This process is done in order to get your attention and to let you know that we are not playing with you. I tend to use this process with people who are alright in business but have lost sight of the bigger picture of working with their partners. This business, after all, is all about partnerships, trust and working relationships. The mere fact that I am in front of you now means that you have forgotten that you have a working relationship with Don Jorge. Don Jorge must like you because you are still alive. He just does not like the fact that you have not made your scheduled payment accurately and or on time. So, I have been sent here to bring you back into the fold, so-to-speak. I am here to collect the outstanding balance that you owe Don Jorge and to give you the opportunity to correct your issues with payment going forward. I don't want you to look at me as if I am the bad guy but rather as a consultant to get you back on track. Do you understand what I am telling you thus far?" Zeke asks with a serious face. Both men again nod their heads yes.

"I need to ask you both a question. Going forward, will you fall in line and do what you are supposed to do or will I have to come and visit you again?" Zeke asks them. Bob, the leader, decides to finally speak up, "Yes, we will do whatever it takes to make the relationship work. We just want to go home to our families. We didn't mean to make Don Jorge upset." "That is good to hear but as I am looking over the notes that were given to me by Don Jorge, it seems as if you have an outstanding balance of forty million dollars. I am not going to ask you why you have not paid Don Jorge. All I want to know is are you ready to pay him right now?" Zeke asks the men.

Ed, the backup, decides it is a good time to open his mouth, "We have paid Don Jorge the money that we owe him. He ain't getting another dime from us and that is that. How is he going to demand that we pay him for sales of a product that we got from someone else? When we picked up from his people the last time, our load was intercepted by the feds. Is that fair business?" "I don't know if it is fair. That is not my job. My job is to get his money. Plus, in this game, if our people deliver the product and your people take possession, then you owe the money simple as that.

Do you know and understand why it is wrong to play with the Don's money?" Zeke asks. The guy, Ed, decides it is time for him to speak again and says "Look, we told his people that the relationship was over and that the last payment was the last payment. So, I really don't understand why you are here." Zeke looks at him funny, takes a breath and says "Well, let me explain to you why we are here. I can't believe I am taking the time to explain myself but I will do it just for shits and giggles. You may not remember this, but the Don set you up in this city. You had competition and the Don took care of that for you. You needed help with the police and we helped you. You had no smuggling routes and we set you up through our connections in Canada. You had no startup money and the Don fronted you half a ton of coke. He did this not because he liked you or because he was dating your sister. He did this because he looked at it as a partnership for the long haul. Now that everything is set up for you and running smoothly, you want to end the partnership? Is that any way to treat your business partner? I don't think so, and that is why I have been sent here to make sure you understand that this partnership will continue uninterrupted from here on out. Now that I have explained a bit more clearly, do you feel as though you can comply with the demands of this partnership in the future?"

Bob answers with "Yes, we can continue with the partnership as outlined in the beginning but we have no money to give to the Don. All the money has been spent and accounted for." "Hmmm, I see, and this is your final answer?" Zeke asks. Then out of nowhere, Ed, the idiot, starts running his mouth again, "It may be cool with him but it's not cool with me. I am not paying the Don shit that I don't owe him. Our load was taken by the feds and the Don needs to understand that. We started using a new connection because someone from his side snitched to the feds and got our load taken."

Ed continues with "So, we don't trust him or your organization anymore. So, you can tell the Don to go fuck himself." "Go fuck himself is that what you said?" Debbie asks. "Yes, I said go fuck himself because we are not paying him shit. Please, El Diablo or whoever you are, can you have your bitch not address me, I don't talk business with women," Ed says boldly. Debbie, who is standing in the back near Carlos says "Oh is that right?" Ed replies "Yeah, that's right. Don't speak to me and stay in your place." Then Debbie walks up to Zeke and takes the Berretta out of his waist band. She walks over to Ed and says "I was on vacation minding my own damn business and had to stop to come and deal with this bullshit. If you keep running your mouth, I'm going to show you what a bitch is really like." She tells him as she stands before him with a gun. Ed replies with "What, is that gun supposed to make me scared little girl?" Debbie just laughs and says "Nope, not meant to scare you at all. This gun right here is meant to kill you" and she shoots him in the middle of his fucking forehead without warning.

Carlos and Jose turn to one another smiling like proud parents as they give each other high fives. In unison they both say "I like this girl" laughing together because they both were thinking the same damn thing. They give each other handshakes of approval further validating that her killing him was a cool ass move. Zeke is left shaking his head as his baby walks back over to him. "Baby, I'm sorry, his mouth was a little bit too much for me to take. I wasn't going to kill him but the mouth just kept running and he left me no choice. Baby, will you forgive me?" Debbie asks him. Zeke says "Yes, baby, it's fine. Don't even worry about it. You told him to watch his mouth and we see he didn't listen." "Thanks for understanding, dear," she says as she hands Zeke his gun back.

"Ok, now that all of that is over, do you feel as though we can continue with business as usual," Zeke says to Bob. Bob who, at this point, is scared out of his mind says "Yes, yes, yes we can continue." Zeke asks him "Your partner being silenced; is that going to be a problem for you?" "Hell no, he always ran his mouth with no regard to who he was talking to. Someone just finally closed that mouth for him," Bob tells Zeke as he looks down at his partner's dead corpse. I guess it was an easy decision for him since he had Ed's blood and brains all over him.

Zeke tells him "I'm happy that the business partnership can continue. There is just the matter of the forty million dollars that is outstanding on your account. If you go ahead and pay me now, we can leave and you can get back to your life." Zeke motions for the laptop to be brought over for the transfer of funds. "That is just it, I have no money to pay the Don. All of the money has been reinvested or spent," Bob says with a quiver in his voice. Zeke just kind of looks at him and says "Wait, you mean to tell me you still don't want to pay? You have been made into a box lunch, your friend has been killed and you still want to claim you are broke? Come on now, you made too much money with us over time to be broke. Hold on a second, I will be right back," Zeke tells him as he walks outside.

Zeke walks outside and calls the backup team. The backup team has been dispatched to Bob's house. They have been waiting for Zeke's call. Zeke gets the team on the phone and tells them to start the live feed. Zeke walks back into the building and addresses Bob. "You know, Bob, I like you and I am trying to work with you. I am going to give you one last chance to get on this laptop and transfer the money. Either you transfer the money or I will use the laptop for something else, you choose," Zeke tells him. "I have no money and I can't give you what I don't have," Bob tells Zeke. "Ok, you don't have it. Well, I have something for you," Zeke tells him as he fiddles with the laptop keys. Then, all of a sudden, Zeke spins the laptop around so that Bob can see the screen. Bob instantly starts to cry as he sees his wife and kids all tied up, sitting on his living room floor with bags on each of their heads. "Ok, ok, please don't hurt my family. I will do anything. Just don't hurt my family," Bob screams aloud.

"So, now you want to pay me? I am happy you changed your mind. Now, get on this laptop and send me the cash," Zeke tells him. "I don't have the money but I don't want you to hurt my family. I will give you five million dollars to let my family go. Please just don't hurt them," Bob pleads. "You have five million? I promise if you give me the five million your kids can go free," Zeke says to him. "Yes, there is five million dollars in the basement of my house. Just have your men go and get it so that they can leave my family alone. Please don't hurt my kids," Bob says again as tears now run down his face.

Zeke calls the backup team on the phone and tells one of them to go to the basement and look for the money. "Bob, you know that if there is no money at the house, then, there are going to be problems," Zeke tells him as he sips on a beverage. Zeke's cell phone rings and he says hello. The voice on the other end of the phone tells him that they can't find any money. Zeke just looks at Bob and asks him, "Bob, are you playing games again? My people tell me that there is no money in your basement". Bob quickly replies with "Tell them to move the deep freezer. The money is hidden in the floor underneath the deep freezer. If they move the freezer, they will see it for sure." Zeke tells the voice to check under the deep freezer. A few minutes pass by and there is another call to Zeke's phone and the voice tells him we have the money. "Yes" Zeke says aloud. "See, Bob, that wasn't hard at all. I told you I keep my promises and as a measure of good faith your family will not be harmed at all. I knew I liked you, Bob. You are honest with me and I am honest with you. I will let them go as soon as we finish our little bit of business," Zeke tells him.

Bob, now wet from tears, sweat and blood, pulls together enough energy to say "I have kept my word and gave you the five million, now, please let my family go." Zeke turns to him and says "Well, Bob, I want to but you have one more thing to do for me. You still need to transfer the forty million dollars and until you do, we are not letting them go. I will give you two choices, the first is, you can transfer the money that you owe now and we leave. The second is, we can take your family with us and just wait for you to transfer the money. When the money is transferred, your family will be returned. I will give you a few moments to decide which one is better for you. Oh, and by the way Bob, when I say take your family with us, I mean back to Columbia," Zeke tells him to really get his attention.

Bob takes a hot second to think about it and says "Fine, I want my family back. I will transfer the money now. I just need the account number and routing number of the bank you want it sent to." Zeke smiles and says "I'm glad we could come to some type of peaceful resolution. Here are the account and routing numbers to the Cayman National Bank. Once the transfer is complete, we will be on our way," Zeke tells him smiling. Zeke turns the laptop to Bob again so he can make the transfer. Bob asks a dumb question "I only need to transfer thirty five million because I just gave you five million in cash right?" Zeke laughs and says "No, you owe the entire forty million dollars. That original five million was for you wasting my time with bullshit and not killing your family because of that bullshit."

About two minutes go by and Carlos says "Sir, the transfer is complete; I can see the money in our account now." "See Bob, that was not so hard now was it? I just wish we could have done this from the start to save time and all this drama. Now, Bob, so that we are clear on a few things, first, things will be back to business as usual from here on out. Second, you will not be dealing with your new supplier. And most important, you will not hold up any more payments to Don Jorge, are we clear on that?" Bob, still in pain answers quickly, "Yes, I understand, no more problems from me." Zeke says "One more thing, Bob, we don't have to worry about you and your wife contacting the police do we? I mean, we can always come back and pay you another visit, if you think there is going to be an issue." Bob replies "No, no, you don't have to worry about a thing from here on out. I will keep her inline, trust me." "Bob, you have been fantastic and thank you for your deposit. I hope I never have to see you again," Zeke tells him as he rubs Bob on the top of his head.

Zeke turns to Carlos and whispers "Tell Rodrigo to kill this fucker. He saw Debbie pop dude and we can't have any witnesses. But have him break a few bones and see if he has more money to transfer first. Keep using his family for leverage. After you tell him what I want done, I want you to go and get the five million from backup team and meet us back at the airport. Before you come back to the plane, give one million to the guys so they can split that up and bring the rest to the jet. Jose, Debbie and I will be waiting for you there." Carlos replies "Yes, boss, right away." Carlos walks out as he picks up the phone to call the second team and let them know of the plan.

Zeke turns to Debbie and says "Baby, our work here is done. Let's get back to the jet and wait for Carlos to arrive. It has been a long day and I am tired. I am sure you are too." "Yes, it has been a long day but very interesting, to say the least. I just want to get out of this smelly ass barn and away from all this nonsense," Debbie tells him. The three of them head back to the transport vehicle so they can be taken back to the jet. It takes them no time to arrive back at O'Hare. Carlos soon arrives after them with duffle bags filled with cash. The plane is loaded and soon takes off headed back to Florida.

NOTHING LIKE A BONUS

When the plane levels off at thirty thousand feet, Zeke asks the hostess to bring bottles of champagne and glasses for everyone. She complies and gives everyone filled glasses of the bubbly. Zeke clears his throat "Here's to a successful hop after so much time off. Not only was it successful, we also got a bonus on top of our standard twenty percent. I would say that is a good day for everyone, don't you agree?" Everyone is smiling and nodding their heads in agreement. Zeke continues with "Since it was such a good day, I am going to treat it like the old days. Carlos and Jose, you two take a million each and leave Debbie and I the last two million. You will still get your normal cut just like the other guys do. There is no reason all of us can't enjoy this little bonus."

"Alright now, that is right on time! I have been eyeing that new LaFerrari that just came out. There were only four hundred and ninety nine of them made. They come fully loaded at one point two million dollars. This is just the excuse I need to go and pick it up," Jose says. "What excuse is that?" Carlos asks. "The free money excuse, of course," Jose says laughing. The entire group busts out in laughter after that. Glasses continue to be raised in celebration. "Carlos, what are you going to do with your bonus?" Zeke asks. "I really haven't had time to think about it, you know. I think I need a small house in the mountains this time. Somewhere nice and peaceful with nature all around, you know, for the wife and kids," Carlos says. "Awe that is so sweet. You are a very nice man, Carlos. Your wife is so lucky to have you in her corner," Debbie says.

"And what about you baby what are you going to do with your bonus?" Zeke asks. "Wow, I get a bonus? I was just tagging along, you know," she replies. "But, in fact, you ended up putting in most of the work. Your actions activated him into giving up the bonus money in the first place," Zeke says. "I just wanted to go and get to know all phases of you. I want to know you inside and out. Now that little issue back there with that guy, he was just getting on my damn nerves with the mouth. He was being counterproductive and hindering progress. More importantly, he called me a bitch more than once. So, I needed to show him what kind of a bitch I can be. That was for me and not for the money," Debbie replies.

Carlos and Jose immediately look at each other and get to shaking hands again. They are giving each other approval once again. Carlos says "I told you I like this girl." "Oh, we got a keeper for sure," Jose chimes in. "All that aside, baby, I want you to take a million and splurge. It is bonus money. We have a tradition of always splurging the bonus money we get. Do sound investments with the salary from the hops and fun with the bonus. Now, come on, what do you have in mind for fun?" Zeke asks her.

Debbie takes some time to think as she takes another sip of champagne. She puts her glass down and sits up in her seat and says "I know you're going to think I am crazy but I think I have a way to secure our happiness forever. I will whisper it in your ear and if you think it is a good idea, then, I will tell Carlos and Jose too. I am just too embarrassed to say it aloud. Is that an ok deal for you?" "Sure, slide over here and tell big daddy your secret," Zeke says smiling. Debbie slides closer to Zeke and whispers in Zeke's ear for a couple of minutes. After she is done she leans back and asks "Ok, so what do you think? Is that crazy or what?" Zeke thinks to himself for a moment about what Debbie has told him. He picks up his glass and takes a drink. He pauses for a moment and says "I like it and I think it will work. Damn, you are a smart woman! That is why I love you!" Zeke says. He picks up the phone that connects to the pilot's cabin. When the pilot answers, Zeke tells him "We have a change in plans. We need to go to Washington, D.C., can you change course and let me know an approximate arrival time? Thank you." and he hangs up the phone.

He then says "Gentlemen, this lady is a genius. We are headed to D.C. now to get rid of both of our spouses. This is going to be a good day," Zeke says as he kisses Debbie and then looks at her smiling. "Are you really going to try it?

It was just a crazy idea and nothing more," Debbie says. "I know but, in reality, it sounded so good I wanted to see if it could work today. I could not have thought of anything better than the way that you have come up with. Plus, doing it your way, I have clean hands of the situation," Zeke says. "That is what I was thinking too. After today's events, I know peace and quiet in my life is what I need. I might as well wrap up all my problems right now and get it over with," Debbie tells him. "I am with you. Let's just nip it in the bud and get it over with. No need to drag out the inevitable. I can't wait to get to D.C. Looks like this bonus is turning out to be a blessing, indeed. I will call my lawyer now so that by the time we land everything and everyone will be in place," Zeke says.

Zeke picks up the phone and calls the detective that he has watching his wife twenty four hours a day for the last six months. "Hello and good evening, Sir," the detective says. "Where is she right now?" Zeke asks with an authoritative voice. He replies with "She is at her lover's house in bed having shots while watching tv. She has been there for two days. Zeke looks up at Debbie while talking to the detective and says "Oh, she's in bed at her lover's house having shots watching tv, ain't that something. Thank you very much. Just stay where you are and let me know if anyone leaves the house." "Ok, will do, Sir," the detective replies. Zeke hangs up the phone.

Zeke then picks up the phone and calls his wife Taylor. She hears the phone and after reaching over to get it she sees who is calling, it's Zeke. She doesn't want to answer the phone but she knows she has to. She reluctantly answers the phone, "Hello." "Well, hello to you as well and I hope your day is going smoothly. How are you doing?" Zeke asks her. "I'm doing alright just at a girlfriends house doing girl stuff," Taylor tells him. Zeke replies with "At your girlfriend's house, is that right? There is no need to lie. I know where you are right now. You are at your lover's house in Potomac having shots and watching tv. You must be very comfortable, since you are all snuggled up in his bed. Now that you know I know where you are, I want you to stay there until I arrive. I want to speak to you both, do you understand me?" "Yes, I understand, how long will it be before you arrive?" she asks. "Well, I don't know. I have to run an errand or two before I get there. You just stay put. And, Taylor, don't try to go anywhere. You know I have a security team watching you. How else would I know that you've been there for two days," he tells her and then he hangs up the phone.

"Boss, what are you and Debbie up to?" Carlos asks. "Just wait and see, my boy, just wait and see. I think you're going to love it," he replies. Zeke picks up his glass and holds onto Debbie's hand ever so gently. He gazes out of the window thinking about the possibilities that could be.

STOP YOUR WHINING

Meanwhile, back at Debbie and Mitch's Potomac home, Taylor knows she's fucked. She grabs the bottle that they have been taking shots out of and takes a long drink straight from the bottle. She gulps it down, turns to dumbass and says "Turn off the television, we need to talk. We need to talk about the phone call that I just received. Here, take a drink and I mean a good one," she tells Mitch as she passes him the bottle. "My husband just called and he said that he is on his way here and he wants to talk to us both," she says. "He wants to talk to us? Oh, that is some bullshit. I ain't talking to nobody. He is hanging out with my wife and shit, so, we don't have anything to talk about. Who does he think he is, superman or something?" he says laughing.

Taylor replies with "Go ahead, Funny Man, keep laughing and take him for a joke. This time, you are in some shit and your luck may have just run out." "What do you mean? The guy does software development," he says as he is doing the quotation marks thing in the air. He continues with "From what you told me, I don't have too much to worry about. Even if we were to get into it, I can handle myself. I am a grown ass man!" "You know, right now, I wish I could tell you what is real and what is not. I just can't right now. But what I do know is that we need to stay here until he gets here," she says as she takes another shot. "So, Funny Man, did you happen to see those big ass body guards with him?" Taylor asks. "Yes, I saw them but, shit, Bill Gates walks around with security too but I'm not afraid of him either," Mitch says. "Well, let me enlighten you on one thing, you need to be afraid of my husband for sure," Taylor replies.

"Why do I need to be afraid of your husband? What makes him so special? He told me to tell you that you had the 'green light' to tell me who he was. He said you would know what that meant. So who is he anyway?" Mitch finally asks. "Oh, that is what he said? Since you asked, let me tell you. Sure, by day he runs a software development and IT security firm. I told you he travels a lot for business but he actually races boats five months of the year. His business sponsors his team," Taylor tells him.

Mitch replies "Like I said, a nice, quiet, soft dude. Why is he a problem?" "Yeah, real soft guy you think? Well, since it is probably both of our last few hours alive, I might as well tell you. My husband, Mr. Softy, is a collector and enforcer for one of the biggest drug cartels out of Bogota, Columbia. Do you remember when I told you he travels a lot? Well, he and his friends travel the world doing hits, or hops as they like to call them, for enormous amounts of money. He only gets the call if the person has really fucked up and a lesson needs to be taught. His government name is Zeke but his underworld name is El Diablo Negro or The Black Devil." Debbie sees the expression on Mitch's face and asks "What's wrong? I don't see you laughing and smiling anymore, Funny Man? Ten minutes ago you were a grown ass man that could handle his own," Taylor says.

"I didn't know he was some type of mercenary. If I did, I never would have fucked with you. Is he going to kill us?" Mitch asks with a certain amount of bitch in his voice. "Oh, stop your fucking whining already. You wanted some pussy and I gave it to you. You didn't give a shit who or what my husband was all them days you were fucking me. So don't be crying and bitching now. Now, when he gets here, the objective for today is to stay alive. The best way to do that is try not to piss him off. The best way to do that is by not disrespecting him by saying some stupid shit out of your mouth. As a matter of fact, just don't say anything unless you are asked a question. Even then, keep your answer short. The less you say the better," Taylor tells him.

"Did he say when he was coming?" Mitch asks. "No, he said just stay here until he arrives. This is about to be a life altering conversation one way or another," Debbie says as she pours them both another shot.

A FINAL SIT DOWN

The jet touches down at DCA a few hours later. It has been awhile since everyone has been home. There have been a lot of boats, planes, and automobiles since they left. Everyone is pretty much worn out from the shear mileage that has been legged let alone partying, drinking and taking care of business along the way. But with the eight million as the twenty percent collection fee plus a little bonus of another five million, the trip that was a vacation has turned out great. Carlos has scheduled the sedan service to have an SUV waiting for their arrival. Upon taxiing to the hanger, they pull to a gentle stop. The stairs are folded down and they disembark into the awaiting suburbans. It does not take long to get into the trucks. All of their main gear is back in Florida anyway. The hardest part was unloading the money.

Zeke tells the driver "Hit George Washington Memorial Parkway north until you get to the I-495 exit then take it to I-270 north. We will give you directions from there. Oh, man, it is good to be good to be home again." "It sure is nice, too bad it is under these circumstances," Debbie says. "Well, sweetheart, if your plan works, this will be the last troublesome day of your life," Zeke says to her lovingly. "I hope that is the truth. I really do," Debbie says as she leans her head on his shoulder.

Jose is in the second truck with Zeke's lawyer. The caravan heads up the parkway and onto Interstate 495. When they hit Interstate 270, Zeke tells the driver "Please stop at Starbucks in Falls Grove Shopping Center on Shady Grove Road. I need a jolt after that long flight and the champagne." He then nudges Carlos on the shoulder and says "Can you call Jose and let him know of the change in route. Thanks and what do you want to drink today? I know how you are about that pumpkin latte," Zeke says to Carlos laughing. "I never would have pictured you as a latte man. Carlos you like pumpkin lattes?" Debbie asks as she is laughing with Zeke. "Yes, I like a good pumpkin latte, so what? Don't hate me because I have class and sophistication." As soon as the words come out of his mouth Carlos cannot help but burst out into laughter as well.

The team pulls in for a quick pit stop. Zeke sends Jose in the adjoining Safeway to get some heavy duty extra large trash bags. Everyone else heads into Starbucks to get something to drink. Everyone gets what they want. Carlos even has his pumpkin latte. So he wouldn't be clowned about the flavor by himself, he picked up one for Jose as well. Everyone is in a good mood and enjoying life as they pile back into the trucks. At this point, it is just a short ride from Rockville to Potomac. It takes no time for the caravan to make it to Debbie and Mitch's house.

As they are pulling up, Zeke calls the detective to get out and to come into the house with them. When they park, doors are being closed. Taylor and Mitch can hear the sound inside the house. "Here goes nothing and I hope we live through this," Taylor tells Mitch. "Yeah, me too and for what it is worth, you were worth it. You are the only woman besides my wife I have ever stayed with longer than two weeks. We have been together for months and I love you," Mitch tells her.

The door opens and the entourage is deep. Carlos comes in first leading the way making sure everything is kosher. The detective comes in after him with a laptop in hand. The lawyer comes in next with a briefcase. Jose walks in with a yellow box of garden size trash bags. Zeke enters the room and takes a minute to stand there and look around, he then proceeds forward. Last but not least in walks Debbie. She stands there for a minute just looking at her husband then at Taylor. Mitch and Taylor's jaws drop as Debbie walks in. They did not expect her to be with Zeke. That scenario did not cross their minds. I mean, with all that is going on, at the end of the day, Mitch still has another bitch in Debbie's house. That is just disrespectful and Mitch knows it from the look that is on Debbie's face.

Zeke tells them "You two sit together over there on the couch. I am going to sit here." Zeke ends up on the couch sitting across from them both. Debbie takes up a chair to the right of Taylor. Mitch is sitting on Taylor's left. Zeke leans down to put his coffee on the table. He looks at Mitch and asks "Well, Mitch, I take it by now, my wife has explained to you who I am. Is that correct?" "Yes she has told me," he replies. "We are going to ask you a few questions and depending on how you answer those questions, will determine your fate. I implore you to be honest. Do you both understand me?" he asks. They both answer yes promptly. "Well, before I start, I first want to take time out to thank our lovely hostess. Debbie, you have a beautiful home. I have never been inside before and I must say, you have a fantastic style and your decorating is impeccable." Zeke tells her as he is gloating the whole time. Debbie, who is eating it up, smiles and replies with "Thank you, baby, I try to have a comfortable home."

Zeke then turns his attention to Taylor and says "Now, Taylor, can you tell me exactly why you cheated? Why would you step out on me after all we have been through? What exactly did I do wrong?" "That is part of the problem right there. I should not have to tell you what is wrong. But I will, since it seems my life depends on it. I cheated because you loved your other woman more than me. You have a better relationship with Pegasus than you do with me," Taylor tells Zeke. He replies with "What the hell are you talking about? I know you have gone over the deep end now." "Yeah, I'm over the deep end alright. You were always gone. You leave me for five to six months a year while the racing season is going on. It was not like that before. You were gone all the time back in the day but you always came back after two weeks. And that was at a maximum. I know you were just a flight away in Florida. But sometimes I just needed some personal attention without having to get on a plane to get it. I was lonely and I needed the comfort of a man. I don't love you any less and I truly and honestly didn't mean to hurt you." Zeke says "You know what? I can honestly respect your answer. I also believe what you are telling me."

Debbie gets up out of her chair and walks into her kitchen. Everyone is watching her at this point. No one else has gotten up since the conversation started. She opens the refrigerator and gets bottled water. She comes back to her seat and places the bottle on the table. Still standing, Debbie says "Now, before I start, there is just one thing." She turns to Taylor and slaps the living shit out of her. Debbie, still looking at Taylor, says "You might be wondering why I slapped you. I did not slap you because you were fucking my husband. Oh no, that is not it. I slapped you because you thought it was ok to fuck my husband in my bed you trifling bitch."

Debbie then takes her seat back where she was. Then, she says "Now that the small issues are out the way, Mitch why don't you step up and tell me why you cheated on me. I gave you all of me didn't I? You just heard this poor woman pour her heart out and show her true feelings. So, let's hear yours, because I gave you everything. Sure, your career is ok, but let's be real, the money is mine." She looks at Taylor and says "Yes, boo boo, all the money, the cars and nice things are all mine. He was mine too, but whatever." She turns back to Mitch and says "So, please, tell me, Mitch, and don't lie."

Mitch sits there for a minute and then says "I cheat because I like women pure and simple. I don't want to give them up. It is either that or I cheat for the love of the chase. I have what I call the new pussy syndrome; all I want is new pussy. Can I talk you out of your panties is the ultimate goal. I mean, once I get the pussy, the thrill is gone for me and it is on to the next one. But, so many women these days don't wear panties. I think I need to come up with a new goal to achieve." With that last comment, Debbie stands up and punches him dead in his fucking face. She hits him so hard that his nose starts gushing blood. Carlos and Jose just dap each other up as they laugh hysterically saying the normal "I like this girl." Debbie sits back down and says "Stop your sniveling already. I didn't hit you that hard. I don't have to like it but I guess that is your own dumb ass reason for cheating on me and I have to accept it." Debbie takes another drink from her bottled water and sits there with her arms folded.

Zeke stands up and says "This gentleman to my right is my lawyer. The gentleman to my left is the private investigator that has followed you two for the last seven months around the clock. Debbie and I have decided it is in our best interest to leave you. We will allow you to divorce us. I have taken the liberty of having the papers drawn up for official separation and also final divorce. You know, in Maryland, it takes a full year of separation. In consideration of the agreement from you both and to keep from any asset division or long court fight, we are going to pay you both one million dollars. You will sign the papers and walk away. You will both vacate your primary residence. You will not take anything that is not yours and will be done vacating the premises within forty eight hours or less. You also will move off of the east coast entirely. You will do this within seven days. I am paying you one million dollars each, work it out. You will come back to the lawyer's office one year from today in order to finalize any divorce proceedings paperwork. You will not make me look for you, you would rather comply than have me find you. You can either accept these terms or I can have my friend Jose over there start opening up those trash bags he has. I will give you two a few moments to discuss my proposition amongst yourselves to figure out what your best option should be."

Taylor and Mitch begin to talk to each other. "As long as we walk out alive, I don't care," Taylor says. "I think he is pulling our leg about the money, but I am with you," Mitch says. "I guess he is in a good mood. I thought he was going to kill us both," Taylor tells him. "Alright, we have decided what to do. We will take the money and live option," Mitch says cautiously. "That is a fantastic choice there, Mitch. I still can't believe I have to give a guy fucking my wife a million bucks. But, seeing as I have Debbie now, I look at it as a fare trade and no robbery as far as I am concerned. As for you, Taylor, I loved you right up until I found out you were cheating on me. The lawyer has the paperwork for you both to sign. It has been prepared and highlighted where you need to sign. As soon as you sign, you can have the money," Zeke tells them.

The lawyer pulls out paperwork for both parties. Signatures are placed on all the documents by all the parties. The lawyer tells Zeke "I will take these down to the courthouse in the morning and get this process started." "Thank you and you are a life saver. Thanks again for working on short notice," Zeke tells him. "Carlos, give them the money, they held up their end of the deal. Let's get out of here," Zeke says. As they walk out of the living room, Debbie turns to Mitch and says "I loved you a lot, too bad you couldn't appreciate me. When I come back to this house in forty eight hours, I don't want to see you or your little girlfriend ever again." Zeke pulls her by the hand to leave.

WHAT'S NEXT

Jose, Carlos, Debbie and Zeke all jump into the suburban and head off back down 270 towards the city. Carlos and Jose are in the front seats holding it down as usual. Zeke turns to Debbie and says "You are a genius, baby. I am still shocked that it actually worked." "How can I ever thank you for getting that woman out of my life so easily?" Debbie replies "How can I ever thank you? Without your muscle behind me, he would have tried to drag this out in court forever. I know him, he would have figured out a way to have me paying him alimony for screwing another woman. He would have said he was mentally damaged or something because I worked too hard," she says laughing. She continues with "If anything, I need to be thanking you for saving me months of agony and thousands of dollars of legal fees and bullshit court dates." "I am just happy you came up with the plan. We are totally free to be with one another. We are free to build a life with one another," Zeke says as he gazes into her eyes.

Zeke says "Baby, look at me." She looks deeply into his eyes and says "Yes, how can I help you?" "With this new found freedom of ours, what would you like to do next? I mean, what is our next move?" Zeke asks her. Debbie takes a minute to answer. She takes a deep breath and says "With everything we have done in the last few days, how about we get some sleep! I am worn out?" Zeke replies "I think that is long overdue. Carlos, you heard the lady, get her somewhere she can get some uninterrupted sleep for the next few days," Zeke says.

"Yes, boss, I have the perfect place for you guys. Give me fifteen minutes and I will have you there. You guys deserve a break," Carlos tells them. The truck heads off to a nice quiet place.

THE END

17685957R00127

Made in the USA
Middletown, DE
04 February 2015